Something Magical

by J.R. Zimmer

Book Five
Fisher/Lafayette Saga

Badlanders Press

Something Magical

©2020 by Janette Walker

All rights reserved

Cover design by Janette Walker
        With Daniela Brinkmeyer

<u>Fisher/Lafayette Saga</u>

If There Hadn't Been You
Now and Forever
Someone Like You
Spitfire
Something Magical
The Dreamer
Eagle's Wolf
Coming Home (Free Ebook when signing up for my newsletter at
www.jrzimmer.com. Not available anywhere else.)

You can find J.R. Zimmer at:

Web site: www.jrzimmer.com
Facebook: www.facebook.com/jrzimmer.author
Email: jrzimmer17@yahoo.com

For

My Sister

Julie Baltzell

Your heart is so full of love for others.
My wish is for something magical
to come into your life and bless you with joy!

.

Something Magical
by J.R. Zimmer

Chapter one

July 1986

Early Monday morning Tabitha Turner all but stormed into her clinic's waiting room and past the reception desk.

The office manager looked up from the computer she was imputing information into, saw the look on Tabitha's face, and winced. In her six years with this veterinarian clinic, she had faced plenty of angry animals, but she got the feeling she would rather face a Rottweiler with rabies than the clinic's owner and valued veterinarian at this moment.

Tabitha had never shown a temper before, but something had brought it out.

"Umm," Grace was hesitant to say more as she watched Tabitha move behind the desk. Watched as she grabbed the chart with the list of morning appointments, then slam the clipboard back down without looking at it. "May I ask what's wrong?"

"I am so angry!"

Duh, Grace thought, but would not say it out loud. "Forgive me for saying this, Tabitha, but I understood that from your growl when you opened the front door."

Tabitha stared at her for a moment. "I'm sorry, Grace." She took a long breath, blew it out. "I'm not being very professional, am I? It has nothing to do with this place."

"I cannot imagine your adorable little girl caused your upset."

"No, she's happy as a clam because it's Monday, and she gets to spend the day with both of my parents, not just my mom. Who knows what they'll do today to spoil her?" she chuckled because she knew her parents enjoyed doting on their only grandchild.

"Then what's up? Unless you want me to bug off and tell me it's none of my business?"

With a sigh, Tabitha sat down in the chair next to Grace. "You know that empty land on the north side of town I want to buy?"

"The one you have been holding fundraisers for and want to turn into a dog sanctuary?"

Tabitha nodded. "I went to the bank this morning. I have raised enough funds over the past two years for them to take me seriously when I ask for the loan I want, so I could purchase those twenty acres. But guess what? Suddenly some development company called Badlander Builders bought it! That land has been sitting there for years! No one's made any noise about wanting it and now, poof," she snapped her fingers, "some damn construction company buys it."

"What are they going to put there?"

"The bank said the company has no intent on developing it yet, but they sure as hell had the money to squander on it." She took another deep breath, blew it out. "I just want to kick something."

Grace held up her hands. "Aim your foot away from me if you decide to follow through with that desire."

Tabitha blinked. Then a slight smile tugged at the corners of her mouth. "I'll be sure to find a wall that can withstand the impact. And thanks. I needed that small amount of humor."

"I wasn't joking. I don't like pain."

The statement caused both women to laugh.

After a moment, Grace told her, "I'm sorry that happened, Tabitha. I know what that project means to you. And I am not making light of things when I say, you'll find another area."

"Maybe. But I've had my eyes set on that land for so long it's hard to imagine any place else." Her shoulders slumped. "With the way my luck is going today, I'll probably get a call from Mason Lafayette's agency, and they will deny my request to have him be part of this year's fund-raiser. You know darn well girls from miles away would have purchased tickets for the chance to have a date with that twenty-one-year-old model."

Grace shook her head as she chuckled. "I can't believe you reached out to his agency. The odds of them saying yes is astronomical, but if by some miracle you do get him here, I will probably buy more than my fair share of tickets too so I'll have a chance to go out to dinner with him."

Tabitha blinked. "You're fifty-five years old! Good lord, you could be his mother!"

"Well, I'm not his mother. And I have seen those ads for Touch My Bod Jeans." She used a hand as though it were a fan as she let out a dreamy sigh. "That boy is mighty delicious."

"I cannot believe you said that."

"And you cannot tell me you don't think he's to die for. Why else would you have even considered trying to get him for your fundraiser?"

"He's attractive, women swoon over him, and I would have probably raised more money this year than I have in the past two combined. That is the only reason I was trying to arrange for him to participate. I certainly do not think of him in any way that involves a bed."

Grace clucked her tongue. "I said nothing about trying to entice the boy into my bed."

Tabitha sighed. "It doesn't matter. I know it was a long shot. I'll just have to come up with some other scheme."

"His agency hasn't answered your request yet. Don't give up hope before the battle begins."

"I know. But after hearing the bank tell me the land I wanted is no longer available kind of gave my optimism a setback." She leaned back

in the chair, feeling defeated. "I have wanted to do this for Owen for so long it almost feels as though my heart is breaking all over again."

Reaching for Tabitha's hand, Grace gave it a light squeeze. "I know, honey. I know what it means to you. I admire you so much for all you have accomplished since Owen died. You are the strongest woman I know."

Tabitha shook her head, tried not to allow the tears forming behind her eyes to surface. She no longer grieved over Owen's death, though he would always hold a special place in her heart. She was finally moving forward with her life, but the tears were from frustration. Building that shelter in honor of Owen's memory meant the world to her.

"I sometimes don't feel all that strong." She grabbed a tissue from the box sitting on Grace's desk, dabbed at her eyes to remove any traces of moisture that may have slipped past her lashes. "If it weren't for you and Greta, I would have lost this place. You will never know how deeply I appreciate everything the two of you accomplished that first year, and the ones after that. And my parents, for giving up their life to move here and help me out. They sold everything, including their Diner in Clarion, Pennsylvania, because they love me that much. I know I would have been more of a mess than I was if it hadn't been for all of you banning together. You guys helped me make it through. That is the only strength I have."

Grace reached out, patted Tabitha's knee. "You know, Greta and I had no choice. Our jobs were at stake, and we happen to like it here." She grinned.

Tabitha's lips twitched. Greta and Grace, having applied for jobs here all those years ago, was a blessing from the goddess she could never repay.

"And your parents are amazing," Grace continued. "Your dad has some honest to God skills in the kitchen. It was great he got hired at Robbie's Family Diner right away when they moved here. That place sure as hell needed your dad's talent. I'm surprised your dad didn't want to open his own place here."

"Dad's fifty-one and not interested in trying to start over. But thank you for the compliment, I'll pass it along to him when I see him tonight."

Squaring her shoulders, knowing she needed to focus on the here and now and not the past, she stood back up. "Okay, I need to get my head into today's game. Who's my first patient?" Tabitha reached for the clipboard she had carelessly slammed down earlier.

"Bubbles McGillicuddy."

Pinching the bridge of her nose, Tabitha shook her head. "Of course, it would be Mrs. McGillicuddy and Bubbles. After discovering my dream was pulled out from underneath me, I shouldn't have expected anything easy." She looked at Grace, chuckled as she said, "Remember the first time that woman brought Bubbles in?"

Grace nodded. "It's hard to forget when an owner makes a frantic call to say they found lumps on their cat's belly, and they need an emergency appointment."

"It wasn't easy not to laugh when I explained to her that those lumps were the cat's nipples. Seriously, how can you be a pet owner and not know animals have nipples?"

"You've been a veterinarian for almost six years, four of which you have practiced at this clinic, and you are just now coming to the conclusion that a lot of pet owners are clueless?"

"Oh, no. I've known that since I was a little girl and collected strays. Each time I brought an animal home, I'm sure my mom and dad wanted to wring my neck." She grinned, knowing her parents never laid a finger on her in frustration because of their only child's habit of stuffing their garage full of animals she wanted to care for. "And knowing people are idiots was the reason I wanted to build a dog sanctuary. I know I can't save them all but damn it. I wanted to do what I could for those poor things whose worthless owners dump them off somewhere when they don't want them anymore."

She ran her hands through her shoulder-length blond highlighted brunette hair. "Who in their right mind would name their company Badlanders Builders? The name implies they build bad land. Why would anyone want to hire them?"

Grace blinked, though not surprised Tabitha had brought the land back up again. "They must be new to the area. I have never heard of them."

"Well, I would sure like to give them a piece of my mind for having stolen that land from me!"

"Umm, technically, they didn't steal it."

Tabitha narrowed her eyes. "Whose side are you on?"

Shaking her head, Grace turned her attention back to the computer at her desk and began working on a few bills owed to the clinic. "I was only pointing out the fact the land was for sale. I'm sorry they beat you to it, but they purchased it fair and square."

"Boy, you sure are playing the devil's advocate."

Grace finished with the invoice she was working on, began another. "Speaking of which, do you have a sitter for Wednesday night?"

"Fortunately, Greg and Kathy are in town for a few days and want to spend time with their granddaughter. In fact, they're having a sleepover Wednesday night, and they will drop Abby off at my parents on their way out-of-town Thursday sometime."

"Oh boy, Greg and Kathy want to spend time with Abby for a change. I cannot believe you allow them the privilege, especially because of the way they treat you."

Tabitha shrugged. "It's for one night. Who knows when they'll decide to come back? Abby is their granddaughter, and I will not deny her the little bit of time they want to give her."

Grace harrumphed. "You're a lot more forgiving than I am. After the hell they put you through when Owen died-"

Raising a hand, Tabitha cut her off. "Again, I no longer care what they think about me. It is unfortunate they have chosen to have little to nothing to do with Abby, but she can never say I didn't let her see them when she is older. She will know it was narrowmindedness on their part just because of their actions."

"Then, you're going to *Mindy's Over Yonder* with us since you, for a change, will not have mommy duty."

The bell over the door rang, signaling someone entered the lobby.

"Good morning, Mrs. McGillicuddy," Grace greeted the older woman. "You're a bit early…."

"Bubbles is pregnant!" the woman announced, setting the cat carrier onto the counter with a bang.

Tabitha shook her head. "Mrs. McGillicuddy, Bubbles cannot possibly be pregnant. She's spayed. We did that last year. Remember?"

"She sure looks pregnant."

Motioning for the woman to follow her, Tabitha led Mrs. McGillicuddy towards an examining room. "We'll do some blood tests and labs to be on the safe side, but I assure you, Bubbles is not pregnant."

"She had better not be! You charged me plenty for that procedure!"

Tabitha glanced over the woman's shoulder, met Grace's eyes, which conveyed the message, here we go again.

"Mrs. McGillicuddy, I did the procedure myself. Bubbles in no way can be pregnant." Tabitha opened the door to the examining room.

The older woman placed the cat carrier onto the examination table and opened the front grate to allow the cat out. Not that Bubbles had any desire to exit the container willingly. She was already hissing at the prospects of this visit.

Tabitha wished her assistant were here because this cat would not come out of that crate without the use of gloves or getting it wrapped in a towel to prevent it from scratching and biting. But Tabitha tried a soothing voice, regardless of knowing it would not do any good. "Come on out, Bubbles, so I can take a look at you."

Hiss.

Sigh.

"Have you allowed Bubbles outside recently?" Tabitha asked the pet's owner.

"Certainly not! I would never allow my Bubbles out of the house! She could get hurt!"

"Did you get another cat? A male, to be precise."

"What?" Mrs. McGillicuddy looked into the carrier, cooed, "Bubbles is the best cat in the world. I would never think of causing her stress. She might become jealous if another cat were in the house."

"Then, how in the world could she possibly be pregnant?"

Mrs. McGillicuddy stared at her. "How should I know?! You're the doctor!"

Tabitha looked up at the ceiling, counted to ten. The woman was beyond ridiculous.

"One moment," Tabitha told her. "I'm going to see if Greta has arrived yet so she can assist me with Bubbles." She stepped out of the room before Mrs. McGillicuddy could answer.

Grace looked up from the computer when she saw Tabitha heading her way. "How's the patient?"

"I'm sure Bubble's is fine. Her owner, on the other hand, always leaves me speechless. My patience left me about three minutes ago. Please tell me Greta's here."

Grace pointed over her shoulder toward the back of the clinic. "She came in the moment you closed the door to the exam room. I believe she's hiding as I told her who was with you in the room."

"I don't blame her one bit, but I need her. Please tell her to bring the gloves so we can look at Bubbles. That cat will not cooperate, and I need to examine her regardless of suspecting it's a phantom pregnancy."

"You're a saint, Tabitha," Grace told her, pushing away from the desk and standing up. "I don't know how you maintain your cool with that woman."

Tabitha grinned. "Trust me, Grace. In my head, I've kicked her in the knee several times."

Laughing, Grace moved toward the back room to tell Greta to prepare for battle while Tabitha walked back to the examination room.

Chapter Two

That same morning TJ Fisher eased his faded blue Chevrolet truck onto the crumbling driveway of the three-bedroom 1,240 square foot house he intended to restore. Turning off the truck's engine, he sat back in the seat as he eyed the property through the cab's front window. It was not the first time he had viewed the run-down house, but seeing it today, he wondered, what in the hell had he been thinking when he bought the place?

True, it would turn a tidy profit once he refurbished it. He had gotten a great deal from the seller. The old lady he purchased it from was entering a nursing home at the time of the sale and wanted to get rid of the property as quickly as possible.

TJ suspected he had been the only one to have put in an offer since she accepted it without fuss. He'd offered far below the asking price, giving him enough wiggle room as he'd expected a counteroffer.

She had not opposed the bid.

Looking at the building now, TJ wondered if the woman's children were worthless pieces of shit. Probably, he thought. They allowed their mother to live in the house when it clearly had been falling down around her. It appeared as though they hadn't bothered to help her with fixing the place up.

He made a mental note to visit the nursing home to see how she was doing. It bothered him when the elderly were treated poorly by the children they poured their hearts and souls into while raising them. He would also check with the nursing home staff. If the woman, Doris, needed something, he wanted to make sure she got it if her useless children would not help her.

Looking at the run-down house made it apparent, in TJ's mind, that Doris's children would not provide for her.

Why he cared about the old woman was a mystery to him. Perhaps values instilled in him by his parents were rooted deep.

He was glad he had taken the trip back to North Dakota a few weeks ago to see his parents. None of his siblings would allow their parents to go without. Donald and Barbra supplied their children with a roof over their heads, clothing on their backs, food to eat, and all the love a child could need. It was only fitting children returned the favor when their parents grew old.

Too bad Doris's children had not felt the same way.

He shook the gloom away, telling himself to get to work. That house would not fix itself.

He swung the truck door open, stepped out, walked around to the tailgate, and unloaded his tools. He had a list of priorities. The place needed to be rewired, the plumbing brought up to date and- He glanced up at the shingles, shook his head. Definitely, the roof needed replacement. The people he hired for those projects should begin arriving soon to start the work. In the meantime, he would roll out the plans his architect drew up to remind himself what this place would look like at the end of its facelift.

He could probably pass the time while waiting for the crews to arrive by beginning the bathroom's demolition.

Thankfully, the porta-potty and dumpster container for the debris had been dropped in the yard sometime yesterday or earlier this morning before he arrived.

He estimated the wiring, plumbing, and roof would be completed by the end of the week. It would have taken longer if he'd chosen to do it all himself, but he was not an idiot. He wanted this project done in one to two months. Hiring out would save him time, though it would cost a tad more than he hoped to spend. He would make the rest up by doing the remaining portion of the remodeling himself. The payoff would come when he resold the place.

Glancing around the neighborhood told him that once finished, he could sell it for four times as much as he paid for it, and the bottom line was, he would make a sizable profit.

This was a pleasant neighborhood. The only eyesore on the block was the place TJ now owned. Property values would go up when this project was complete.

As he placed the first load of tools down on the filthy carpet in the living room, he looked around the space, making a mental note of what areas of the room needed repair. The rug was on the list of things to go into the trash. There was a beautiful hardwood floor under it. He knew it was there because there was a sizeable chunk of carpet missing from one corner of the room, and he could see the wood under it. Why someone would cover a hardwood floor was a mystery to him, but once he refinished it, it would stand up to everyday living.

But the living room could wait.

It was low on the list of priorities.

TJ walked back outside to gather another load of tools from his truck. Once there, he paused for a moment and took a deep breath. It was promising to be a beautiful day, and he stood for a moment soaking in the neighborhood's quiet. The south side of town where he lived was also peaceful. Hell, the entire town was quiet compared to the rat race he'd lived in for seven years.

He liked the quiet. After living in New York City, with its hustle and bustle, he could now appreciate a slower pace. While growing up in Bismarck, he believed he was living in the middle of nowhere. There was nothing to do there unless you were into hunting, fishing, and camping. But once winter hit, even that small amount of entertainment dwindled.

As soon as he was old enough, he'd taken off for New York City, thinking the bigger metropolis would be a lot of fun because there would always be plenty to do.

Well, it had been fun. At least in the early years, while TJ built up his business to the roaring success it had been, he'd enjoyed the fast pace. But then he'd gotten a rude awaking that had shaken his world enough that he sold everything, including the business, and moved out of the area.

Moving to Binghamton, New York, a few years ago, gave him the distance he needed from the Big Apple. But if he wanted to take in a Broadway show or some other entertainment form, it was only a three-hour drive to get there. Other than that, he had no desire to set foot in Times Square or anywhere else in that place.

He liked this state, just not that city.

The roofing company drove up as TJ reached his truck. He spoke with the man in charge of that group for a moment, confirming the job's expectations. They parted ways as the roofers began unloading ladders and climbed onto the roof to start removing shingles.

TJ unloaded the last of the tools he brought with him, placed them in the wheelbarrow he would use to move rubble out of the house to the dumpster, and made his way back into the house. He would bring his larger power tools over once the electrician, plumber, and roofer would be out of his way, and he could work in peace.

Now, there was an oxymoron. There was nothing quiet about construction.

Glancing out the dining-room window gave him a view of the house next door. It was a tad larger than this house, and it looked as though whoever lived there gave a shit about their property because the lawn was trimmed, and the area was clean.

Whoever lived there would probably be thankful when this project was complete. At least the neighbors would no longer have an eyesore right next to their perfect little home.

He heard a car door slam and walked outside, hoping it was the electrician or plumber, or both, here to begin their part of this remodel.

13

Nope. Sigh. The slamming door belonged to the vehicle parked in the driveway of the house next door. He watched the older couple climb out from the car, and the woman help a small child out from the backseat. Perhaps three years old, the child was all energy as she ran to the front door of the house. The woman called the child back as the older gentleman opened the trunk of the car. They handed the child a small bag of groceries before each of them hefted out two more sacks and followed the child into the house.

Grandparents and granddaughter, TJ assumed, then shrugged. It was none of his business.

Time to take a sledgehammer to the bathroom walls.

TJ had two walls in the bathroom down by the time the electrician arrived.

The bathroom's plaster walls had been too far gone to repair cost-effective wise. Which was a shame as plaster gave better insulation and didn't harbor mold because mold could not grow in it. But TJ was unwilling to spend the money on its repair, so he would use cement board around the tub to help prevent mold in that area.

The plaster in the rest of the house he would salvage. He knew enough about repairing it, so he would not have to hire out for it.

He liked saving money by doing the work himself and enjoyed working on projects like this.

Besides, the decorative plaster features of the ceiling in the living room were beautifully detailed. TJ did not want to destroy something a skilled plaster expert had painstakingly put together thirty-six years ago when the house was built in 1950.

"Yo, TJ," Quinn Bultman called out to him as he stepped from his own company vehicle.

"Quinn," TJ acknowledged. He stopped a moment to wipe the sweat from his brow with the sleeve of his shirt, leaving a smudge of dirt across his forehead that would not be the first nor last of the dust he would carry home with him tonight. "Glad you could make it before the sun went down."

The electrician was an hour late from his scheduled time of arrival.

"Yeah, yeah. I know. It couldn't be helped. I got an emergency call on my way here. A guy noticed humming coming from his electrical breaker box. Since I didn't want to take the chance the guy would like, you know, go boom, I thought he took priority over your little rewiring job."

TJ smiled. "Good choice." And because Quinn was a friend, and a hell of an electrician, he teased, "I hope you figured out what the problem was."

With a straight face, Quinn said, "Na. I told the guy to hum along with it until I got back."

They laughed.

The plumber pulled up to the curb in front of the house soon after the humor faded.

"Hey, Glen, glad you could make it to the party," TJ waved. "Why don't you both come on inside, and I'll roll out the plans, and you can get started."

Glen shook his head. "This place looks like a dump. Why in the hell would you waste your money on it?"

"She might look rough around the edges," TJ said, referring to the house as the three of them entered it, "but once she gets a facelift, I won't have any trouble selling her."

"If you say so," Glen said. "But it's your money. I guess you can throw it away however you want."

"You'll see," TJ told him. "I've been doing this kind of thing for a long time. The market is ripe for this little lady."

Quinn followed the two others into the house. "Obviously, Glen, you don't know him."

Glen shrugged. "I know he's the guy who hired me. As long as he can pay the bill, I won't question what he wants to do with his money."

Quinn shared a look with TJ. Apparently, Glen had no idea as to TJ's net worth. Even if the house did not sell, Glen would get paid.

TJ rolled out the blueprints for the house on top of the small kitchen island. "All right boys, take a look." And he broke down for them which areas of the house he wanted to be done first to last.

The sound of the roofers removing the shingles was music to his ears as he went back to work while Quinn and Glen got started on their projects.

TJ took a break at two in the afternoon. His stomach kept reminding him he hadn't eaten since early that morning. Everyone else had taken their lunch breaks while he'd continued with the demolition of the bathroom walls.

He walked out of the house, grabbed the cooler from inside his truck, and climbed up on the tailgate. The workers for this project had driven off to eat at a fast-food joint or a Diner earlier, but TJ always packed his own lunch and stayed on site. It made the end of the day so much sweeter. When he left here, it was the end of the day, and he'd be heading home for a shower, and maybe he would grab something to eat along the way and bring it home with him.

He chuckled to himself as he thought of the house he lived in now. He loved it. It had five bedrooms, three bathrooms, and was in a quiet neighborhood. He had landscaped and fenced in the backyard and added a pool and hot tub, which he looked forward to soaking in later tonight. If the people he knew in New York City would see the place, they would probably believe he had lost his mind to have given up the sixty-five-million-dollar penthouse he had owned on Park Ave.

The view from the living room floor to ceiling windows had been spectacular.

But that had been a few years ago when he thought he wanted that lifestyle, and before the betrayal.

Since that dark day, five years ago, TJ had been more than happy to put that life behind him. Now he spent his days working on hobbies, one of which was breathing new life into houses he believed were worth the investment.

Easing himself onto the tailgate, he reached for the cooler and pulled out the sandwich he packed that morning. On the menu this afternoon was a peanut butter pickle sandwich accompanied by a nice cold beer.

He sat, watching the quiet neighborhood's tenants going through daily life as he ate. A few houses away were a handful of teenage boys playing basketball in the driveway. A few younger children were riding their bikes on the streets while fathers mowed the lawn, and mothers were inside the homes doing whatever they did or were outside helping with the yard work.

With fondness, TJ remembered his own carefree days of riding his bicycle around his hometown of Bismarck. During the summer, he and his friends would ride their bikes three miles to the Elks pool to splash in the water at the public facility. The ride down to the pool was a piece of cake. Downhill all the way. Coming back had been a bitch. Uphill, mostly. But he and his friends always fueled up after the afternoon swim by stopping by the Dairy Queen located less than a block away from the pool and ordered banana splits. They'd eat the treats in the Custer Park across the street from the swimming pool before taking on what they had jokingly called the mountain leading home.

The garage next door opened. TJ's eyes moved in that direction. He watched as the three-year-old he had seen earlier in the day shoot from the garage on a pink tricycle that had matching pink streamers coming from the handlebars.

TJ almost laughed at the pure pleasure on the girl's face as she pointed the three-wheeled trike down the sidewalk and took off at high speed.

The woman TJ assumed was the grandmother followed the child on foot as far as the driveway. She stopped and watched to be sure the child only went as far as allowed before the woman turned and walked back into the garage, emerging within moments with a few gardening tools. She began working in the flower garden in the front yard while the child rode her trike up and down the sidewalk.

Closing his eyes for a moment to stretch his arms and arch his back, he did not notice when the child from next door stopped on the sidewalk in front of him until she said, "Hi."

He eyed her. Cute as a button, with huge amber-colored eyes that seemed to stare into his soul. There was an innocence about her, and he had the uncanny urge to shelter her from the world.

"Hi back," he said. "Didn't your mom tell you not to talk to strangers?"

She rolled her eyes and nodded. "All the time. So do gramma and grandpa."

"Then, should you be talking to me since I'm a stranger?"

She ignored that and asked instead. "What's your name?"

"TJ. But you shouldn't talk to people you don't know-"

"I'm Abby. Abby Nicole. We aren't strangers 'cause I know your name, and you know mine." She grinned.

He damn near laughed at her logic.

"Well, Abby. I suppose that's one way of looking at it."

Abby nodded. "Do you want to play ball?"

"Sorry. I've got lots of work to do."

Her shoulders slumped. "My mom says that too."

He almost felt guilty for not taking her up on her offer. "I think you need to go home now."

She shook her head. "I can't. Mommy isn't here to get me yet."

Obviously, she did not live next door. But when TJ glanced in that direction, he saw Abby's grandmother watching this conversation. He could tell by the woman's body language she was coiled to spring into action if he laid a finger on her granddaughter.

"Your grandma would feel better if you were over there with her, rather than talking to me."

Abby let out a forlorn sigh. "Okay." The word came out sounding like a grumble.

Little Abby turned her tricycle toward her grandparent's house, and TJ watched her slowly making her way down the sidewalk.

He wanted to reassure the grandmother he wasn't some psychopath who kidnapped children. The only thing he could think to do was to give her a quick neighborly wave.

The woman gave a hesitant wave back before turning her attention back to the child.

Dismissing the older woman and the child, TJ picked up the empty wrapper his sandwich had been in, carried the cooler into the house, and finished the beer.

He smiled as the image of Abby Nicole formed in his mind, and he laughed now at her claim they were no longer strangers because they knew each other's names.

No wonder her grandmother was watchful. The kid did not appear to have a shy bone in her body.

Chapter Three

"Mommy!" Abby exclaimed the moment Tabitha walked through the front door of her parents' home. She was sitting on the couch with her grandfather, allowing him to read a book to her as he pointed out the letters and words as he read.

"Hi Scooby-Doo," Tabitha said, opening her arms as her daughter climbed off the couch and ran to her. "Boy, I sure missed you. I didn't get one Scooby kiss all day!" She lifted her daughter up, nuzzled her close before kissing her on the cheek. "So much better," she said, smiling.

Abby placed her hands on both sides of her mother's cheeks and proceeded to give her a quick kiss on the lips. "That's a Scooby kiss, silly mommy."

Tabitha laughed and set her daughter back down. "So, what sort of nonsense did grandma and grandpa make you do today?" She took her daughter's hand, led her back to the couch. Sitting down next to her father, she placed Abby on her lap.

"Your mother and I spent the day abusing her," John Stevens answered as his wife Angela entered the living room from the kitchen.

Tabitha looked at her daughter, playfully gasped, "Is that true, Scooby?"

Abby had played this game often enough. She giggled and said, "I had to go shoppin' with them."

"No!"

Abby nodded. "And they made me play at the park!"

"How dare they?!" Tabitha looked at her parents. The smile on her face was at odds with her outrage.

Angela Stevens sat down on the recliner. "Next week Monday, if the weather cooperates, grandpa and I will take you swimming, so make sure mommy brings your bathing suit."

"I wish I could go tomorrow," Abby grumbled, sticking her lower lip out in a pout. She loved the water and planned on being a mermaid one day- if she could figure out how to change her feet into a tail.

"Tomorrow is Tuesday. Grandpa has to go to work."

"I could go with grandma," was Abby's solution.

"Grandpa will have the car. Besides, I think grandpa would feel bad if he couldn't go with both of you," Tabitha said.

Abby didn't complain, but the pout didn't go away.

"Wednesday, you get to spend the day with grandma and grandpa Turner and have a sleepover with them. Won't that be fun?"

John Stevens rolled his eyes. His wife pressed her lips together in an effort not to say what she thought of the idea.

Abby shook her head.

"They want to spend time with you, and I think that is nice of them." She said cheerfully, regardless of the fact she had no love for Owen's parents. They traveled year-round in their motor home, and she could count on one hand the number of times the couple bothered to come to Binghamton and ask to see Abby. The couple's prejudice against any-thing outside their religious beliefs kept them away and prevented them from showing more than a smidgen of affection for Abby. They be-lieved Tabitha, and Tabitha's parents, who had raised their own daugh-ter in their faith, were evil, and Abby was tainted.

They were narrow-minded, and it was their loss if they wanted to be judgmental fools. But as Tabitha had told Grace earlier in the day, she would not deny the Turner's time with Abby whenever they deemed her worthy enough for their attention.

She tried not to hate them.

Tabitha's mother stood up, took Abby by the hand. "Come on, my little one. You can help me set the table. Your mommy is probably hungry, and we don't want her to blow away in the wind, now do we?"

It was Angela's way of telling her daughter she thought she needed to gain a little weight, but Tabitha had always had a slim figure regardless of what she ate.

"So," her father said as he sat back on the couch, "how was work today?"

"It was business as usual, which is fine by me. It's nice to only have to deal with regular checkups on the pets." Unless Bubbles McGillicuddy was brought in. Its psycho owner was more challenging than that cat was. Not that Tabitha would tell her father that. It was not professional to talk to anyone outside of work about the patients and their caregivers.

"That's good to know," John told her. "I know you're also working on the fundraiser you want to hold at the end of August. Is there anything mother and I can help you out with on that front?"

Tabitha slumped. "I don't even know if there will be a fundraiser this year."

"Oh? Why not?"

She told him about the land having been purchased by someone else and was no longer an option. "Maybe the dog sanctuary isn't meant to be."

"That doesn't sound like my daughter talking," John told her. "My daughter has always had a spirit of determination, no matter what." He reached over, patted her knee. "What's really going on, buttercup?"

"I don't know," she sighed, knowing that was not true. Knowing she was feeling lost and alone lately, regardless of having the support of her parents and friends. When Owen died, she had not had time to think, and raising Abby, whom she loved beyond words, took up the time she had when she wasn't at work.

And forget dating. Even if she were to find someone she was attracted to, he probably wouldn't like the fact she already had a child. She was not free to go somewhere unless she found a sitter, and babysitters cost money she felt was better off put into savings for Abby's education. She also refused to take advantage of her parents more than she already did. They watched Abby Monday through Friday, except Wednesday mornings, every week.

"If you need help with anything, all you have to do is ask."

"I know, daddy. If it hadn't been for you and mom, I don't know what I would have done. You two gave up everything to move here and help me out. I love you both so much."

He took her hand in his, squeezed it gently. "You're just lucky you're an only child. We probably would have disowned you the day you brought a snake into the diner when you were six years old and began showing it to all the customers." He winked.

The memory made her laugh, which was his intent.

"You know," John said as another memory took hold. "I recall a day when you were eight and brought a stray cat into the Diner."

"I was always bringing animals into the diner."

"True. But you talked a man and woman into taking it, and I heard that cat was given to Grant Davidson, the artist."

"Seriously?" Grant Davidson was a well-known artist from Clarion. Despite being born with down syndrome; he was famous for his ability to make sketches so lifelike people often thought the images were photographs. His artwork was often showcased in a well-known New York City art gallery and sold at top dollar. "How come you never told me that before?"

Her father shrugged. "Maybe because I forgot about it. But I was thinking, maybe you could reach out to him for a donation for your fundraiser. Have you heard from that Lafayette fellow yet?"

"I'm not holding my breath I'll get a positive answer, but you've given me another option. Thanks, dad. I think I'll write Grant a letter after Abby goes to sleep tonight. It doesn't hurt to ask."

Abby ran into the room and announced, "Gramma said time to eat."

They gathered around the dining room table, lit five candles, and joined hands for the mealtime blessing. When it was over, they passed around the parmesan chicken over spaghetti noodles, which her mother had prepared along with a side salad.

As they ate, the conversation turned to the house next door.

"Not sure what's going on at Doris's old place," Angela said as she cut into her chicken. "Seems to me like it's being remodeled, though why anyone would want to spend that kind of money on it, I do not understand." She smiled at Abby. "I think the two of us should visit Doris sometime next week. I'm sure she would like to see you, little one."

Abby nodded. "I miss Doris. She always gave me a nickel."

Angela chuckled.

"Well, I'm glad someone is fixing the place up," John said. "The house has a good foundation. I'm sorry Doris had to sell, but she couldn't keep up with the place, and her kids never helped her out."

"I would never do that to you and mom," Tabitha told her parents.

Her mother smiled at her. "We know, baby girl."

Abby laughed. "Mommy isn't a baby!"

Angela smiled at her. "Your mommy is always going to be my baby."

Abby rolled her eyes. Obviously, grandma did not know the difference between a baby and a mommy.

"Anyway," Tabitha said, pushing her plate away and noticed her mother was eyeing it to see how much she had eaten. Which was all of it. The chicken had been good, and she had been hungry. "I'll help you with the dishes, then Abby and I need to head home."

Tabitha began clearing the table while her father took Abby back into the living room to read another story to her.

When Tabitha walked into the kitchen, her mother was running warm water into the sink and adding dish soap into the water. "I'll wash. You dry," her mother said. "And you know you don't have to help me. Your dad is more than capable of doing this chore."

"I know, mom. But I want to help. You cook dinner for Abby and me every evening. It's only right I help as much as possible."

Angela chuckled. "I have to make food for your father and me, anyway. It doesn't take any effort to double a recipe."

"How did I get so lucky to have you for a mother?" Tabitha asked, plucking the clean glass her mother had just washed and rinsed from her hand and began drying it.

"Well, it certainly wasn't luck," her mother abolished. "I've told you before, the universe has a way of putting people together if they trust it enough."

Tabitha managed not to roll her eyes. At one time, she'd believed in her parents take care of nature, and it will take care of you philosophy. She felt a connection to animals at an early age, loved to plant gardens and feel the earth on her hands and feet, but when Owen died, her sense of that natural magic seemed to have gone to the grave with him.

"Honey," her mother continued, "you need to start dating again."

"Sure, with all the free time I have, I'll get right on that."

Her mother stared at her. "Tabitha June," she said in her abolishing voice, "there is no need for sarcasm."

Tabitha grabbed a clean plate from the drain, dried it, and put it away in the cupboard. "I'm thirty-two years old, mom. Using my middle name when you're upset with me doesn't hold the power it once did. And I wasn't being sarcastic. I work Monday through Friday from seven in the morning until five or six at night. And that depends upon what's going on at the clinic at the time. I come here, pick up Abby, eat, go home. The weekends are my time to spend with her."

Angela's eyes looked upward as she shook her head, took a deep breath, and mumbled, "Goddess help me."

This time Tabitha did roll her eyes.

Angela stopped washing the dishes, turned toward her daughter, put a hand on her hip, "Tabitha, I love you. And because I love you, I'm going to say this. You need to stop making excuses. It's been over three years. You've grieved, you've cried, and you have bounced back.But I also know you are lonely. You need to date, and your father and I are certainly willing to watch Abby for a few extra hours so you can have time with your friends and find your soulmate. I know he's out there for you, but you need to stop hiding from him."

"Mom! Please don't start that Owen wasn't the one the goddess meant for you, crap."

Angela pressed her lips together and went back to washing dishes.

Tabitha sighed. She knew her mother meant well, but they'd been over this before. "If it will make you feel better, I'm going out Wednesday night to Mindy's Over Yonder with Grace and Greta."

Her mother turned to her, smiled. "That's wonderful! I'll light a pink candle for you and say a wish."

"I'm still surprised Greg and Peggy called and want Abby to spend the night with them. On the bright side, you'll have the entire day free, and Thursday morning since she'll be with them. They'll drop her off here Thursday afternoon."

Her mother, usually a rational person, hissed. "Oh, my. What's the occasion that they want to spend time with her for a change?"

"Who knows? But since they called and asked to see her, I won't deny them."

"You should. I've met no one as closed-minded as the Turners are. I don't dislike many people, but I'm glad those two don't come around often. Abby is better off without them and their silly opinions." Angela set the last dish in the drain. "I hope they won't try to convince her you're an evil witch."

Tabitha smiled. "Don't worry, mom. My little girl is too smart for them, and I'll make sure she wears her black kyanite necklace to help repel any negative energy they might give off."

Angela put her hand over her heart, tapped her chest lightly. "You make me proud. I've been afraid you'd forgotten your faith."

Tabitha could only shrug. She may not believe as she once had, but she was willing to have some when it came to Abby's protection.

Once the last dish was put away, Tabitha walked into the living room. "Come on, Scooby. We need to head home so you can take a bath, and I'll read you a story before tucking you in for the night."

"Can we read One Fish, Two Fish, tonight?"

"Of course, as long as you remember to brush your teeth after your bath."

"Do I have to?" she wailed.

"Yes, you do."

Abby made a face. "Fine. But I won't like it."

With a smile, Tabitha told her, "That works for me. I don't care if you like it or not."

As mother and daughter reached Tabitha's Honda Accord, Abby's eyes moved to the house next door. She was hoping to see her new friend, but there were no lights on in the place, and there were no longer any vehicles parked in the driveway or on the street.

She almost told her mom about her new friend but decided to keep it a secret. Mommy would probably get mad, and she did not want mommy mad at her for talking to TJ, even though, in Abby's mind, he was not a stranger. She knew his name.

By ten o'clock that evening, Abby was bathed, had her teeth brushed, read too, and was sound asleep before Tabitha tiptoed out from her daughter's room and turned off the light.

This was the time of the day Tabitha dreaded. During this time, before she crawled into bed, was the loneliest of them all. She wanted someone to curl up on the couch with. Maybe watch a movie or have an adult conversation that had nothing to do with work.

And most of all, she wanted to be held during the night in a man's arms again.

All right. Her mother was right. She was lonely and knew the only way she could move on was to begin dating again.

Goddess, help her.

Chapter Four

Wednesday afternoon, around four, TJ quit working on the remodel early. It allowed him enough time to drive home, shower, and change before meeting with friends at Mindy's Over Yonder Bar and Grill. It was a bar with a country-western theme and reminded him of some bars in his hometown.

He and a few friends tried to meet up every Wednesday night for drinks and a good meal.

The place had a dance floor, although if it wasn't the weekend and you wanted to dance, you had to slip some money into the jukebox because there would be no live band playing until Friday night.

The group TJ was with preferred coming here on Wednesdays because it wasn't as busy as the weekends. You could hear yourself talk and not have to shout to be heard over the music.

Normally. Tonight, however, it appeared as though it was Binghamton's only hot spot. The booths and tables were crowded, and there were already a few drunks sitting near the bathroom entrance.

Probably a wise decision for them.

TJ and his friends managed to find a table toward the dance floor without too much difficulty. Once seated, they ordered a round of drinks and skimmed through the menus kept at the tables.

Their group was comprised of three men, two of whom were married, and they had brought their wives along. That left TJ the odd man out since he was single and had no date, but it didn't bother him to be the fifth wheel.

Quinn Bultman, the electrician working on TJ's remodel, slipped his arm around his wife's shoulder and asked her, "What looks good on the menu?"

"I think I'll have the ham and cheese sliders," Penny answered.

"Honey, you have those every time we're here. Don't you want something different for a change?"

"Nope," she set her menu down, turned to Linda sitting on her right, and married to Ray. "How 'bout you, Linda?"

"Yum, I'm in! I love those too."

Her husband shook his head but was wise enough not to comment.

TJ laughed, earning him a sharp look from Ray.

"One day, Fisher," Ray told TJ, "It's going to be you sitting here with a girlfriend or wife, and then we'll see who has the last laugh."

With a grin, TJ said, "I almost went down that road, you know. Fortunately for me, I dodged that bullet."

That statement had both women at the table looking at him as though he was a lost cause.

Linda glanced at Penny. "We need to set that boy up with someone," she claimed.

TJ put up his hands, palms out, to ward off their claim. "No, thanks. I'm happy as a clam to remain single. And besides, if I want a woman, it doesn't take much effort to get one."

Linda shook her head. "Seriously, TJ? Just because you're as handsome as sin doesn't make you attractive to a woman."

Ray's eyes moved to his wife, and he cocked a brow. "What do you mean he's handsome as sin? He's uglier than hell."

Linda patted his arm. "Honey, you're so cute." She loved her husband dearly, but TJ was better looking. Not that she would tell that to Ray. She had a good marriage and planned on keeping it that way.

"Let's just forget about TJ's sorry excuse for a face," Quinn said, "and get someone over here to take our order." He began looking around for a waitress, signaled when he found one.

The conversation progressed from the weather to sports while they waited for their food and sipped their drinks.

While the men talked, Linda reached into her large purse and pulled out a magazine. Flipping it open, she showed Penny what was on the page without the men paying attention to what they were oohing and aahing about. The men assumed it was some frilly girl thing and could not care less.

Until at some point, Ray heard his wife say, "God, he is so hot."

That got Ray's attention away from the heated discussion about which pro baseball team was the best. "What are the two of you looking at?" he asked and tried to reach for the magazine.

Linda held it close to her chest and out of her husband's reach. "You guys just go back to talking about your silly ol' sports and leave Penny and me to do what women like to do."

Ray cocked a brow. "Now you have my curiosity up. You're acting like you're looking at porn or something."

His wife's face flushed.

"It isn't porn!" Penny exclaimed. "For heaven's sake, why would you think we would bring something like that here?"

Ray shrugged but continued to stare at his wife.

Quinn held out his hand. "The two of you might as well share what's got you looking guilty."

The two women shared a look before Linda slowly handed him the magazine.

Glancing down at the ad they were enthralled with Quinn's eyes widened. "Good God, it is porn!"

"What?!" Ray exclaimed, yanking the magazine from Quinn's hand to view the offensive photo for himself.

And because TJ was sitting next to Ray, he could see plain as day the ad for Touch My Bod Jeans.

He had the uncanny urge to slither out of the chair he was sitting in and try to leave with no one noticing when he saw who the model was.

Mason Lafayette, his shoulder-length raven black hair, was disheveled as though someone had moments ago been running their hands through it. He stood shirtless against a backdrop of light blue with swirling mist. He was in a pair of jeans that were so tight they had to have been sewn onto him. But that wasn't what made the photo provocative. It was the fact the jeans were unzipped, and Mason's hands were poised as though he were about to slip them off, and it was clear as day he wasn't wearing any underwear. The photographer had strategically cast shadows over the area that would have easily shown Mason's groin behind the zipper. The jeans were riding low enough on the hips to appear as though they were about to come off.

Seeing the image made TJ a tad uncomfortable. Not because he was a prude, but because he knew the model. Knew him personally and had held Mason as a baby a time or two when the Lafayette's visited North Dakota once a year.

He honestly did not want to hear his friends talking about Mason's seductive photo.

Excusing himself from the table, he headed toward the jukebox. Maybe if he got the music going, it might get the two couples at the table more interested in dancing than the photo of one of his nephew's best friends.

TJ wove around some tables, managing to avoid being backed into by a guy standing by a group of people telling them some story as his arms flew about as though he were swatting flies.

Once he reached the jukebox, TJ studied the selection, and as he did, his mind wandered. When a picture of little Abby from next door came to mind, he grinned at the memory.

Earlier in the day, when he took a break from the construction work in the project house, the garage door from next door opened. Once again, Abby peddled that trike of hers at lightning speed from the space. It had amused TJ as he watched the child turn the corner from the driveway onto the sidewalk as though it were a hairpin curve.

He'd also found it almost eerie that for the third day in a row, that garage door opened at the same time he took a break and sat on the tailgate of his truck and drank ice water. One would have thought the neighbors somehow knew when he would be free long enough to allow Abby to say hello to him.

Which was ridiculous, of course. They would have no way of knowing when he would stop working for a short time, and he chalked it up to coincidence.

But Abby wasn't shy about coming his way once she saw him when she'd turned back around and started coming back up the sidewalk. She grinned and pumped her legs as fast as she could to make the trike move faster; excited to greet him.

"Hi, TJ!" she'd said. "Look what grandpa gave me last night!" And she reached into the small basket attached to the front of the trike and pulled out a medium brown Gund teddy bear. Snuggling it against her neck, she told him. "I love him."

"That was nice of your grandpa. To give you a gift. What did you name him? -Or is it a her?"

Abby giggled. "Silly, TJ. He's a boy! See his blue bow tie?"

"Yep," he did once she pointed it out to him. "So, what's his name?"

She shrugged. "I don't know," she admitted. "He hasn't told me yet."

With a smile, TJ told her, "He's probably shy since he just met you."

With a shake of her head, she laughed. "He's not shy! He told me you know his name!"

Shocked, TJ exclaimed, "Me? Why would I know his name?"

Abby just shrugged, then held the bear out to him.

TJ supposed he'd named enough bears in his life, one more wouldn't hurt him. God knew his multiple nieces had given him plenty of practice in that department.

"All right," he said, gently taking the bear and studying it. Knowing how to play the game, he held the bear up to his ear as he told it, "Okay, Mr. Bear. Tell me your name."

Oddly enough, the name Eddy popped into his mind.

He handed the bear back to Abby. "His name is Eddy. Eddy the Teddy."

It wasn't long after that weird naming ceremony when Abby's grandmother called her back to the house next door.

Shaking the memory away, TJ's eyes once again went back to the jukebox. He was debating between choosing Stevie Nicks hit song Talk To Me, or Kim Wilde's You Keep Me Hanging On, when he thought he heard a woman from the hallway leading to the bathrooms shout, "Back off or I'll kick you in the nuts!"

He damn near laughed.

Then he thought he heard something hit the wall in the hallway, and a man's voice exclaim, "You little bitch! That wasn't nice!"

Okay. That TJ couldn't ignore. If the guy was drunk and harassing a woman, he was going to shut that shit down. He did not tolerate men, drunk or not, bullying a woman.

He dropped the correct amount of change into the music box, pushed the button for Talk to Me, and moved off toward the hallway.

When he entered the dimly lit corridor, he paused at the entrance as he took the scene in. There was a tall, burly man with massive arms standing in front of a woman. His huge hands were planted firmly on the wall on the opposite sides of the woman's face, which was hidden in shadow because the guy was blocking the small amount of light that came from the single bulb in the ceiling.

She, the woman, obviously was not happy to have him crowding her space. When she tried to move, the man laughed and said, "Come on. A pretty thing like you would know how to please a man."

"You're drunk!" the woman, whose height did not reach the man's chin, raised her hands, placed them on the guy's chest and tried to push him out of her way regardless of the fact she must have known her effort wouldn't budge him a fraction.

The guy chuckled. "You sure are a feisty one."

TJ cocked his head as he considered how he wanted to play this out. He could simply walk up to the guy and sock him in the face. Though it would be satisfying on a personal level, he had reached the age when opting for violence right off the bat was not his first choice. At thirty-six, he'd learned he did not recover from a brawl as quickly as he had when he'd been in his early twenties.

Option number two. Walk up to the guy and tell him to leave the lady alone.

Ha, like that wouldn't lead to option number one. The man appeared drunk enough to take a swing at him if his answer was no.

Option number three. Play ignorant as though the big fellow wasn't there and hope the woman would be smart enough to go along with the unrehearsed plan. If not, option number one would undoubtedly play out.

He sighed, prepared for the worst, and hoped for the best.

TJ began walking forward down the hallway. As he did, he exclaimed, as though he did not see the man practically holding the woman captive, "Honey! There you are! We were beginning to think you got lost!" Bold as could be, he stepped toward the woman and placed his hand around her arm, and said, "I think next time you need to use the ladies' room, I'll have to send somebody with you to help you find your way back.

But I found you. Our song is playing, and I want to dance." He looked at the drunk, laughed as he winked, and said, "My wife sometimes can't find her way out of a paper bag." He tugged the woman toward him, and surprisingly, the drunk stepped back.

When the shadow moved off from the woman's face, TJ could see her clearly, and he felt as though he had been sucker-punched. Her past the shoulder brunette hair framed a lovely oval face. Her huge amber-colored eyes were outlined with black liner, blended into a soft shade of dark brown eye shadow. She had gorgeous pouty lips glossed with some shade of light pink lipstick, and her doe eyes were staring at him as though caught in headlights.

He figured she was probably wondering if he was just as drunk as the other guy was, but man, she was beautiful in her confusion.

It took him a second before he could come out from the spell she'd somehow woven around him. She was at least a foot shorter than he was, so he had to lean down to whisper in her ear, "It's all right. I've got you."

He stood up and smiled at her, trying to reassure.

There was only a moment of hesitation before she nodded. She put her hand in his, and when she did, it felt as though an electric spark passed between their two hands.

They both jerked but kept their hands linked.

"What in the hell was that?" TJ asked her.

She shook her head. "I have no idea, although I assume it was static electricity." Gripping his hand tighter, she began to lead the way out from the hallway. But what she did know for certain was she would never tell her mother about that electric charge that had sparked. Her mother, without doubt, would tell her it was a sign she'd found her destiny because that was precisely what her mother had told her years ago lit the fires between her parents the first time they'd met.

"Hey now," the drunk said, and TJ winced. He should have known the guy would not make it easy on himself and end his pursuit of the woman. "If she's your damn wife, where's her wedding ring?"

Oh good, an observant drunk.

It was the woman who was quick with an answer. She did not stop her forward motion as she looked over her shoulder at the man and told him, "I left it at the jewelers to be cleaned. Jackass."

TJ had to bite his bottom lip so he would not voice the laugh that bubbled up.

That seemed to satisfy the drunk. At least he did not follow them, although TJ could feel the man's eyes on them as the woman, still gripping his hand, led him out of the hallway.

He tugged her toward the dance floor where others were dancing to Talk To Me.

"I'm with-" she managed to get those two words out before TJ took her by the waist and reeled her into him as he began moving to the beat of the music.

"That guy's still watching us," he said. Reaching for her hand, he gave her a spin. Pulling her toward him, he gave her a killer smile. "So, we'll dance for a bit until he gets bored and then I'll escort you back to-" He frowned. "Are you here with a boyfriend? Husband? I should have asked."

"No," she told him breathlessly as she tried to match his steps. "I mean, yes. I'm with some friends."

He grinned. "Good. For a moment, I thought I might have to look out for someone else who would be heading my way other than the drunk."

"What?" she asked, bewilderment in her tone.

The song was coming to its end.

"I think your admirer from the hallway wants to cut in."

She glanced over her shoulder as Janet Jackson's hit song Nasty began coming through the jukebox speakers. Indeed, the man from the hallway was swaying his way toward them. But she had no time to panic as TJ swept her behind him in one smooth move that left her wondering if they were still dancing, or if this man were taking her out of harm's way if that drunk decided to make a scene.

The drunk stopped within a foot of them. "Hey," he said, "it's my turn to dance with her."

"Buddy," TJ said, "get lost. No one dances with her except me."

"Says who?"

TJ shook his head, knowing no one could reason with a drunk. "That would be me."

"Hey, lady. I want to dance with you."

"No," she said, and it was a firm no.

"There's your answer," TJ said. "Back up, turn around, and walk out the door."

"I want to dance with her!" he reached for the woman, but TJ grabbed his hand.

"I tried to be nice, but since you don't seem to have a lick of sense, I'll help you along." TJ moved forward in a flash, wrapped his fists in the man's shirt, pivoted his hip, and flipped the man to the ground.

The dancers stopped as their eyes turned to the person lying on the wooden floor, surprised to see him there.

The drunk lay there, dazed.

"Whoa, Fisher, that was one smooth move," Quinn said at TJ's side. "Didn't know you knew that kind of martial arts shit."

"I have a nephew who insisted everyone in the family learn some basic moves," TJ explained, then looked around the crowd for the woman. He wanted to know her name. Hell, he wanted her phone number. For the first time in a very long while, he was interested in someone he thought he'd like to get to know.

He spotted her standing perhaps six feet away with two women he'd seen here on other nights when getting together with Quinn and Ray. Maybe they were the friends she mentioned moments earlier?

Taking a few steps in that direction, he was able to hear one woman say to her, "Are you sure you're all right, Tabitha?"

TJ grinned. Her name was Tabitha, and the name suited her. The only other time he heard that name was from the TV show Bewitched and oh yes, this Tabitha was definitely enchanting.

He'd almost reached her when someone shouted, "Look out!"

Spinning on his heels, he managed to duck the punch directed at him. But this guy was not the one he'd moments ago introduced to the floor.

"That's my friend you knocked down," the guy shouted.

TJ backed up, held his hands up with his palms up. He chastised himself for not checking to see if the drunk had friends who might take the confrontation farther. In his mind, he could hear his nephew Hunter, a top-ranking martial artist and Navy Seal, telling him he was a fool. He'd always said, "Don't turn your back on the enemy until you know for a fact there's nothing more coming at you."

"Hey," TJ told the guy, "This doesn't need to go any farther. Your friend was harassing a woman and wouldn't take no for an answer."

"That doesn't give you no right to hurt him!"

TJ could see over the man's shoulder that the drunk was already on his feet and did not appear any worse for the wear. "He's fine. Why don't you take your buddy outside and cool off?"

"You need a lesson in manners," the guy hissed and was obviously as drunk as his friend.

Seriously? TJ thought. "Listen, pal, this is ridiculous."

Quinn and Ray appeared, flanking TJ. "We've got you're back, Fisher."

"I can handle one guy," TJ told them.

Quinn pointed. "Apparently you failed to notice the four others with these two imbeciles."

TJ glanced to his right, saw the four men coming his way with fire in their eyes.

"Hell," TJ sighed. If he were his nephew, he'd be able to handle them, but he wasn't Hunter, and he'd need Quinn and Ray's muscle if he were to come out of this without too many bruises.

"You guys need to take this outside!" the bartender shouted.

Everyone in the place had their eyes on the tense situation taking place in the middle of the dance floor.

"Come on," TJ tried to reason. "There is no need for this. Let's just all get back to having a good time."

"It's going to be a good time once we show you what we do to people who hurt one of our own."

"For the love of Christ," TJ murmured, regretting having not knocked the drunk out first thing when he'd come upon him harassing the woman named Tabitha. He could have left him lying in the hallway with no one here the wiser.

"Outside, or I'm calling the cops," the bartender shouted to be heard.

The four others joined the one confronting TJ, and the original drunk found his courage in numbers because he joined his buddies.

"Asshole," drunk number one exclaimed. "I'm going to teach you a lesson!" And he charged straight at TJ.

The dance floor suddenly housed a different kind of dance as mayhem broke out. There were screams and shouts from the women as their men grappled, pushing and punching each other in a knock the opponent out battle.

TJ's last glimpse of Tabitha, before he was swallowed up in the pandemonium, was of her and her friends walking out the door.

* * *

"Oh my God! Tabitha, what happened in there?!" Grace exclaimed as she and Tabitha, along with Greta, exited Mindy's Over Yonder.

"I have no idea!" Tabitha cried as the three of them all but ran for Grace's car. "When I came out of the bathroom, there was this drunk in the hallway and I became the center of his unwanted attention." She wove around one car, then another. "Things like that don't happen to me!"

"That really sucks. Damn drunks," Greta griped.

"Never mind that!" Grace rummaged through her purse for the keys to her car. "Who was that hot, and I do mean hot, guy you were dancing with?"

"I don't know!" Tabitha exclaimed, glancing back at the bar's entrance. "He just suddenly appeared in the hallway and pulled me onto the dance floor and away from the drunk."

Grace opened her car door, stared over the roof at Tabitha. "Tell me you at least know his name."

Tabitha shook her head. "Maybe I could go back in and ask him?" She took a step in that direction.

Greta stopped her. "Don't be ridiculous! You can't go back in there. Not now, when there's a fight going on and the cops will probably be here any minute. The clinic does not need the bad press if you're seen in there. And I won't even mention what could happen if you, for whatever reason, got arrested!"

"Me?! I didn't do anything! It was that crazy drunk that started the whole thing."

"And until that gets sorted out, they could plaster your picture all over the front page of the morning's paper."

Tabitha bit her lip, gave one last longing look at the bar's entrance. She had been having the time of her life dancing with a man she'd connected to in ways she had not experienced before, not even with Owen. She wanted to know who that handsome guy was.

But sensibility stopped her. Greta was right. She had her practice to think of and above that, Abby. Tabitha could just envision the conversation she would endure with Owen's parents if she were to get arrested. It wouldn't matter to them if she was innocent of wrongdoing. Abby's judgmental grandparents were always looking for something to condemn her for.

"By the stars, a curse on that drunk!" Tabitha exclaimed, pulling open the passenger door.

Her companions stared at her for a beat, then burst into laughter.

"Do you know how long it's been since we've heard you use that, by the stars, curse?" Greta asked, opening the back-passenger door. "Normally you just say phooey when you're mad."

"I'm beyond mad," Tabitha admitted, climbing into Grace's car.

Grace chuckled, "Gosh, I'd hate to hear what you'd say if you were full out furious."

"Well, it wouldn't be fiddlesticks, I promise you that," Tabitha claimed, which brought forth another round of laughter.

"So," Grace said, easing her car out of the parking lot. "Now we have a mystery on our hands." She glanced at Greta through the rearview mirror. "We have to find out who that guy is for our Tabby."

"I hate that nickname, you know," Tabitha said.

"I know." Grace grinned.

"I think I've seen him there before," Greta told them. "We'll have to stake out the place from now on."

"Oh god, that is so teenager," Tabitha groaned.

"I know, but it would be fun. And who knows, maybe we'll get lucky."

A police car raced past them, going in the opposite direction, with lights and sirens going full out towards Mindy's Over Yonder.

"I hope he's okay," Tabitha said, glancing behind her toward the bar.

"Maybe he'll get arrested, and his name will be in the paper."

"Grace! As much as I want to know who he is, I certainly don't want him put in jail! Especially because he was trying to protect me from that dumb drunk."

"I was only trying to look for a silver lining."

Tabitha shook her head at her friend's logic.

Settling back into the seat, Tabitha crossed her fingers. She could only hope no one, especially him, would be hurt or thrown into jail tonight.

Chapter five

TJ ached all over. Spending time in his hot tub last night after his unplanned trip to the police station hadn't helped a bit with soothing the soreness. It was precisely why he had not wanted to fight that damn drunk, whose name he found out during the arrest, was Kip Bachmeyer.

He hated the aches and pains that came with fighting.

And what pissed him off the most was the fact the very person he'd been drawn into a fight over had vacated the building without a backward glance.

Those enormous amber eyes of hers sucked him in before he realized it. He'd instantly wanted to protect her, which was absurd. He was no one's champion. Not that he would standby and allow a man to harass a woman, but something happened when he'd taken her hand. Some emotion he could not identify jolted through him. A connection to her he never felt with Heather, and he had thought he was in love with that bitch. So much so he'd given her a ring, and they set the wedding date.

The dance with Tabitha caused his heart to pulsate, and not because the dance was vigorous. She'd been so in tune with his lead it felt as though she were an extension of himself.

How was that possible? He had experienced nothing like it in his life.

He'd been detained at the police station for over an hour while the officers decided whether to book him for whatever reason they could find would stick. Fortunately, they let him go before he called his lawyer, who happened to be his brother. Aaron would have been annoyed to receive a call from him at 2 AM, and even less excited about the idea of flying all the way from North Dakota just to deal with this mess.

What he wanted now was to find that woman. He wanted to know if last night's connection was because of the circumstance, or if there really was an attraction between them.

Not that he was looking for a permanent relationship. Having almost gone down that road once had soured him on marriage, but he was not opposed to dating, as long as she understood it wouldn't go any farther than the bedroom.

That vivid dream of her he'd had last night promised the sex would be good. They'd made love on a sunny beach until the tide came in.

He'd woken up with an erection hard enough to cause a tent in the sheet.

The hammer he was using on the nail going into the sheetrock in the bathroom of the project house missed, and a large hole appeared in the new wall, bringing his mind back to the job.

"Son of a bitch," he yelled.

Quinn, running wire past the doorway, glanced in. "Ouch," he said, viewing the sizable hole.

"Not a word," TJ told him.

Quinn shrugged. "I don't know what you're complaining about. You're not the one with the black eye."

TJ grinned. "Well, I'm not jealous of the one you got."

"At least my wife had some sympathy for me last night. We played doctor-patient, and I wasn't even feeling this shiner by the time she was done."

"I don't think I want to hear about your sex life."

"Why? Because you missed out?" Quinn burst out laughing at TJ's scowl. "I'm not sure how Ray fared. I haven't talked to him today."

"I did. He told me the same thing. Linda made his boo-boo go away."

"It's too bad that lady got away. I'm sure she could have done something about that bruise on your cheek and cut on your lip."

TJ grunted as he stood up.

"Anyway," Quinn continued. "The kitchen wirings done. I'm moving into the living room next. Looks as though I should be finished up with everything by tomorrow."

The hammering from the roof was a steady beat above them as the new shingles were nailed into place by the roofing company. They and Glen had told him the same thing. Everyone would be done with what he hired them for by quitting time tomorrow.

"Great. Fine." TJ set the hammer down and walked out to his truck. There was too much activity taking place at the house, so he opted to sit on his truck's tailgate while he drank some water and tried to get that woman out of his head.

A car he had not seen before pulled into the driveway next door. An older gentleman stepped out at the same time an elderly woman did from the passenger side. They opened the backdoor of the vehicle and out popped Abby.

TJ frowned. Hadn't he seen this scenario play out on Monday? But this older couple were not the same ones from that day.

They were halfway up the driveway when the front door to the house opened, and the woman he'd guessed was the child's grandmother, and lived next door, stepped out.

"Grandma!" Abby's joyous shout reached his ears as her little legs raced to the woman and threw her arms around her grandmother's knees.

She was the cutest kid he had ever seen, and he was an expert on children considering he had forty-five nieces and nephews and was a great uncle to eighteen others.

He loved children and had hoped to have a house full of them one day, but when he called off the wedding to Heather, that dream vanished along with the bitch.

The couple stood on the front lawn, speaking with the lady who lived next door. Abby ran for the garage and was out in a flash, riding that tricycle of hers as though she were flying on it.

TJ grinned. He could not seem to help himself as the little daredevil cruised down the sidewalk as fast as her short legs could pump the peddles. He could appreciate her enjoyment of feeling the power of going fast. Whenever he was in his Porsche and on the open road, he pushed the limits.

Abby spun the trike around and headed back up the walk.

What she needed, TJ mused, was one of those Big Wheel things. They were lower to the ground and safer for those sharp turns she liked to make and were less likely to tip over.

He wondered why Abby's dad hadn't gotten her one. Surely the guy knew his daughter liked speed and would want to keep her safe.

And she needed a helmet to protect her head if that trike tipped over.

The more he thought about it, the angrier he got regardless of the fact Abby was none of his business. He was not a fan of irresponsible parents.

As expected, Abby made a beeline toward him.

She was smart enough to stop five feet away from him. He was unsure if that was because he had told her she should not get too close to someone she didn't know, or if perhaps her grandmother issued a warning.

"Hi, TJ!" She waved her little hand at him. "What'cha doing?"

"I'm taking a break from my work," he answered, making sure he did not move a muscle as he could see they were being watched by the group on the lawn. "And drinking some water. What did you do today?"

She wrinkled her nose. "I was with grandma and grandpa Turner."

It was easy enough to read between the lines. It was apparent Abby was not a fan of that pair of grandparents.

"They have a winno bagle."

He cocked his head to the side as he tried to decipher that. "A what?"

"A winno bagle!" she exclaimed in an exasperated voice, as though he should understand what that was.

"Oh, right!" he said, though he had no clue. "What did you do with the winno bagle?"

"I slept in it last night." She lowered her voice as though conspiring. "In a campground."

"Oh!" he threw his head back and laughed. "A Winnebago!" It was obvious now she was talking about a motorhome.

She looked at him as though he were an idiot. "That's what I said! A winno bagle."

"So, you did."

She eyed him. "What happen to your cheek?"

Gingerly, he reached up and touched it. "I ran into something." He would not tell her that something had been a fist.

"What?"

"What?"

"What did you run into?"

"A door," he told her as it was the best explanation he could come up with put on the spot like that.

"Ouch. Did your mom kiss it? My mommy kisses my ouwies."

He shook his head. "My mom lives far away."

She frowned. "Did the door cut your lip?"

"Yes," time to turn this conversation around. "Did you have fun in the campground?"

Abby shook her head. "Grandma and Grandpa Turner don't know how to have fun." She sighed dramatically. "Grandma Turner wants me to sit next to her so she can read me her dumb stories and pray."

"Reading's a good thing, Abby." He tried to encourage her.

She shook her head. "Not when Grandma Turner reads to me."

"What does she read to you?"

Abby wrinkled her nose. "She read me a story about witches being evil." She rolled her eyes. "Dumb book."

TJ stared, cocked his head. To his mind, that seemed to be a strange subject to read about to a three-year-old. "What else does she read to you?" Hopefully there was something the child enjoyed.

"About Badlands. She said they were going there and would take me with them."

He did not find it unusual for grandparents to want to take a grandchild on a road trip. "I like the Badlands," he grinned. "Did she mention where they were?" The Badlands spread out among the states, but he knew the ones in his home state.

"Northdah Koda," Abby told him.

He chuckled. "Those are the best ones."

Again, she shook her head and rolled her eyes. "Boring."

He changed the subject because it was apparent she had no interest in learning about geography. "You spend a lot of time with the grandparents that live next door. They must babysit you when your mom and dad are working," he hedged, trying to understand why she spent the day with the older couple.

Okay. He was using the kid as an informant. Sue him.

"Yep. Mommy works all day."

"And what does your dad do?"

She shook her head. "No daddy. Only mommy and me."

Well, that answered his question as to why her father had not thought about her safety.

He wanted to quiz her more but bit his tongue.

"Well, sometimes all you need is a mom," he told her. "And now I think you need to go back because your grandparents seem a little nervous that you're over here talking to me. So, off you go before one of them comes over here and socks me in the nose for talking to you."

She giggled.

But she did not argue. She turned the trike around and headed back toward her grandparents.

Jumping from the truck's tailgate, TJ realized talking to Abby was a highlight in his day, and with a smile on his face, he went back to work.

* * *

Tabitha was kept busy Thursday morning.

She repaired a wound a husky received cutting its back open three inches on the bumper of a vehicle. The bumper had a sharp edge the owners had not bothered to fix as they felt their truck was old and not worth the repair cost. Once they got the bill for this procedure and paid for the dog's prescription to help prevent infection, they would wish they had fixed the damn bumper to keep animal and human safe.

Idiots.

After that procedure, a couple brought in their Yorkshire Terrier because it fractured its right leg jumping from their back porch. Thankfully, it was a clean break and would heal nicely.

Then there was the German Shepherd that swallowed the cap that belonged on a plastic bottle. Fortunately, the cap had not lodged in its throat, but she'd had to remove it surgically.

It appeared the animals in Binghamton were hell-bent on finding trouble today. They kept her active with one mishap after another. Which was fine by her. All of it kept her mind off the mystery man from last night.

Worst of all, he invaded her dreams, and she had woken aroused beyond belief. Every part of her had tingled from desire with no way for immediate release because work called. They needed her for an emergency Caesarean section and there was no time to indulge in any self-pleasure. She had not done something like that since she'd been a teenager, but she would have willingly done it this morning had the damn phone not rung. For the first time in a long while, she would not have to fear Abby would suddenly come into her bedroom since she spent the night with the Turners.

Closing time came before Tabitha realized the hour.

Greta was working on sanitation when Tabitha walked into the dispensary.

"I'm pooped," Greta said, placing the last of the sterile instruments into their proper place.

"Tell me about it," Tabitha stretched out her back. "All I want to do is go home and crawl into bed, but I still need to pick up Abby from my folk's. I hope she had fun with Owen's parents. She didn't want to go with them, but I talked her into it."

"Poor kid," Greta grumbled.

Tabitha threw her hands in the air. "Could you cut me some slack? I'm doing the best I can where they're concerned."

Greta sighed. "I know, and I shouldn't have said that. The truth is, I admire you for attempting to keep peace with them when they don't deserve any olive branch at all from you."

"It was for one night, and knowing them, they will leave by tomorrow. Who knows when they'll show up again? And I'll cross that bridge when the time comes. As often as they come around, Abby might be a

teenager by then and can make her own decision if she wants to see them or not."

Greta shrugged, not knowing how to respond.

Grace walked into the room. "The front doors are locked, and I declare it the end of the day."

"You don't have to tell us twice." Tabitha grabbed her purse, dug out her car keys. "We just have to make it through tomorrow, and then we'll have the weekend to recover."

"What kind of exciting things do you have planned for you and Abby this weekend?" Grace asked as she set the building's alarm system.

"Maybe we'll go to the park. We'll see what she wants to do."

They walked out of the building, locked the door, and headed toward their cars.

"So, Tabitha," Grace said, "About that hot guy last night."

Tabitha held up her hands to ward the conversation off. "Seriously, I do not want to talk about it." She did not want that man popping into her head and invading her dreams again tonight.

"Maybe someone at Over Yonder knows who he is," Grace continued, ignoring Tabitha's declaration. "I could ask around. Find out who he is."

"Oh. My. God," Tabitha stopped walking in mid-step. "Do you think I'm that pathetic I need someone to find a man for me?"

Grace's eyes widened. "What?! No! Tabitha, God no. I just want to help! We all saw the sparks flying between the two of you, and it was nice to see you with someone…" she trailed off as Tabitha's eyes continued to stare at her.

"Listen," Tabitha said, gentling her voice. "If it's meant for me to see him again, it will happen."

Grace touched Tabitha's arm. "I'm sorry. We just want you to be happy" She trailed off again. "I'm going to shut my mouth now before I totally screw our friendship up."

Tabitha smiled. "I know you care about me, okay?"

"But he sure was hot," Greta sighed dreamily, causing them to laugh, and Tabitha would not deny that truth.

Without much more conversation, they parted ways and drove off in their separate directions.

When Tabitha arrived at her parents, it was just in time to see the tail-lights of a truck backing up from the driveway next door and head down the street away from her.

She had to admire the dedication that person had to their job. It was after six in the evening.

"Mommy!" Abby exclaimed with her usual gusto when Tabitha walked into the house.

"Hi, Scooby. Were you good for grandma and grandpa Turner?"

"I let grandma read her dumb books to me."

Tabitha's lips twitched. "It was nice of you to let her do that," although she knew her daughter did not enjoy anything the Turners wanted to engage her with. She moved into the living room, but her mother told her supper was ready, and she might as well come into the dining room and sit at the table.

She was so fortunate not to have to cook after work.

"What kind of book was it?"

"Evil witches and Badlands." Abby sighed dramatically. "Dumb books," she repeated.

Tabitha glanced at her mother, narrowed her eyes, and firmed her lips. She would not bash Peggy Turner in front of Abby, but the fact the woman would dare read to her about witches being bad caused her to see red. It also confirmed her suspicions that the woman still believed their son married an evil witch, and that was why he was dead.

Having been raised Wiccan did not make her a witch, although her parents practiced the craft, and Tabitha had too. It was not the kind of sorcery the Turner's faith twisted around and deemed evil. Because of their ignorance, they believed Tabitha and her parents were heathens.

Pagan yes. Heathen, absolutely not.

Angela cleared her throat. "When they dropped Abby off this afternoon, they announced they were going to stay in Binghamton for a little while and would call you to set up another overnight with Abby."

Tabitha tried not to make a face. "That's surprising," she managed to say without sarcasm.

Then her mind clicked with something else her daughter mentioned. "Did you say Badlands?"

Abby nodded.

There was that word again, reminding Tabitha of the construction company, Badland Builders.

"Why did they read to you about the Badlands?"

Abby shrugged.

"Well," John Stevens said, "It never hurts to learn about other places. That's why it's important to learn to read," John told his granddaughter.

"TJ said reading is good," Abby announced, taking a biscuit from the basket when her grandmother held it out for her.

Tabitha stared at her daughter. "Who is TJ?"

"My friend."

Tabitha looked at her mother, waiting for an answer.

"I believe he is the man working on Doris's house. I keep meaning to go over and introduce myself to him, but I haven't made it there yet. Abby likes to talk to him when she sees him taking a break."

"Mother!" Tabitha exclaimed. "You let Abby talk to some man you don't know? For the love of-"

"I keep my eye on them. He keeps his distance, and he sends her back to me after five minutes."

Like that was okay? "Have you lost your mind? What if he's some kidnapper?"

"I don't get that kind of vibe from him," Angela told her daughter.

Tabitha gasped. "A vibe? Seriously?!"

"Oh now, honey," her mother said, "you were always talking to people you didn't know. I kept my eye out when you were little. You didn't get kidnapped."

"Things were different then!" Tabitha threw her hands up in the air, unable to believe her mother saw nothing wrong with allowing her granddaughter to talk to a stranger.

"Tabitha, I wouldn't let anything happen to her!"

"But you still let her talk to a complete stranger without being with her."

"I told you, I keep my eye on them."

Tabitha made a sound of disgust. Obviously, her mother did not realize the man could scoop Abby up in seconds and drive off with her before her mother could do anything about it.

"Tomorrow, you need to tell him to stay away from Abby."

"Mommy!" Abby whaled. "TJ is nice to me!" She stuck out her bottom lip.

Abby rarely had tantrums, but Tabitha could sense one brewing.

"You cannot visit him without grandma being with you," she compromised.

Abby hung her head. "Okay," her voice showed her disappointment.

"I'll introduce myself to him tomorrow," Angela promised. "Besides, I've been wanting to get a closer look at him. From a distance, he looks vaguely familiar, though I can't seem to place where I may have seen him before."

"Probably on a top ten wanted poster," Tabitha grumbled under her breath.

"Very amusing, young lady," her mother sat down. "I promise, tomorrow I will speak to him."

"And you won't allow Abby to be anywhere near him without being right next to her."

It was a decree.

Angela tisked. "You act as though I don't know how to raise children. I seemed to have done a fine job with the one I had."

Now she had hurt her mother's feelings, and she felt guilt over it.

"I'm sorry, mom. I know you would not willingly allow something to happen to Abby. I'm just asking you to be a little more careful."

Chapter Six

TJ's plan for an early start on the remodel was set back a half-hour. He received an unexpected phone call from his youngest brother. Colten stunned him by announcing he and his wife Jacqueline were planning to drive up from North Dakota in a few weeks to visit him.

The declaration rendered him speechless for almost an entire minute. Colten and Jacqueline hardly traveled outside of North Dakota together. Not because they hadn't wanted to. But they feared Jacqueline's step-brother, Pierre Bellefeuille, would discover the hitman he hired to kill them twenty-four years ago was unsuccessful in accomplishing the mission. If Pierre found out the truth, there was no doubt in anyone's mind, the man would come after them intending to finish the job.

"I'm honored you want to visit me," TJ said at last, "and I have the room for you at my place so you won't have to stay at a hotel, but why would you risk traveling?" he asked his brother.

"Well," Colten said, "After all these years, everyone involved believes it's safe enough for us to leave the state. And I don't have to worry about running the ranch since my son-in-law is capable of overseeing everything. Hell, Jake's so organized and efficient I'm feeling like a fifth wheel around here."

TJ laughed.

"So," Colten continued. "My wife and I decided it was high time we drove to Pennsylvania and visit the Davidsons instead of them coming here to see us. Besides, the two of us are long overdue for a vacation together. And since Binghamton isn't that far from Clarion, so my wife tells me, we might as well come that way too and see my baby brother."

"I suppose since Jacqueline attended college in Clarion, she knew that off the top of her head."

Colten chuckled. "She told me she may have attended some parties in Binghamton with some friends during that time, but she'll deny it if I tell the kids that tidbit about their mother."

Now it was TJ's turn to laugh. "When can I expect you?"

"In about a week. Maybe a week and a half? We'll finalize the plans and let you know when we've pinned down the exact day."

"I'm looking forward to it."

TJ hung up the phone with a smile on his face.

He gathered up the power tools, and portable table saw, placed them in the back of his pickup, and headed toward the project house. Now that the wiring was complete, he was in no danger of blowing a fuse when he plugged in something requiring a lot of power into a socket. And it was nice to have the bathroom functioning. He no longer had to use the porta-potty whenever he needed to relieve himself.

Pulling up into the driveway of the project house, he glanced at the home next door and wondered when Abby would make her appearance today. He guessed it would be around two, as that seemed to be when she was typically allowed out of the house to ride her trike while her grandmother worked in the yard.

Maybe today he would get a glimpse of Abby's mom, and why he wanted to know what the woman looked like he could not say, but the interest was there.

Was Abby's mom divorced?

And damn it. Why was he speculating about Abby and her mother? They were none of his business.

He forced himself to concentrate on the business at hand and worked through the morning, finishing texturing the bathroom's drywall. It would be good and dry by the time he painted it later next week.

When he was ready for a break, knowing he was timing it according to when Abby usually came around, he went outside and sat down on the front porch to wait. As he reached into the cooler he set there earlier, he smiled to himself when he heard the garage door open. Looking up, he grinned when Abby, like clockwork, shot out from the garage like a bullet leaving a gun on that trike of hers.

However, this time, she did not make her usual path down the street but made a beeline toward him. More surprising, he saw her grand-mother walking his way as well.

The grandmother, if that was who the woman was, seemed young. Per-haps in her fifties. TJ's own parents were both in their eighties. He had been an oopsie baby. His parents had not planned on having more chil-dren after Colten was born. After three sets of twins and three single births, Barbra and Donald had more than fulfilled their dream of having a house full of children. But eighteen years after Colten's birth, Barbra Fisher, who had been forty-five at the time, surprised her husband by informing him he was going to be a father once again.

So much for their plans to be empty nesters. They had to wait another eighteen years before they were free to travel without children or ar-ranging a sitter for him, although usually one of his brothers or sisters took on that roll if need be.

Fortunately, Barbra and Donald had not resented that fact. Otherwise, TJ's life might have been a lot different. But his parents had been ex-cited to have another child to raise. He never lacked for love, but he had not been coddled.

"Hi, TJ!" Abby waved and stopped her trike on the sidewalk in front of him. "My grandma wants to meet you."

TJ smiled, stood up, and nodded to the woman who was just catching up to her granddaughter. "Hi," he said, walking forward and extending his hand to the woman. "I'm TJ Fisher."

J.R. Zimmer

Angela reached out, shook the offered hand. "I've been meaning to come over here and introduce myself." Before Angela released TJ's hand, she turned it over, examined his palm. A smile curved her lips as though pleased at whatever she'd seen in his calloused palm as she said, "I'm Angela Stevens."

Weird, was TJ's thought as he brought his hand back to his side and felt as though he'd just had his future read. "It's nice to meet you," he said, wondering if the woman was a bit eccentric.

Angela's smile didn't fade as she told him, "It appears my granddaughter enjoys talking with you. I hope she isn't a bother when she gets to talking your ear off."

TJ laughed. "Ma'am, I have numerous nieces and nephews, and one of my nephews has autism. He is high functioning, but he obsesses over the darndest things. He will tell you about whatever he is obsessing over at the time on a constant repeat. One little girl couldn't possibly talk my ear off."

Now it was Angela's turn to laugh. "That explains why you seem to be so patient with her. And I appreciate it that you keep your distance and send her back to my place after five to ten minutes."

TJ shrugged. "I'm a stranger. I asked her that first day if anyone has told her she shouldn't talk to strangers. Then she asked my name and claimed we weren't strangers since we knew each other's names."

"That sounds like her," Angela stated.

"Grandma," Abby patted the woman's pant leg, "Can I talk to TJ now?"

He looked down at the little cherub and smiled. "Grandma wants to make sure you're safe, and I don't blame her." He met Angela's eyes and grinned. "I have references if that would make you feel better. They can tell you I'm not a psychopath. Or you can lay the ground rules. I don't mind talking to Abby during the day for a short time."

60

Angela was silent for a moment. Every instinct she had told her she could trust this man, but Tabitha would be furious if she mentioned that again.

"Do you have children, Mr. Fisher?"

"Call me TJ and no. I have no children."

"Are you married?" Angela almost blushed when she realized she said that out loud.

"No." There was a chuckle in his voice.

"I'm sorry. I don't mean to give you the third degree."

"I understand completely. You want to keep the little munchkin safe."

She breathed a sigh of relief. "Thank you. I appreciate you understanding."

"Not a problem."

"Can I ask you another question?"

"Sure," TJ said, chuckling.

"You look vaguely familiar to me. Have we met be-fore?"

"No, ma'am."

She frowned, trying to picture where she had seen him before, but the more Angela tried to bring up the image, she got the impression it was someone she had seen a long time ago.

An image of a cowboy hat formed in her mind, and as she observed TJ, she could almost see the person she thought he resembled.

And then the memory was gone.

With a shrug, Angela let the recollection fade.

As she continued to converse with TJ, she wished Tabitha could meet this man. His palm revealed he was trustworthy and kind to others. If Tabitha could talk to him, she would see for herself he was no threat to Abby.

Good looking too.

And single.

She grinned as the idea formed, and she said, "If you don't have plans for this evening, perhaps you would like to come to my house for supper? We eat at six."

Abby nodded her head, clapped her hands with enthusiasm. "Please, TJ? Mommy can see you are not on a wanted poster." She frowned, looked up at her grandmother. "What is a wanted poster, grandma?"

The sound Angela made was somewhere between a laugh and a groan. It embarrassed her that Abby would bring up that comment Tabitha made last night.

TJ knelt so he could be at Abby's eye level. "A wanted poster is what law enforcement uses to display pictures of bad men."

Abby frowned, shook her head. "You're not a bad man. Mommy is silly."

"I think your mom wants to keep you safe." He looked up at Angela. "It would be my honor to have supper with you tonight, Mrs. Stevens," he told her, surprising himself. He did not understand what prompted him to say yes, but he could do that much to ease the woman's mind. If they got to know him, he would no longer be in the stranger category.

"My husband and I will look forward to it. And it will put Tabitha's mind at ease."

TJ, in the process of standing, he almost stumbled upon hearing that name. "Tabitha?"

Angela laughed. "My daughter. Abby's mother." She held up her hands, "and yes, I know. Naming her Tabitha when our last name is Stevens wasn't the best choice. But that television show Bewitched didn't come out until well after she was born, but she heard enough jokes about being the daughter of Samantha Stevens growing up. She wished she had magical powers so she could turn everyone into toads."

He was still trying to wrap his head around the fact Abby's mother's name was Tabitha.

It could not be the same woman from Over Yonder, could it?

He shook his head as though he were answering his own question. But this time, when he looked at Abby, he could almost see a resemblance to the woman he danced with Wednesday night. They both had huge amber-colored eyes that sucked him in.

Or perhaps he was only seeing something that was not there.

Abby climbed off the trike, ran up to TJ, and hugged his legs. The gesture surprised both Angela and TJ. "Yeah! I'm so happy! And mommy can see you are not a napper!"

TJ glanced at Angela. If the woman's flushed face was a sign, he figured he could assume there had been speculation about the man who talked to Abby, and if he might kidnap the child.

"No," he said, patting the top of her head, and felt a strange emotion in his heart at the feel of this little girl holding him tight, "I am not a napper."

"Come along, Abby. I'm going to need your help to get things ready for when Mr. Fisher comes over tonight."

"Okay!" Abby exclaimed, twirling a little as she almost danced back to her trike.

TJ waved goodbye and went back to work with a smile on his face. He wasn't sure if the smile was because Abby had thrown him a kiss as she turned her trike around, or because he was hoping her mother was the same woman from Over Yonder.

* * *

Tabitha was running late. A last-minute emergency prevented her from leaving the clinic on time. A car had hit a dog, and its frantic owner rushed the poor animal to the nearest veterinarian clinic. The dog's back leg had been broken in three places. That was the bad news. Fortunately, the Border Collie had no internal bleeding or other life-threatening injuries that would require the animal to spend the night at the clinic.

Now, as she eased her Ford Taurus into the driveway of her parent's house, she noted there was a black 911 Turbo Porsche parked in the street in front of the house, and she wondered who it belonged to.

She exited her vehicle, dismissing the Porsche. However, she wondered who her parents knew who had that kind of money to afford the beautiful car.

As she reached for the doorknob of the front door, it opened before her hand touched the metal.

"Mommy!" Abby exclaimed, hugging Tabitha's legs briefly. "We have been waiting for you!"

"I know, Scooby-Doo. I'm sorry I'm-"

"TJ is here!"

"What?"

"Grandma asked him to come eat with us!" She did a little spin to show her excitement.

Tabitha glanced at the couch where her father sat with their guest.

She visibly jerked when her eyes met his.

"Hi," TJ said as he stood up. "It is nice to see you again."

John Stevens glanced between them. "You two know each other?"

"We met Wednesday night at Over Yonder," TJ explained as he took a few steps toward Tabitha. His eyes held hers captive. "Unfortunately, she left before we were properly introduced. And I was a little busy at the time of her exit to stop her."

Tabitha had no words. It was a shock to her system, seeing the man who invaded her dreams these past two nights standing in front of her. And that bruise on his face reminded her why she'd allowed Greta and Grace to remove her from the premises that evening.

She should say something to at least acknowledge he had rescued her from that drunk. "I do appreciate what you did for me." It was a lame opening line, and she knew it.

His smile showed his teeth. "Which part? My getting into a brawl because of that drunk I rescued you from or helping you out of that situation in the first place? After you left, they escorted me to the police station." He sighed. "That was my least favorite part of the entire night, believe it or not."

She winced and felt both of her parents staring at her.

"Tabitha!" her mother exclaimed, "You didn't mention there had been a fight at the bar Wednesday night!"

TJ knew he should not have put Tabitha on the spot like that, but he'd been a tad upset she would just walk out the door without a backward glance when the whole thing had been about her. Granted, there had been a chance she would have gotten hurt, so he should be glad she hadn't been, but it still grated she'd left before he'd obtained her phone number.

He looked over his shoulder at Angela Stevens. "Just a small one," he assured the woman, although that was a whopper of a lie. Mindy's Over Yonder had been forced to hire a crew to clean up the damage and lost half a day's business as the place was put back together. They'd had to set up temporary tables to replace the three that suffered damage from being overturned and their legs broken off to be used as clubs.

Tabitha cleared her throat. "There were reasons I needed to leave," she murmured, taking Abby's hand in hers when her daughter came up alongside her.

TJ glanced down at Abby and considered that she was likely one of those reasons. He could understand why she wouldn't want to be discovered at a bar while there was a fight going on. "Then I look forward to finding out what those reasons are. But not now. I will consider it water under the bridge if we can both agree to begin anew. I was hoping to run into you again, and I guess we have Abby to thank for wanting to be my friend. It is an amazing coincidence to discover you are her mother."

John Stevens chuckled. "There is no such thing as coincidence's, young man. It was fate. Obviously, Abby was drawn to you for a reason."

Tabitha absolutely did not want her parents starting a conversation about chances and omens. "I can agree to start over," she told TJ.

He grinned.

"The food's ready, so perhaps we can all move to the table and share a meal?" Angela suggested.

"I want to sit by TJ," Abby declared.

"Why don't you sit here," John told his granddaughter as he rearranged the chairs, placing the one that held her booster seat between two others. "TJ can sit here, and mommy can sit there. That way, you can sit next to both of them."

"Yeah!" Abby said and wiggled herself up onto her chair.

TJ held out his hand toward the table. "Ladies first," he said, and held the chair for her as Tabitha sat down at her spot at the table.

John and Angela shared a look between them.

"I'm sorry I'm late, mom," Tabitha managed to say although she was still dazed.

"It's all right. We know sometimes you get delayed because of work."

"What kind of work do you do?" TJ asked as he sat down next to Abby.

Abby sat up straight and said proudly, "Mommy is a Narian."

Placing his attention on Abby, he said, "A what?"

"A Narian," Abby repeated as though everyone knew what a Narian was.

Tabitha came to his rescue by saying, "Veterinarian."

"Oh!" TJ laughed. "I was trying to figure out what a Narian was."

"You're silly," Abby told him. "Narian's help animals. Do you have a pet? Mommy would take good care of it if it got sick."

"No. No pets."

Abby's eyes grew enormous, and she used an accusing tone as she asked, "You don't like animals?"

Why he felt the need to defend himself to a three-year-old, he would never know. "Yes, I like animals. Dogs, cats. Even horses. One of my brothers owns a horse ranch in North Dakota, and I've learned to ride one, but I don't have the time to give a pet the attention it deserves."

"Thank you," Tabitha said quietly.

His eyes went to her, and he raised a brow. "Thank you for-?"

"Being responsible. So many people get a pet without realizing the commitment needed, then are irresponsible dweebs and discard the animal when they no longer want the job of caring for it. They drive out to the country and push the animal out of the car and assume it will fend for itself." She sat back, shook her head. "I'll stop with that. Otherwise, once I get started, I get a little heated over the injustice."

TJ agreed with Tabitha. He had no place in his life for people who discarded pets as though they were disposable commodities, either.

Wait a minute. "Did you just say, dweeb?" TJ asked.

Tabitha gave a quick nod. "Yes, I did. The word I wanted to use is not suited for my daughter's ears."

With a twinkle in his eye, TJ laughed. "Understood."

John stood up, lit the white candle in the center of the table. "It is time for the blessing," he said, picking up the candle. He brought it to the white tea candle set at the top of his place setting, lit it, and passed the candle to his wife. She did the same with the tea candle at her place setting.

TJ watched Angela pass the candle to Tabitha. She mimicked her parents, lighting the candle at her place setting, then passed the candle to TJ.

He wasn't sure what this ritual was, but he followed along and lit the candle at his setting. Not knowing what else to do, since all the candles seemed to be lit, he placed the larger candle back in its holder at the table's center.

John grinned; clapped his hands. "Now that the circle is complete let's eat."

"Blessed be!" Abby exclaimed.

"Blessed be," Tabitha and her parents echoed.

As far as prayers went, TJ thought, that was the shortest one he'd been privy to. Nor had he heard it closed without an Amen. Not that he cared. He was not a spiritual person.

"Did you say you are from North Dakota?" Angela asked as everyone once again sat down and began passing the food around.

"Yes, ma'am. Born and raised in its capital, Bismarck. I moved to the Big Apple twelve years ago, but I moved here when I discovered I no longer liked the rat race there."

"We can agree on that, young man," John told him. "I have no use for the place myself."

Something Magical

"Mommy," Abby pushed the peas around on her plate as she tried to figure out how she could hide them with no one knowing. "Can we go to the zoo tomorrow?"

"If you clean your room and help me with laundry, yes."

It was fun to watch Abby's face as she struggled between having to do the dreaded chores, yet knowing it led to a trip to the zoo. "Okay," she said, in that dramatic sigh of hers. "Can TJ come too?"

All the adults froze, surprised Abby would make the request, although they shouldn't have been. For whatever reason, Abby was drawn to TJ.

Tabitha was the first to unthaw. "I'm sure TJ has a lot of things he wants to get done tomorrow."

"You know what," TJ said, "Where I come from, our zoo is fairly small, but it has a Kodiak bear who is considered the world's largest bear in captivity. He stands nine feet tall and weighs almost 2000 pounds. His name is Clyde; his wife's name is Bonnie."

"Mate," Tabitha corrected.

TJ chuckled. "Not much difference. They're stuck together regardless of what you want to call their relationship."

Tabitha stared at him.

Abby was looking up at him with those huge puppy dog eyes of hers. "Will you come with us? To the zoo."

God, those eyes could pierce his heart like nothing else could. And yet, he could admit they were not the only reason a trip to the zoo with mother and daughter appealed to him. It would give him more of an opportunity to spend time with Tabitha. He wanted to explore what it was about her that reached out to him.

He asked Abby, "Will you help your mom without complaining about it?"

Again, that climactic sigh passed the girl's lips, and TJ thought about introducing Mason Lafayette's mother to this little ham. Rosalinda would appreciate the child's ability to create an effect. "Okay," she said.

"All right then, if your mom does not object, I'll go to the zoo with you tomorrow."

John and Angela glanced at each other. A slight smile curved their lips. There were no coincidences. The goddess had drawn Abby to TJ. Now they needed to trust the powers of nature to do its magic.

Chapter Seven

Tabitha agreed to have TJ pick her and Abby up at her house at two the following afternoon. She wrote down her address and phone number for him and wondered at the same time if it was a wise decision.

Now that Saturday afternoon was here, and lunch was over, the clock showed the fast approaching pickup time.

Tabitha took the last towel from the dryer, folded it, and set it on top of the stack she'd already created. Scooping the pile up, she walked them into the bathroom and put them away in the cupboard.

Then she looked at her reflection in the mirror and silently asked herself how a stranger was wiggling his way into her life so quickly.

It was because of Abby. Somehow fate had chosen TJ to work on Doris's old house, knowing his kindness would attract her daughter to him. Abby, Tabitha knew, was looking for a father figure.

All of Abby's friends at the daycare she went to on Wednesday mornings, as that was the day her mother went out with friends to have coffee and catch up on whatever the latest gossip was, had dads, and Abby begun to wonder why she did not have one.

"Sally's dad picked her up. Lifted her high in the air!"

"Tommy's dad took him fishing. I wish I could go fishing."

"Amanda's dad took her to the park, and they played in the sand."

"Jeff's dad took him to a ballgame! He said it was fun! I want to go to a ballgame."

"Dawn's dad-"

"Enough!" Tabitha hissed at her reflection as her mind replayed all the conversations about dad's Abby was bringing up lately. She thought she was prepared for when and if her daughter would begin bringing up the lack of a father in this house. But she had been wrong. And it didn't help that Tabitha's own attraction for TJ Fisher was tangible.

God, she had not had sex for so long she was going insane!

And he owned a Porsche. She had no idea how in the hell he could afford it. The subject of what he did for a living did not come up last night. But since he was working on that house next to her parent's place, he obviously did construction work though she did not know which company he worked for.

But that car was as hot as he was.

And now she was expected to spend the afternoon with the man because her daughter finagled him into saying yes to a trip to the zoo.

Tabitha could not believe TJ hadn't made up some excuse to turn Abby down. But it was apparent he had the patience of a saint. What other man would put up with a three-year-old stranger interrupting his day? Then spend time talking with the child when he had every right to tell her to get lost.

She told herself the lure pulling her toward a man she basically just met was nothing more than lust. TJ Fisher was beyond handsome. There was no denying that. The first time she'd seen him at the bar, her libido was affected like never before when her eyes met his and felt herself falling into the darkest brown eyes she'd ever encountered. And that stubble of a beard and mustache he favored gave him a sexy come join me in bed appeal.

Tabitha moaned. His image formed in her mind and caused her skin to tingle.

"Mommy, are you okay?"

Jerking her forehead off from the bathroom mirror, where she had lowered it in her distress, Tabitha stared at her daughter. "What?"

"You made a funny sound."

Oh. God.

"I'm fine, Scooby-Doo." She truly could use a cold shower. "Did you finish cleaning your room?"

Abby nodded.

"Is it ready for inspection?"

With a small salute, the child said, "Yes!"

"All right. Give me a moment, and I'll be right there."

"Okay!" Abby scampered off.

Tabitha grabbed a washcloth from the vanity, ran it under cold water, rang it out, and held it against her face. She would need to redo her make-up but did not care.

The doorbell rang just as Tabitha finished reapplying cosmetics to her face. She took a deep breath and prayed she would make it through this outing without doing something foolish by pouncing on the guy.

Her biological urge was under control by the time she opened the door. TJ, stood outside her front door, leaning against the door frame gave her the impression he was a man of easy confidence. But his tight-fitting jeans and T-shirt stretching across his chest, outlining a sculpted physique, did little to assist her in maintaining that self-control.

Then he smiled and she swallowed the urge to say, yum.

There should be a law about having a smile that was killer enough to cause her knees to go weak.

"Hi," he said. "If this is awkward for you-"

He had no idea how true his statement was but she managed to come out from the ridiculous fantasy she'd just had.

"No, it's fine," she assured him. "And Abby would be upset if you backed out now."

"She's a great kid."

Tabitha nodded. "She is. Now, if you'll excuse me one moment, I was about to inspect her room. She told me it was clean, but I suspect she threw a few things under the bed."

He laughed. "That would be what I would have done."

Tabitha opened the door wider. "Come in. You can wait in the living room if you would like. This won't take long." She motioned toward the living room area and moved off to inspect Abby's room.

While Tabitha was busy with her daughter, TJ entered the living room, scanned the space; pleased to note it was neat and tidy.

There were photos on the wall—all of them of Abby at some stage of development. And even as a baby, Abby had been adorable.

He slowly walked around the room, looking for other photos. Strictly to pass the time while he waited. Not because he was looking for clues about Abby's dad, although when he spotted a framed photo on the side table next to the couch, he noted a younger Tabitha smiling at the young man standing with her in the picture.

Was this Abby's dad?

He was about to reach out to grasp the frame and bring it closer for a better view, but mother and daughter walked into the room, preventing him from doing so.

For some odd reason, TJ felt as though they caught him doing something sinister, though he had done nothing wrong.

"TJ!" Abby exclaimed, running to him.

When she leaped, instinct had him reaching out to catch her before she went crashing onto the floor.

She giggled and wrapped her arms around his neck.

Tabitha tried hard not to be jealous of her daughter being held by the man.

TJ set Abby down. "Are you ready to go?" His eyes locked with Tabitha's. Even with that deer in the headlight look she gave him yesterday when she'd entered her parents' house and discovered he was there, he thought she was appealing in ways other women he'd been around weren't. She was slender enough that he knew if he were to put his hands around her waist, he could probably touch his fingertips against each other at the small of her back.

Those gorgeous eyes were outlined with black liner smudged into some shade of light brown eye shadow, creating a smoky effect. Her long lashes held black mascara. Combined with the hint of blush and pink lipstick, she reminded him of a goddess. The crescent-moon pendant around her neck, the long golden earrings, and the off-the-shoulder blouse tucked into the flared chiffon skirt completed the look of mysticism.

No doubt about it. She had to be a witch, and whatever spell she cast on him was doing its job. He was drawn to her like a moth to a flame and as ridiculous as it was, being near her felt familiar; as though they'd known each other in a past life.

He was aware of the fact he was close to being in the danger zone but did not know if he had the will to resist the temptation.

Clearing his throat at the same time he tried to clear his head, he asked, "Are you sure you're all right with this?" He meant if she was comfortable with their going to the zoo together, but he acknowledged the attraction between them.

It was palpable.

"I promised Abby," Tabitha cleared her own throat because damn it, the words came out huskier than they should have.

She felt the air between them sizzle.

"Mommy, can we go now?"

J.R. Zimmer

Abby's voice was a much-needed splash of cold water. Tabitha jerked out from the trance she had fallen into while looking into TJ's dark as sin-colored eyes.

She cleared her throat again. "Yes. That would be a good idea," she told her daughter and dared not look at TJ for fear of becoming hypnotized again.

TJ took Abby's small hand in his larger one and said, "Then, let's get this show on the road."

When they moved outside, TJ asked, "I know Abby needs to be in a car seat. If you would rather take your vehicle, so we don't have to transfer it to my Porsche, let me know."

Tabitha almost laughed. Was there even a debate about this? "I've never been in a Porsche," she hinted.

He grinned. "Then show me how to buckle her booster seat in correctly, and we'll take my car."

It took almost no time to switch Abby's car seat from Tabitha's vehicle into the Porsche. Once everyone was buckled in, and TJ started the engine, Tabitha sat back in the seat and closed her eyes. "Listen to it, purr," she sighed. "It's a god among cars, and it knows it."

TJ could not believe she just voiced his own thoughts regarding his Porsche, and he might have felt his heart quicken to have met a woman who could appreciate his passion for the German automobile. "You're into cars?"

"Not really," she opened her eyes, looked at him. "But when I see one that has the right to be idolized, I can give it the respect it's due."

He might have fallen a little in love with her at that moment.

Without a word, he shifted into gear and pulled the Porsche away from the curb.

They arrived at Ross Park Zoo, located on the northern face of Binghamton's south mountain a short time later. The 90-acre plot of land housing the zoo had been donated to Binghamton's city by a wealthy businessman named Erastus Ross, with the stipulation the land be used as a park for all the community to enjoy. The zoo officially opened in 1875 and was now the fifth oldest zoological institution in the country.

Entering the building where guests paid for entrance into the zoo, TJ automatically reached for his wallet to pay the admission fee, but Tabitha touched his arm. "I do not expect you to pay our way. Abby invited you. It is only right I pay for your passage into the enclosure."

That surprised him, but he shrugged and allowed her to reach into the fanny pack fastened around her trim waist and pay for the tickets. The women he knew, the non-related ones, were always content to let him spend his money on them and never reciprocated.

Well, to be fair, that had been when he'd first moved to New York City and had been naïve. He'd wised up darn quick after Heather. And he reminded himself, Tabitha did not know he could afford to buy the whole place if it went on sale. He wanted to base their friendship on who they were, not on each other's bank accounts.

While mother and daughter browsed a short time in the small gift shop, TJ located the donations box. He knew this was a non-profit organization, relying heavily on donations, grants, and other funding to keep the facility running. He slipped a couple of large bills into the box without hesitation, knowing every contribution helped with the place's upkeep.

After a short amount of browsing at the souvenirs for sale, Abby was ready to head outside and into the zoo. If they walked the whole thing, which was the plan, it would be approximately a one-mile journey.

TJ could not help comparing it to the Dakota Zoo in his hometown. He estimated this zoo was probably about two acres larger, but it did not have the largest bear in captivity, which, in his mind, made the zoo in Bismarck a lot more impressive.

Okay. Admittedly he was a snob when comparing things to memories from childhood.

He walked beside Tabitha as Abby skipped along beside them. "How long have you been a Narian?" TJ broke the silence between them as they stopped to allow Abby to watch the Ring-tailed lemurs moving through the trees.

Tabitha chuckled at him using Abby's pronunciation of Veterinarian from last night. "For about six years."

"Did you attend the University of Pennsylvania, School of Veterinary Medicine?"

"No, though I grew up in Clarion. My parents owned a small diner there, but by the time I was ready to head off to college, I wanted to see another part of the country. I graduated with my Bachelor of Science in Microbiology, with a minor in Chemistry from Texas State in 1976. After that, I spent another four years at Iowa State University, graduating from there in 1980." She shrugged.

Her accomplishments impressed him. The fact she was from Clarion amazed him.

"It's a small world," he told her.

"Excuse me?"

"That you're from Clarion. One of my sisters-in-law attended college there, and the couple she stayed with during that time still live there. I've passed through there a few times myself and often stop by to say hello to them. I guess you could say I've developed a friendship with them, too."

She smiled. "You're right, it is a small world."

"So how did you wind up in Binghamton, New York, and not so far from the Pennsylvania border?"

Abby lost interest in the lemurs and dashed to the next exhibit.

The adults followed at a leisurely pace. As long as they could see the child, they allowed her the freedom to roam.

Tabitha did not appear in a hurry to answer his question, and he decided she had deemed the subject closed. But as they watched Abby eyeing the vulture's, the answer came out quietly. "My husband was from here."

"Was?" TJ's stomach clenched. It was her tone that alerted him that the man had not deserted her and Abby.

"Owen, that was his name, died in a car accident a little over three years ago. He was going too fast, the highway patrol told me, and the roads were icy."

"I'm sorry," he said and glanced at Abby as he tried to calculate exactly how old the child was. He wondered if she was older than he thought. And considering the fact she had a good grasp of holding conversations with adults, it was possible she was older than her size suggested.

Abby was off to the tortoise exhibit, and they moved along with her.

Tabitha took a deep breath. After all these years, although no longer painful, the ache was below the surface. "I had just found out I was pregnant. On the day he died. I sat in the doctor's office, being told we were going to have a baby, and when I got home, there was an officer and minister knocking on my door. What they told me took away the joy I'd had less than an hour earlier."

"Geezes," TJ said. "I don't know what to say."

"It's all right. As I said, it's gotten easier." She stopped walking, looked at him. "I did not tell you that to get sympathy from you. I've gotten through the worst of everything, and the last thing I need or want is pity."

He began walking when she did. "I get that, but I admire your courage. You came through tragedy and are raising one hell of a kid."

"My parents have helped with that. They sold everything, including the diner, and moved here as soon as they could to help me out."

"What about Owen's folks?"

She shrugged. "They grieved, of course. But they are not interested in staying in one place. They travel. They were both retired when Owen died, and helping to raise Abby was not in their plans." She would not mention that Owen's parents disliked her and blamed her for their son's death, claiming she sentenced him to death on the day she married him because she was not a Christian.

"It's God's punishment!" Peggy had screamed at her. "We warned Owen not to marry you! You worship the devil!"

Tabitha certainly did not worship the devil. That ancient belief was so outdated it was laughable.

TJ's opinion of Owen's parents went considerably low. He could not grasp how they could leave their daughter-in-law during that difficult time.

He and Tabitha moved on to the cougar cage as Abby headed in that direction. They were content to walk along the path for a while without talking.

After a time, TJ stopped, touched her arm. She looked at him, questioning. "I'm sorry about the other night. I wish that frickin' drunk hadn't been hell-bent on causing a scene. And I wish I had gotten your phone number before the guy came at me. I was interested in getting to know you better. I still am."

Tabitha stopped walking, turned to him. "I wanted to stay. I was having fun. But all things considered, my friends convinced me it was better if I wasn't seen there. I own the clinic I work at. I cannot afford that type of publicity."

TJ laughed, raked a hand through his short dark brown hair. "Oh, yeah. I know what unwanted publicity can do for a person." A few people he knew in the Big Apple had gotten terrible reputations because of screaming headlines.

"And I had to think of Abby," Tabitha told him. "She was spending the night with Owen's parents. The relationship I have with them is strained. Had I gotten arrested, it would only add to their opinion of me."

"If they don't think you're amazing as hell for everything you've accomplished since Owen died, they're dumb asses."

Tabitha stared at him for a beat, then burst out laughing. "I think that was a compliment," she chuckled.

"It was." He grinned.

What that smile did to her insides was scandalous.

"Mommy!" Abby exclaimed, and suddenly the girl was pulling on Tabitha's hand. "Let's go see the monkeys!"

"I don't know if that's a wise idea," Tabitha told her daughter, keeping her face somber. "They might become jealous when they see the biggest monkey of all out of her cage."

"Mommy!" Abby giggled, "I'm not a monkey!"

Tabitha chuckled. "Okay, Scooby-Doo. We'll be right behind you."

She watched her daughter take off like a rocket. After a moment, she glanced at TJ and said quietly, "I guess maybe you and I can start over." She held out her hand. "I'm Tabitha Turner."

"TJ," he said, taking her hand and giving it a shake. "TJ Fisher."

The tattoo on Tabitha's upper shoulder, covered by her sleeve, felt as though it suddenly became hot, and she tried to ignore it the best she could.

When she would have taken her hand from his, he did not relinquish it.

Tabitha cleared her throat, "I think we better join Abby before the monkeys take her," she said, and this time TJ allowed her to ease her hand from his.

The three of them moved on, continuing to enjoy the zoo. At the half-way point was the concession stand. TJ wanted something cool to wet his throat, and he asked Tabitha, "Would you two like anything?" He pulled out his wallet. "My treat."

They ordered, then found a table and sat down to enjoy the refreshment. As Abby began eating her bowl of ice cream, Tabitha's eyes moved to TJ. "You know what I do for a living. Obviously, you work construction. What company do you work for?"

"I'm self-employed." He wasn't ready to tell her his back history. "When I find a house, I know has the potential to make a profit once it's remodeled, I fix it up and resell it."

"Is there a lot of money in that?"

He laughed. "I drive a Porsche."

"Touché," she conceded.

"To be fair, if a person doesn't know what they're doing, and have no clue how to read the market, they can lose their shirt. Fortunately, I'm good at analyzing markets and numbers." Which was an understatement. He'd been a geeky kid who, from the time he'd been ten years old and discovered stocks, bonds, and real estate, began studying and analyzing trends.

It had motivated him to begin investing. He'd mowed lawns throughout Bismarck in the summer and shovel snow in the winter. He saved the earnings, spending little on himself, and placed most of it in the bank. His goal had been to raise seven thousand dollars by the time he turned sixteen, to invest a thousand dollars into several different companies he believed would become hot items.

He reached his goal a year early, and the stocks he had gotten his parents to help him invest in hit big. After that, he set his eyes on real estate. That, too, had struck gold. The combination had made him his first million by the time he turned twenty-one.

"Lucky you," Tabitha told him. "I struggled through college with math, but I was determined to graduate at the top of my class. I managed it, though."

She earned another point with that declaration.

He took a drink of his coke then asked, "So, when can I see you again?"

Chapter Eight

"Oh my god, Tabitha! You're kidding me!" Grace exclaimed Monday morning before the clinic opened for business.

"I swear to you on the stars it's the truth."

"The same man you danced with at Over Yonder is the guy remodeling the house next to your parents?"

"And talking to Abby. I about died when I walked into mom and dad's house Friday night, and he was there."

Grace sat down in the chair at her desk, stunned. "And you went to the zoo together on Saturday?"

Tabitha nodded.

"Are you blushing?"

"Stop it! I'm not!"

Greta chose that moment to walk into the clinic, reporting for work. She glanced at Tabitha and asked, "Why is your face red?"

Tabitha choked.

"She's blushing because she found the mystery man from Wednesday night. And they went to the zoo together on Saturday," Grace informed the newcomer.

"Get out of town!" Greta's eyes bulged.

Tabitha shook her head. "I'm sure we have work to do. What time is the first appointment?"

"You've got fifteen minutes to spill the beans before you can use the excuse you're too busy to talk." Grace leaned back in the chair. "So, start talking."

"There's nothing to tell. TJ went with Abby and me to the zoo, and that's all."

Greta and Grace shared a look.

"Tell me you're going to see him again!" Greta exclaimed.

"He's coming to my house for supper this Wednesday night. Since that's the night we're closing early, I'll have time to cook before he arrives, and he claims he's a champion Candy Land player. He challenged Abby to a game."

"He's going to play Candy Land?! What guy does that willingly?"

Tabitha shrugged, having a hard time believing it too. She cautioned herself not to fall too quickly for a man she just met, but it wasn't easy.

TJ Fisher seemed like a dream come true, which meant she needed to guard her heart and use caution. It wasn't only her feelings that would be impacted if this tentative friendship moved forward, then soured. It would hurt Abby. She'd already lost her heart to the man.

"Could we just move on?" Tabitha suggested. "Who's the first patient? —and don't you dare say Bubbles."

Grace laughed. "Fine. If you don't want to talk about that hot guy you spent the day with, we won't drill you. For now. But you know we're going to want all the sordid details Thursday morning." She reached for a chart. "And no, Bubbles is not scheduled today."

"Thank the stars," Tabitha said, taking the chart from Grace. She walked into the backroom with it, unaware she was humming to herself.

Grace and Greta bumped fists.

"If he turns out to be a jerk and breaks her heart," Greta said, "I'm going to track him down and stick a needle in his neck."

"I know what you mean. I haven't heard her hum before. Not ever. She deserves someone special in her life who can bring a sparkle to her eye."

When closing time arrived at five o'clock, Tabitha was ready to call it a day. Not that anything demanding came up. It had been a peaceful day with no unusual mishaps. But the weather had been sunny and bright all day and she hoped to be able to feel the sun on her face, if only for a little while. Maybe her mother would serve dinner tonight on the porch and they could breathe in the fresh air before it was time to take Abby home.

Walking out the clinic's side door with Grace and Greta, she stopped in her tracks when she saw TJ standing by his work truck. He was casually leaning against it with his arms folded over his chest. When he saw her, he smiled.

"Hi," he said, straightening to his full height of six feet two.

Tabitha tried not to be as giddy as a schoolgirl, but she wasn't able to hide her grin.

"Hi back," she said and rolled her eyes when she heard her two companions sigh as though smitten.

To be polite, she introduced the two women to him.

"Nice to meet you," he told them, then turned his attention back to Tabitha. "I'll confess I asked your mother what time you normally got off work."

"What are you doing here?" she asked.

"Well, I was wondering if I could take you to dinner. Your mom said she had no problem watching Abby for an extra hour tonight if you said yes."

There were collective sighs from behind her again.

She turned around. "Shouldn't the two of you be heading home?"

"Before hearing your answer?" Greta told her. "No way."

Tabitha looked at TJ. "I'm still in my scrubs."

He shrugged. "And I'm still in my work clothes, though I tried to dust most of the dirt off. I'm not talking fancy restaurant. Simple food with a view."

"Where?"

He stepped back, opened the passenger door of his truck. "You have to get in to find that out."

She could see the dare in his eyes.

"Maybe I should double-check with my mother," she told him, then laughed because that sounded too much like a teenage girl and not the thirty-two-year-old woman she was who could make her own decisions.

"All right," she told him. "I don't know why I'm okay that you set this up with my mother without asking me, but I am."

"Good," his eyes twinkled.

He helped her into the truck, closed the door, and shot a wink toward her friends as he walked around the vehicle to the driver's side.

Both women thought they would swoon.

Once TJ turned the truck onto the street, she asked, "Okay. I'm here. Where are we going?"

He chuckled. "Patience must not be one of your strong points."

She lightly slapped his arm with her hand, which only caused him to laugh outright.

"Sit back, relax, and enjoy the ride. I realize this beauty isn't the Porsche, but it's faithful."

Tabitha leaned back in the seat, folded her hands in her lap. "I can be patient. I won't ask again. In the meantime, while you're taking me to wherever this secret place is, let's talk about your name. Is TJ your actual name?"

He glanced at her. Smiled. "The one I was born with? No. They are the initials of my first and middle name."

Tabitha felt the hairs on her arms raise, and the tattoo she had on her upper left shoulder tingled.

"Everyone has called me TJ since I was twelve years old. Well, except my folks. They still insist on using the one they gave me."

"Which is?" she asked.

Again, he took his eyes off the road long enough to wink at her. "I don't share that with anyone, but if you guess it, I'll let you know when you hit the bullseye."

"Tom Jones," she said.

"Not even close." He turned right at an intersection.

"Travis Jackson."

He shook his head.

She kept trying as he drove, her guesses becoming more and more outlandish as they neared their destination. "Come on!" she said at last. "Give me a hint. At least tell me your first name!"

He glanced in her direction as he considered, however; he hated his name enough not to say it. Even for her, but he was enjoying her frustration. "Nope." He slowed down and made the turn into Otsiningo Park, found a parking spot at the half-way point just past the children's play area. Turning off the motor, he opened his door and said, "Come on. It's a nice evening. We'll sit at a table and watch the Chenango River flow by.

"I thought you said something about food."

She watched him exit the truck, move the driver's seat up, and reach behind it.

Withdrawing something that looked suspiciously like the picnic basket her mother owned, he told her, "Tah dah." He grinned. "Your mom put this together for us. It smells like fried chicken, but that's only a guess as I didn't see what she put in here. If there aren't paper plates, napkins and silverware, blame her."

Tabitha couldn't help her laugh.

He moved around the truck to the passenger side, opened the door. "I'll let you pick out the place we're going to sit."

Sliding from the cab, she told him, "How kind of you. And I hope my mother included something to drink in there. I'm a little thirsty."

"Actually, I'm providing the beverages. If you look behind the passenger seat, you'll find a small cooler. I stopped by my place on the way to the clinic and picked us up a few beers, and some bottled water if you don't like beer."

Tabitha retrieved the cooler, looked inside. "Weihen-stephaner Hefe-weissbier?" she said, though suspected she probably pronounced it wrong. "What in the heck is that? I was expecting a Bud light or something of that nature."

"Ugh. Seriously? A Bud light?" He closed the passenger door, locked the vehicle, pocketed the keys and they began walking toward a table. "The beer in that cooler is a world-class import from Germany."

"Maybe I should just stick with the bottled water. I'm not sure if my taste buds could handle something that expensive." She told him.

She moved toward a table where she felt the scenic beauty would surround them the best, and they set about taking items from the picnic basket. Once they were seated across from one another, they began eating the meal provided for them.

"This chicken is amazing," TJ commented as he consumed a chicken thigh. He wiped his fingers with one of the napkins Angela included along with the plates, then reached into the cooler for a beer. "Your mom could sell this recipe and make a fortune." He popped the lid off the beer and drank.

"My dad," she told him, eyeing the beer.

"Excuse me?"

"It's my dad's recipe. He's the chef. People came to their Diner in Clarion just for that chicken. And his caramel rolls. They melt in your mouth."

"Well, it's obvious your dad is a food wizard. Does he miss working at a restaurant?"

"He still cooks. He was able to get a job right away when they moved here. Not that he had to, as they made a good profit from the diner's sale and the house I grew up in. But he loves to cook. He works part-time at Robbie's Family Diner." She leaned forward, lowered her voice as though about to tell him a secret. "Sunday mornings are the day he makes the caramel rolls, but you'll need to put your order in by Friday afternoon, or you can forget getting any."

"I'll keep that in mind." He held out his beer to her. "Want to give it a try?"

She eyed it skeptically, but when he wiggled the bottle, as though dangling a prize, she accepted the offer.

The first thing she did was sniff it.

TJ threw his head back and laughed. "It's not poisonous, I promise."

The humor in his eyes was enough challenge for her to put the bottle to her lips and take a long pull.

"Oh, my god!" she said, bringing the bottle down and looking at him wide-eyed. "I've never tasted anything like that. It's good!"

He reached into the cooler, brought out another bottle, and popped the lid. Tapping the bottle to hers, he told her, "I told you. You'll never want a Bud light again."

She took another pull on the bottle. "I shudder to think about how much this cost."

He shrugged, then stood up as he began repacking everything they hadn't used back into the picnic basket. "We still have a little time left before I need to take you back so you can pick up Abby. Would you like to go for a short stroll?"

Tabitha gathered up what was garbage and put it in the nearby trash container. "Yes," she told him. "I think that would be nice."

TJ picked up the basket and cooler. "I'll lock these in my truck and be right back."

She watched as he walked away and liked the way his broad shoulders tapered down to his slim waistline.

He was back within moments.

They followed the walking path as it wound around lush trees and cut through the green grass. The Chenango River was to their right, but they only caught glimpses of it through the thick trees lining its bank.

"Will you tell me about Owen?" TJ asked softly, breaking the silence.

The question surprised her. And it touched her that he would acknowledge a man who had been an important part of her life once, rather than pretend he never existed.

"What did you want to know?"

"Anything you want to share. How did you meet him?"

"He was attending Iowa State University at the same time I was," the memory took her there for a moment. A small smile curved her lips as a memory of the first time she saw Owen when he'd walked into the pre-clinical classroom she was enrolled in. "He wanted to specialize in small animals. Especially dogs. When he was a boy, he would bring stray dogs' home with him." She laughed. "We discovered both of us had that in common. I was always bringing home strays, but I didn't limit myself to dogs. As far as I was concerned, if it was an animal and breathed, it needed a home. I brought my fair share of garter snakes into

J.R. Zimmer

my parent's diner when I was a child." She looked at TJ, humor in her eyes. "I assure you; my mother was not happy about that."

"I bet not," TJ agreed, amused, and pictured Tabitha as a young Abby and could see her doing exactly that.

"Owen and I," Tabitha continued after a moment, "became engaged the year I graduated, and we married the following year. We both dreamed of owning our own clinic, specializing in small animals. In the first year of our marriage, we worked on our business plan, found a building in a great location, and figured out the equipment we needed and staff requirements. By the following year, we had gotten the bank to loan us the money, and we opened for business."

TJ was silent as he listened to her. "How long was the clinic open before Owen passed away?"

"Almost two years." She reached up and plucked a leaf from a low-hanging branch from the tree they passed under. Holding it to her nose for a moment, she breathed in its aroma before playing with it in her hands.

He thought about what she said and imagined the determination Tabitha must have had to keep the place running through the tragedy and giving birth to a child. Even now, she would still have a loan to pay off, and she had a house that would also have a mortgage.

"Your clinic must be doing well," he commented.

"It is. It was a little shaky those first few months after Owen passed away. I owe a lot of gratitude to Greta and Grace. Grace is a very efficient office manager, and Greta is my assistant. The two of them have amazing skills when it comes to marketing. And Grace talked a few veterinarians in the area into volunteering at our clinic twice a week to fill those gaps when I couldn't be there. And because of them, and the resourcefulness of those two women, my clinic is running in the black."

As a businessman who had run a multi-million construction company in New York, he was more than impressed.

"Enough about me," Tabitha decided. "It's your turn. How did you wind up in New York from North Dakota?"

"My hometown doesn't offer a lot of choices for entertainment," he told her, surprised at how easy it was to talk to her. "I guess you could say I was a quirky kid. I read The Wall Street Journal at a young age."

"How old?"

"Ten."

She stared at him. "Are you pulling my leg?"

He laughed. "Nope. I told you, I was a quirky kid." He waved that away. "Anyway, I guess because it is based out of the Big Apple, I had it in my head that was the place to be."

"Obviously, something changed your mind to have you move from there to here."

He shrugged. "I guess the small-town atmosphere couldn't be shaken." And he was more than happy to be away from Heather and Rick.

He glanced at his watch. "I should probably take you back to the clinic to pick up your car so you can get Abby. I wouldn't want your mom mad at me for bringing you home late."

She laughed. "She hasn't grounded me in years."

Before he knew he was doing it, TJ took her hand in his as he laughed, and they began walking back toward his truck.

They walked in silence, comfortable enough with the other to enjoy being together without conversation.

TJ took his keys out of his pocket once they reached his truck. Unlocking the passenger side, he paused before opening the door.

"Tabitha," he told her. "I'm going to kiss you."

She got that deer in the headlight look he was beginning to find adorable, but she didn't object as he slowly leaned in to brush his lips over hers.

He intended for the kiss to be whisper-soft. A quick meeting of lips, but the moment his mouth touched hers, her hands came up, and she wrapped her arms around his neck, drawing him closer.

The kiss took on a life of its own. TJ opened his mouth, used his tongue, and she matched him thrust for thrust.

They broke apart, panting.

Tabitha placed her fingertips over her lips, unable to believe the heat they had created. And she could admit to herself that as much as she had loved Owen, he had never built a fire in her with a kiss alone.

TJ leaned his head down, touched his forehead to hers. "I don't understand what's happening, but I'm making you a promise here and now." He placed his hand on either side of her face, cradling it. "One day we're going to finish what we just started. You can count on it."

Chapter Nine

Tuesday morning, needing to purchase a few supplies from the hardware store, TJ took an early break from working on the project house. While he was running errands, he made a stop at the nursing home to check on Doris and see how she was adjusting to her new surroundings.

Entering the facility, he stopped by the nurse's station first to inquire if Doris needed anything. The woman behind the desk smiled up at him and said, "At the moment she's all set up, and she's especially enjoying that television you gave her. She loves watching The Price is Right and refuses to miss Wheel of Fortune." The woman chuckled. "Doris claims she never realized those shows weren't in black and white because she never owned a colored television before."

TJ smiled. "I'm glad she likes it."

"That she does. And it's so sweet of you to think of her. Are you related to her?"

He shook his head. "Nah. She just seems like someone who could use a helping hand, and sometimes I'm a sucker for an older woman." He winked, then laughed at the nurse's expression. It was easy to see what she was thinking. That he had a fetish for women beyond his years.

"So," he said, not bothering to correct the nurse in her assumption. "Do you know if Doris is in her room? I was going to say hello to her before going back to work."

"I believe she's outside in the garden area."

"Great. Thanks." And he moved away from the counter to head in that direction. He'd been through this facility once before when he'd first checked in with Doris to see if she needed anything.

When he arrived at the garden area, he paused at the door long enough to allow an older couple coming back in to make it through the door.

J.R. Zimmer

One of them had a walker, and the other a cane, so it took them a bit of time to shuffle past him, but he wasn't in a rush. Besides, there was no point in getting mad at older people the years had stolen their youth from. Everyone in the world would one day have the same aches and pains if they lived long enough to reach old age.

Passing through the doorway into the area that offered residents a place where they could enjoy the outdoors and still remain within a fence's safety, TJ paused in his search for where Doris might be.

"TJ!" he heard his name called out and was shocked upon hearing Abby's voice.

Turning toward the sound, he watched as Abby ran toward him from where she had been sitting with her grandmother, visiting Doris.

"Hey, munchkin," he said, reaching out and ruffling the girl's hair. "What are you doing here?"

She pointed toward her grandmother. "We're visiting Doris!"

"I came to say hello to her too."

As though she had the right to do so, she reached up with her hand and captured two of his fingers with it. "Come on, silly!" she said, and led him toward the two older women. "Grandma!" she called out, "I found TJ!"

Angela Stevens smiled and waved at him. "This is a nice surprise," she said when he got closer.

"I came to check up on Doris." He turned toward the woman whose skin was almost paper-thin because of her age. "Hey, Doris. How's your day going?"

Doris, sitting in one of the metal chairs the home provided for residents to sit on and enjoy viewing the various flowers planted in pots, and cascading on terraces, reached for his hand and gave it a squeeze. She was surprisingly strong for a woman of ninety. "Well, sonny. Now that I have a handsome man to look at, I'm doing mighty fine!"

96

Her grin was toothless, but the smile was contagious.

"I hear you're enjoying the television I got for you," he said, sitting down next to her as Abby picked up the stuffed bear she'd brought with her and climbed onto his lap without an invitation.

TJ glanced at Angela, but the woman only shrugged as though he shouldn't be surprised her granddaughter was staking a claim on him.

"I love that television! My goodness, TJ, you are too good to me! You're fixing up my house and are taking care of me better than my rotten children ever did. Bless your heart. I don't know what I did to deserve your kindness but thank you all the same!"

TJ cleared his throat and wondered if Doris understood the house in question was no longer hers. "It's a beautiful home," he told her. "And sometimes, a beautiful woman needs someone to look after them." He smiled at her and would probably never fully understand what had drawn him to that neighborhood and that house.

Other than the fact, the price of the house had been a great deal.

Doris looked at Angela. "You said the right person would come when you lit that candle and said that spell."

In his mind, TJ questioned why Doris used the word spell in place of the word prayer. But after having dinner with the Stevens last week, and witnessing their ritual using candles, he assumed Angela had prayed for Doris's house to sell and a candle was used during it.

Catholics did that, didn't they? Lit candles as a sign of gratitude to God for answered prayers. And used them as a symbol of the light of Christ. Or they were used in a way to both extend your prayers and show solidarity with the person the prayer was being made on behalf of.

TJ had not been raised Catholic, so he was only guessing at why the Stevens used candles. Not that he cared. It was their routine, and they were welcome to it.

Abby, settled on his lap as though she had sat there a thousand times before, held her bear up for Doris to see. "Grandpa gave me a teddy bear," she proclaimed.

"And it's a fine-looking bear," Doris told her. "You keep that little rascal safe, and he'll be good to you."

"I will," Abby promised and snuggled the beloved bear under her chin.

The adults spoke for another twenty minutes before TJ picked Abby up from his lap as he stood and placed her feet on the ground. He told the small group goodbye, needing to get back to the project house. He'd always prided himself on finishing jobs within the allotted deadline he gave himself. Just because he was now only accountable to himself, he still liked his schedules.

Whistling a tune he remembered from his childhood, but could not recall the name of, he exited the nursing home, got in his truck, and headed back to Doris's former home.

* * *

"Mommy!" Abby cried the moment Tabitha opened the front door of her parents' home that evening. "Grandma and I saw Doris today. And TJ too!"

"That was nice," Tabitha said, assuming Abby had seen TJ during the usual afternoon break the man took in the afternoon. "How is Doris?"

"She liked my teddy bear, and she had a nickel for me!" Abby reached into the front pocket of the pink shorts she had on, held up the treasured coin for her mother to see.

"Another one to add to your piggy bank," Tabitha smiled.

Abby nodded.

"My granddaughter told us TJ is coming to your house tomorrow night," John said, standing up from his recliner.

There was no denying the grin on her father's face.

Something Magical

For some strange reason Tabitha couldn't fathom, she felt a blush creep up her cheeks. "I invited him over," she admitted.

"He's going to play Candy Land with me!" Abby beamed.

"Oh?" John asked, glancing at his daughter.

Tabitha shrugged. "He asked if we had the game."

"Time to eat!" Angela called from the dining room.

The family gathered around the table, said a blessing, and began to eat the stuffed peppers Angela had prepared.

"Mmm, so good. Thanks, mom. These are my favorite."

Angela smiled. "I know, honey. I'm not that old to have forgotten what your favorite dishes are." She took a bite of the pepper she served herself, chewed, then asked, "and what are you going to make for TJ tomorrow night?"

There was a singsong to her voice Tabitha knew meant she wanted to ask more questions, but with Abby sitting in her chair taking in the conversation, those questions couldn't be asked.

"I'm not sure yet," Tabitha answered, which was the truth. She hadn't thought that far ahead.

"Well, if you need any help, you just let me know," her mother told her.

Tabitha chuckled. "I haven't forgotten how to cook, mom."

"I just thought I'd offer."

"It's appreciated, but we're closing early tomorrow because there aren't any appointments late in the day. And Grace has already told me she's going to keep it that way because I'm having a guest tomorrow night."

John grinned. "One day you'll have to give that woman a raise for looking out for you."

"I think both her and Greta are conspiring in this since I told them this morning I'd invited TJ for supper."

"Good for them," Angela said.

"TJ bought Doris a TV," Abby announced out of the blue, effectively changing the subject without realizing her mother was glad for the new topic.

"He did what?"

Angela nodded. "We found that out today while Abby and I were visiting her."

"What?" Tabitha was having a hard time following the conversation.

"TJ. He bought Doris a colored television."

Taking the confused look on her daughter's face as a sign, Angela knew she needed to explain. "Apparently the man is looking out for her. The nurse told me when Abby and I were leaving, TJ asked them to contact him whenever Doris needs items that are not supplied by the home."

Tabitha sat back in her chair, stunned to discover the man was more kindhearted than she'd believed.

All too easily, she could lose her heart to him if she wasn't careful.

"That's really nice of him," was all she could think of to say.

"That it is," John agreed.

"Now," Angela said, pushing her plate away. "Not to spoil your appetite, but have you heard from the Turners? Are they still in town? I haven't seen them since they dropped Abby off last week, I thought maybe they've left the area."

Tabitha pushed her own plate away, no longer hungry. "They're still in town. Peggy called the clinic this afternoon to say they had some things to take care of this week before leaving, but they want another sleepover with Abby. She didn't say when, though."

Angela sighed. "I hope they finish their business sooner rather than later and be on their way down the road."

Tabatha could not have agreed more. She couldn't shake the feeling that this visit from the Turners was different than the other rare occasions when they stopped by to see Abby.

Chapter Ten

Wednesday afternoon, Mason Lafayette strolled into the waiting area of Sizzling Concepts' American branch of their worldwide modeling agency as though he were on a mission. The twenty-one-year-old six-foot-three hunk seemed not to notice the sea of hopefuls waiting for their interview with Connie Fay, the company's ace talent agent. Nor did he acknowledge the sighs of appreciation for his physical appearance following in his wake as the handful of women, and two men, in the reception room almost fainted as he passed them by.

Mason Lafayette had the face of a mythical god and the toned body of a chiseled statue brought to life.

He was so accustomed to being lusted after he did not give it a second thought as he walked past the receptionist and straight into Connie's office.

The secretary didn't bother to try to stop him as she'd been down that road before.

Connie wasn't alone. He hadn't expected her to be, nor did he care. He walked straight to her desk and threw the packet of photos he'd carried with him onto it. "I picked these up from Ray. They suck. He ess a horrible photographer. I will not work with him again."

Connie sighed and glanced down at the six glossy images that had fallen out of the packet. If the man standing before her were anyone else, she would have chalked his anger up to a model who had more drama than talent. However, in this case, it was the opposite. She could see the women posed with the man in the photos looked awkward, and the lighting was terrible.

"I apologize, Mason. They assured me Ray was an expert."

"My eleven-year-old sister could do better," he told her.

Connie eyed the nineteen-year-old sitting across from her, looking wide-eyed up at Mason. "Candy, you are excused. Close the door behind you."

The girl scrambled to her feet and raced for the door.

"I am sure you are right," Connie picked up the conversation with Mason as though no interruption had occurred. "But your father taught your sister, and no one can compete with Charles Lafayette's talent for capturing images on film." After all, he was a famous movie director from France who had won countless theatrical awards for his work.

Connie looked down at the images once again. Although the quality was that of an amateur, the male model's talent leaped off the paper. There was no denying that the lens of the camera had a love affair with him.

It was the same love the camera gave Mason's mother. In her early years, Rosalinda Lafayette modeled products for companies until they cast her in her first film, and then it was the lens of the motion picture world that embraced her.

"Mason, you know I would never purposely make you unhappy," she soothed. He was a goddamn goldmine, and she planned on being a part of this gravy train for as long as possible. She would walk over broken glass spread over hot coals if he asked it of her, and he probably knew it.

He motioned to the 27×40-inch poster of himself that was the current ad for Touch My Bod jeans hanging on one wall in the office. "I will work with Jon. He knows how to take a picture that sells."

Connie glanced at the photo and knew it wasn't only Jon's talent that sold that image. It was the hard body combined with that face, framed with shoulder-length blacker than sin hair, and cat-like green eyes that had women buying up magazines by the dozen to own the image for themselves. Not to mention those same women were buying up Touch My Bod jeans for their boyfriends and husbands because they were delusional enough to hope those jeans would transform their man into the hunk in the photo.

"Yes, he does. And I promise you, he will be the only photographer we'll pair you with from now on." She motioned to the chair in front of her desk. "I'm glad you are here, Mason. I have been wanting to have a meeting with you. I want to advance your career. Make you a household name beyond Touch My Bod jeans."

He cocked a brow, but he did not sit. "Connie, I have been a household name since the day I was born."

She had to concede that point. Having been born to Rosalinda Lafayette gave him fame as a birthright. All of France adored him because of who his mother was. But here in America, he was not as well known. Which was what she told him. "You are not looking at the big picture, Mason. I want people in the United States to know who you are beyond that jeans ad."

This time when she motioned for him to have a seat, he obliged her, intrigued enough to hear her out.

Turning in her chair, she reached into a box she had set next to her earlier in the day. From it, she withdrew more than a dozen paperback books and lined them up in front of him.

He stared at them, then at her. The covers of the books had couples featured on them, all in various poses and dress. Some more risqué than others, but the apparent theme of them all was sex. "Are you reading porn books now, Connie?"

His smile was sensual yet amused.

She laughed. "These are not porn…" she thought about it a moment, reconsidered. "Well, I suppose you could say they are soft porn. They are romance books with sex sprinkled in throughout the story. Not all of them have hot and heavy sex scenes, but a few do, and women buy these up like candy."

"Stories about romance." He said slowly, as though he did not understand it, and not because English was his second language.

"Boy meets girl. Through the story, they fall in love and have a happy ever after."

He shook his head. "Absurd."

"Now, do not be a snob, Mason. Your own parents create movies centered around love stories. These are no different than those."

Mason eyed the books once more. "What is your point, Connie?"

She pointed to the ad poster of him. "Women want you, Mason. Look at the men on these covers. Although good looking, you have that sex appeal women are drawn to. With Jon's eye and your ability to create a pose that looks so natural, I really believe you could make a fortune modeling for romance books."

He laughed and shook his head. "You want me to pose for a romance cover? I think you have lost your mind."

"Mason, I have been working out a deal with Citnamor Books. They are the number one publishing house for these types of works, and they are very interested in having you come down for a cover shoot."

"Mon Dieu, Connie. No one would take me seriously as a model-"

Connie scribbled a sizable figure onto a small notepad, tore it off, and handed it to him. "This is what Citnamor Books have agreed to pay you."

Mason glanced down at the figure and was not impressed. "I made more than that last year with the work you provided for me."

"Per cover, Mason. Not per year."

"Scare bleu!" He stared at the figures for a moment, unable to believe someone would pay him that much to pose for a romance book's cover.

"Well?" Connie asked.

Slowly, he took his eyes off the paper and put them on her. The smile he gave her had her wishing she were thirty years younger. Good lord, that boy could cause a woman to become aroused without trying.

"Tell me when and where and I will be there," he told her, rising out of the chair.

"One more thing, Mason. On top of the fee, you have exclusive rights to choose who you work with. That includes photographer and lead female model if they require an image of a couple."

He was speechless.

Now Connie rose from her chair. "With those God given looks, Mason, you will have a long career ahead of you." She scribbled once again on another piece of paper and handed it to him. "Here is the where and when. As you can see, they scheduled it for next week. You are free until next Monday. Enjoy your mini vacation."

Mason could not hide his grin as he took the paper and walked out the door, through the lobby, and to the elevator.

When the elevator doors opened, the older man who delivered the mail to the office slowly pushed out the cart loaded down with the day's mail. When he saw Mason, he grinned. "Hello there, Mr. Lafayette. I have a letter for you. I was going to drop it off at the agency, but since you are right here let me find it for you."

About to tell William not to bother as he did not doubt it was fan mail, the letter appeared in front of him before he could get the words past his lips.

"Here you go, Mr. Lafayette. Have a good day."

Automatically Mason took the envelope, and William continued past him to deliver the rest of the mail.

Stepping into the elevator, Mason pressed the button for the garage level, then glanced at the return address, knowing he would not know who this person was. His friends and family knew his home address in New York City. They would not write to him at the agency.

He recognized the city the return address was from. He knew someone there he considered an uncle. But this was not from TJ Fisher. It was from a place called More Than Little Paws Veterinary Clinic.

Curious as a cat -and what was the irony in that? -he opened the envelope, pulled out the letter, and scanned the paper as the elevator continued its descent.

By the time the elevator doors opened onto the garage floor under the building, he was laughing. He gave the business credit for coming up with the idea. A date with Mason Lafayette. That was the name of the fundraiser this Doctor Turner was hoping he would consider participating in. She hoped to raise funds for a sanctuary for unwanted dogs she was determined to build one day.

Apparently, his popularity was more widespread in America than he realized.

His hand dipped into the front pockets of his jeans. Withdrawing the small note Connie gave him that pro-claimed the salary Citnamor Books would pay him for each cover and knew the answer. They would never consider paying someone without a following that much money.

The elevator doors opened as he contemplated his parent's reaction when he told them how much he would earn. It may not be the millions they made from each movie his father produced, and his mother starred in, but it was impressive enough.

As Mason walked toward his red Corvette, his thoughts turned to what Connie said in her office about his looks. Sometimes it bothered him he had inherited his looks from his biological father. He had not met the man to know if that were true. Nor did he want to see the man in the flesh to discover for himself if they were indeed mirror images, as he'd been told. He, Mason, existed because he was a byproduct of a heinous crime committed against his mother.

He struggled for a few years after discovering the truth about his conception. He had been devastated to realize the man he'd believed sired him was not blood-related but secretly adopted him and gave him his name. Charles and his mother never intended for anyone other than a select few to know the truth. But as Mason grew older, his features revealed he was not Charles' son and forced Rosalinda to come forward with the truth.

Over time Mason was able to accept Charles once again as his father in all ways that mattered.

Thinking about the letter from that woman gave him pause. He had a few days off. Why not head home, pack a bag, and drive the three hours to Binghamton and surprise TJ with a visit?

He could not wait to see the man's face when he arrived unannounced.

Almost to the Corvette, he watched the shadow detach itself from the garage wall and begin following him.

Mason sighed. After all these years, he should be used to having someone watching him at all times, but it did not mean he liked it.

When he had been a child, he'd grown accustomed to having bodyguards surrounding him whenever his family traveled outside of their home. Not only to keep a watchful eye out for some deranged fan of his mother's that might intend harm. But to prevent his biological father from kidnapping him if that would become the man's intent.

Nothing suggested Pierre Bellefeuille had any interest in him. Even after the press conference his parents held to announce the truth about Mason's conception, there had been no attempts from Bellefeuille to contact him.

That might have something to do with the fact Mason's surrogate uncle, Cadman Benson, made it his mission to keep Pierre constantly on the move. Cadman was the head of a secret United States task force that tracked down terrorists. Cadman had been tracking Pierre since the day the man kidnapped Rosalinda.

To date, Pierre alluded, seeming to always be one step ahead of Cadman. But what was consistent was that Pierre appeared to frequent South America, Africa, Iran, and Iraq with occasional trips to Central America. He had not been spotted anywhere near France, nor the United States in years.

Mason did not believe the extra tail on him was necessary, but because Cadman disagreed, Mason was stuck with the shadow until Pierre was captured or confirmed dead.

"Ray," Mason spoke out loud, speaking to the shadow as he stood with his hand on the Corvette's door handle, "Go away."

"As soon as my replacement arrives, I'll do that," came the reply from somewhere to Mason's right.

Mason shook his head and wondered why Ray remained hidden when Mason knew he always lurked in the shadows.

Cadman's orders, but not Mason's choice.

Replacement? In the middle of unlocking the Corvette's door, Mason hesitated. Ray stayed on duty, riding in the passenger seat whenever Mason left his house and stuck with him like glue. There were only a few places Mason could go without Ray's shadow. Connie's office and the restroom.

Oh. And the bedroom. Thank God.

"Are you ill?" Mason inquired.

Ray materialized. "Nah. Boss told me he had a surprise for you, and I could go once it got here."

Mason cocked a brow, intrigued. "What kind of gift?"

Ray smiled. "A wolf."

It took Mason two full seconds to comprehend what that meant, and with the realization came a grin. Wolf was the United States code word for his best friend, Hunter Sundance Fisher.

As though on cue, the two men heard someone say, "Good god, Ray. How in the world do you keep Mason out of danger? You ignore what's going on around you. I could have killed you three times by now if I'd wanted to."

Ray, a seasoned combat-trained soldier, nearly jumped out of his skin when Hunter materialized from behind the pillar Ray had been standing next to.

"How in the hell do you do that, Hunter?" Ray exclaimed, hand on his heart. It did not appease him to discover Hunter was on crutches as it made the fact he had not sensed him that much worse.

Hunter laughed, leveraged his crutches under his arms, and began moving toward Mason. His right leg was in a long leg cast, extending from the middle of his thigh and down to the base of the toes. It looked as though his face had a few bruises to accompany the broken leg and to Mason's eye, his best friend looked like hell. "A lifetime of training in martial arts and ballet keeps me light on my feet," he answered.

Mason chuckled and was brave enough to point out the obvious. "Apparently someone was quicker than you to have given you a broken leg."

Hunter scowled. "The son of a bitch broke my fibula with a kick I hadn't been able to block."

"You," Mason stressed the word as he could not believe Hunter hadn't been fast enough, "weren't able to stop him?"

"I was busy fighting three other guys at the time, but I can guarantee you I took that guy down before I felt the pain in my leg."

Mason stared at him. "You fought on a broken leg?"

"Adrenaline is an amazing thing."

"Mon Dieu, Hunter! Who were you fighting?"

"A few nasty soldiers of a drug lord in Columbia. They were trying to prevent my team from arresting their boss," he answered as he moved forward with the crutches. "Anyway, I've got about eight weeks downtime. Thought I'd spend some of it with you, then go home to North Dakota and visit my folks."

With a grin, Mason opened the driver's side of the Corvette. "You are just in time. I was about to drive home, pack a duffle bag, and travel to Binghamton and surprise TJ. Where are your bags?"

Hunter maneuvered to the passenger side. "They're already at your place. I stopped by there first." He looked over the top of the Corvette. "Hey Ray, you're sprung from this duty. Cadman says to have fun and then report to him before resuming your post, babysitting Mason."

With a big whoop, Ray took off in search of transportation since he wouldn't be riding with Mason.

"I hate that term," Mason grumbled, sliding behind the wheel.

"You hate fun?" Hunter laughed as he climbed into the passenger seat and buckled in and knew that wasn't what Mason was referring to.

"Salaud."

"You can call me a bastard all you want."

"Damn it, Hunter," Mason backed the Corvette out from its slot. "I am tired of having a constant shadow! I am no longer a child! If Pierre had an interest in me, he would have come for me already. Uncle Cadman can pull Ray off my tail and find something else for him to do. I am done with having someone following me everywhere I go!" He hit the steering wheel with his fist as he maneuvered the vehicle out of the parking garage.

Hunter allowed him to stew for a few blocks before saying, "Uncle Cadman agrees, and so do I. You're a free man, Lafayette."

Mason almost lost control of the powerful car. "What?" Surely, he must have misunderstood.

Hunter repeated it in French and added, "I'd appreciate it if you'd stay on your side of the road."

"You could never understand what it has been like to have someone watching you twenty-four hours a day for twenty-one years." Mason's voice was harsh.

With a laugh, Hunter told him, "You never allowed that to cramp your style. You still tried to sleep with every girl on the planet when you were younger, no matter if someone was watching or not."

Mason glowered. "You know what I meant."

"Yeah, I do." Hunter ran a hand through his medium-dark brown hair that was midway past his ears. He looked out the window to watch the city go by, as Mason weaved the Corvette through traffic.

After a time, Mason asked, "Is there a reason Uncle Cadman suddenly decided to pull my keepers? Or is it only while you're here with me?" He couldn't help his suspicion that this would only be temporary. "Or is it because Cadman received news that Pierre Bellefeuille is dead?"

"Oh, Pierre's still kicking." Hunter's eyes moved back to Mason's profile, wondering how much he wanted to share about the monster who was his best friend's biological father.

Which was none of it. He'd been close to finding Pierre a handful of times since he'd begun working for Cadman. Being on the man's trail gave Hunter a clearer picture of the man's twisted nature. It was so perverted that even Hunter found his stomach rolling whenever he spoke with one of the man's victims when trying to track him. He would never burden Mason with the knowledge. Nor would he ever tell him that the reason Pierre probably was not interested in him was because the man had another son, one who was a year younger than Mason, he kept at his side.

But Mason deserved something, so part of the truth, toned down, was all he would say. "I've gotten close to tracking him a few times. He's a slippery snake. Cadman and I will not stop hounding him until the man's dead. You can bank on that." He shrugged. "But Cadman is fairly confident the fucker has no interest in connecting with you. So, enjoy your freedom."

Mason switched lanes, heading south toward home. "I intend to. And tonight, once we reach Uncle TJ's place, I'm going to get shit faced drunk."

"Now that," Hunter said, trying to get comfortable in the small space, "is one of the best ideas I've heard in a long time."

After a brief silence, Hunter asked, "How are your folks?"

"Good. When they arrived back in France after the annual reunion with your parents in North Dakota, I spoke to them. They had an enjoyable time, as always. Mother told me my sister is becoming very good at horseback riding."

Hunter rolled his eyes. "Your sister is an annoying twirp."

Mason glanced at him. "And you weren't at her age?"

"What?!" Hunter shook his head. "I was never as irritating as she is."

Laughing, Mason took the exit leading to his home and knew better than to tell Hunter that he and Daniela were so much alike it was frightening.

Chapter Eleven

Wednesday night TJ, for the first time since moving to Binghamton, did not join his friends at Mindy's Over Yonder. Tonight, he was having dinner with Tabitha and Abby at their home.

He'd been looking forward to this evening since Tabitha invited him when he'd dropped her and Abby off at their house on Saturday after their trip to the zoo.

That kiss they shared at the park rocked his world. He'd experienced nothing like it in his life. There was something about Tabitha that drew him to her, and if he were a man who believed in witchcraft, he would think there was magic being weaved over him, and Abby was her accomplice. That little girl was wiggling herself into his heart, and he knew that once he completed the remodeling project, he would miss her weekday visits.

Easing his Porsche into Tabitha's home driveway, he cut the engine, jumped out, and grabbed the two bouquets of flowers from the back seat. The largest one, the one for Tabitha, was made up of peach roses, purple carnations, lavender cushion poms, and baby blue eucalyptus. He was not sure what it was about lavender, but the color reminded him of Tabitha.

The smaller bouquet held baby breath and pink roses. It was for Abby.

He walked up the short path to the front door and rang the bell. When it opened, Tabitha stood there in a long black cotton dress that hugged her thin figure and showed the softness of her hips. The dress was cut low, allowing him a teasing glimpse of skin and small cleavage. A pentagram pendant suspended on a silver chain around her neck rested between her breasts.

It brought him back to his earlier thought that she was a witch—a beautiful one at that.

She smiled at him and said, "Thomas Jane."

He laughed. Obviously, she was still playing the name game. "Nope. Besides, he was born after I was; if you're talking about the actor."

"Thomas Jefferson," she tried.

"Nope to that too." He grinned. "I give you an A for effort, though."

She sighed dramatically, and he could easily see where Abby learned the habit. "Come on, can't you give me a little hint?"

"Considering how much I hate my name, triple nope to that."

"It can't be that bad."

"Yep. It can." To distract her, he held out the flowers. "I picked these out for you." His eyes were drawn to the stone in the center of the pendant. It was a purple stone, matching the color of the flowers he'd picked out.

Coincidence? He wasn't sure, but he felt the hairs on the back of his neck rise.

"They're beautiful," she exclaimed, reaching for them. She brought the flowers to her nose, inhaled deeply, and sighed. "I love carnations and roses! Thank you." She leaned in, gave him a quick kiss on his cheek.

"Umm, that is an unusual necklace," he commented.

Her hand reached up, grasped it gently in her right hand. "It symbolizes the five elements of life—fire, earth, metal, water, and wood. The amethyst in the center represents me. I could give you a history lesson if you would like." Her smile was tight. "But it has nothing to do with Satan worship as so many people foolishly believe if that was what you were thinking."

"I said it was unusual," he told her casually. Obviously, he'd unintentionally hit a sore spot, if her stiffened body language was any indication. "I wasn't thinking you were going to change into a bat and land in

my hair. Although, that would be kind of cool." He gave her a crooked smile.

"I'm sorry. The pendant is special to me, and my reaction was uncalled for."

He shrugged. "Apparently, people give you the evil eye when they see it. I was merely making an observation as I have never seen one surrounded by the tree of life before."

Her eyes widened with surprise, but she had no chance to comment as Abby came up alongside her and exclaimed, "TJ!" She grinned ear to ear.

"Hey, munchkin. I brought you a present," he told her and held the second bouquet out for her inspection.

Her eyes widened, and her little mouth made an O shape. "I love flowers!" she wrapped herself around his knees. "Thank you, TJ!" She took the package, showed them to her mother. "Mommy! TJ gave me flowers!"

"I see that, Scooby-Doo. Shall we find a vase for them?" At her nod, Tabitha began walking toward the kitchen. Over her shoulder, she told TJ, "Come on in. You can have a seat on the sofa, or follow us and watch us hunt for something to put these in."

TJ closed the door as he stepped into the house. His eyes were drawn to Tabitha's feet as she walked gracefully away from him. She was barefooted, and he could see the small Triple Moon Goddess tattoo on her right ankle.

He thought it was sexy, and he wondered if she had any other tats on her body.

God, he hoped he'd discover the answer to that sooner, rather than later. Dreaming of her at night was raising havoc on him.

Following them into the kitchen, he said, "May I ask you a question?" He hoped it wouldn't offend her, but he was curious.

"Sure," she rummaged through her cupboards and found a container that would work as a vase for the flowers he'd given her.

"Are you Wiccan?"

Her hand stilled in the process of placing the container under the tap. Looking at him, she asked, "Would it matter?"

He shook his head. "No. I was only curious. I don't know a lot about the religion. As far as I'm concerned, each to their own."

"Do you have a religion?"

He chuckled. "Honestly, no. Nor am I an atheist, as I cannot prove there isn't the existence of a god."

"Agnostic?"

"I can't prove there is the existence of gods either. As I said, each to their own."

Abby opened a cupboard, pulled out a mason jar that appeared to have been découpaged with comics cut from a newspaper. "Can I put my flowers in this, mommy?" she asked, holding it up for Tabitha's inspection.

"That's perfect," Tabitha smiled. "Let's fill them with water, add a few drops of bleach to each container, then cut the stems."

"Bleach?" TJ cocked a brow. "I thought you liked them."

Chuckling, Tabitha explained, "I love the flowers. That's why we're adding bleach. Only three drops, along with a small amount of sugar. It keeps the flowers fresh and prevents the growth of bacteria."

"Umm. I had no idea."

"I'll give you another chemistry lesson some other time," Tabitha helped Abby trim her flowers and arrange them in her container. "But dinner is ready, and I'm not a fan of cold shrimp Alfredo fettuccine."

"I knew something smelled good. Did you make it?"

Tabitha handed him the vase containing the flowers he'd given her, pointed toward the dining room. "You can put these in the center of the table. And yes, I made the dinner. We might usually eat at my parents Monday through Friday, but I'm on my own on the weekends, and I learned how to cook next to my dad in their diner when I was little."

Once he set the flowers where she'd told him to, he helped her bring the food out to the table, then sat down after she did.

"Dig in," she told him, taking up Abby's plate and filling it with a small amount of the pasta dish.

He hesitated, looking around the table for candles.

"Is something wrong?" Tabitha asked.

"No. I guess since that meal at your folks began with some type of prayer, I wasn't sure if there would be a repeat of it tonight."

She shook her head. "That's something my parents do. It's important to them, so Abby and I take part, but it isn't my thing." She glanced at her daughter. "And when Abby is old enough, she can choose her own path and what connects for her." Her eyes moved up, met TJ's. "Unless, of course, you enjoy prayer before a meal. We can do that if you wish."

He shook his head. "No, I'm good." He reached for the bowl of pasta as she handed it to him. "But I'm open to other's beliefs. As long as a person's beliefs don't harm anyone, I stay out of religion."

Tabitha gave him a small smile. "My thoughts exactly. If it harms none, do what you will."

TJ met her eyes. "That's a Wiccan expression."

"It is." She poured Abby some water from the pitcher sitting on the table before continuing. "My parents are more traditional in their beliefs. When I was younger, they were careful with whom they invited into our home. Unfortunately, Wicca is not recognized as a religion in this country yet. However, we are hopeful the United States Court of Appeals will decide shortly in our favor."

"Dettmer vs. Landon," TJ said. "I read about it back in April when the case began. As far as I'm concerned, the courts should decide in its favor because it's entitled to First Amendment protection like any other religion."

"Exactly," Tabitha told him and felt something within herself relax to know TJ truly seemed at ease with her differing from mainstream religion.

She touched her necklace. "How did you know this is the tree of life wrapped around the pentagram?"

He chuckled. "I'm a history geek. I might have gotten that from my grandfather as he loved studying the past. Mostly he stuck with the history of North Dakota. But I enjoy reading up on different civilizations, their cultures, and traditions. Some of my reading was on ancient religions. Because of that, I know Wicca pre-dates Christianity."

Abby spoke up, "Are you really going to play Candy Land with me, TJ?"

"I sure am. You're not scared I'll win, are you?"

She giggled and shook her head.

TJ grinned. "You should be. I have never lost a game of Candy Land." He finished the shrimp Alfredo, helped himself to a little more. "This is fantastic," he told Tabitha.

The phone rang, and Tabitha excused herself to answer it. She hoped it wasn't an emergency call from Greta or Grace to say they needed her at the clinic. Usually, that didn't happen. Once the clinic was closed, it remained that way. Still, occasionally things happened, and a call was made to the clinic's emergency line, which went directly to Grace's home number.

"Hello?" Tabitha said, picking up the receiver.

"Hello, Tabitha. This is Peggy. Greg and I would like for Abby to have another sleepover on Friday. What time shall we pick her up?"

Tabitha pulled the receiver away from her ear, looked at it as though it suddenly sprouted horns. She hated that about Owen's parents. Since last week, they had remained in town but hadn't bothered to see Abby since the previous sleepover, and now they assumed she would cater to them.

She sighed. On the one hand, if she wanted Abby to know these estranged grandparents, she didn't have a choice. "Whatever time works for you," she answered, finding it strange that they stayed in Binghamton longer than usual. By now, normally, they would have been driving down the road to whatever tourist town they were interested in seeing.

"We'll pick her up from your parents' home sometime Friday afternoon. Please make sure she has a change of clothing with her. And do not forget her toothbrush like you did the last time." Peggy hung up without a goodbye.

Tabitha did not resist the urge to stick out her tongue at the receiver. Her former mother-in-law was crazy, and she had not forgotten to pack Abby's toothbrush last time.

"Bitch," Tabitha said in a quiet whisper before walking back to the table and sitting down.

TJ could easily see the strain on her face. "You okay?" he asked, wanting to go to her. To wrap his arms around her and offer support and did not understand why the desire was so strong. They were still strangers getting to know one another.

Tabitha met his eyes. Nodded. Then he witnessed her transform her thin lips into a bright smile as she looked at Abby and said with enthusiasm. "Hey, Scooby. That was Grandma Turner on the phone. They want to have another sleepover with you. They're going to pick you up from grandma and grandpa's Friday."

Abby slumped in her chair, and her head bowed. She shook her head. "Do I have to go?"

The plea in her voice broke Tabitha's heart.

Tabitha swallowed a lump in her throat. She wanted to tell her daughter she never had to see Owen's parents again if she didn't want to, but the problem was, they were his parents, and he would have wanted his daughter to know them.

Regardless of Owen's parents practically disowning him because he dared to marry someone outside of their church, he had loved them.

"Scooby," Tabitha's voice was gentle as she explained, "I'm sure they won't be here much longer. And I know it's hard for you to understand them. Their ways differ from ours. But that does not mean they don't love you." Discreetly, she crossed her fingers under the table, hoping her statement was true.

"Okay," Abby grumbled as she picked up her fork and used it to push the pasta around on her plate. "I hope she doesn't read me a dumb book again."

"Perhaps you can bring a few of yours with you and share them with her," Tabitha suggested, and that idea seemed to brighten Abby's spirits.

TJ watched the exchange between mother and daughter, impressed with the way Tabitha persuaded the child to comply without raising her voice.

"So," he said, attempting to take Abby's mind off the upcoming sleepover with her grandparents. "I'm almost finished eating this amazing meal. How about after we help your mom with the cleanup, you and I," he spoke to Abby, "break out Candy Land and see who's the better player?"

Tabitha smiled; shook her head. She still had a hard time believing this man, who was six-foot-two, ruggedly handsome and had a muscular build, would sit on the floor and play a child's board game.

"If you're trying to impress me-" she began.

TJ grinned at her. "Is it working?" He asked, then laughed at her scowl. "Honestly, I'm used to playing kid games. I told you I have a lot of nieces and nephews. When we have family reunions, I seem to attract the little ones. Probably because I'm their youngest uncle and can keep up with them better than my brothers and sisters."

"How many siblings do you have?"

"Seven brothers. Two sisters."

Tabitha blinked. "Wow. Apparently, your parents kept busy."

TJ laughed. "They told me it was an excellent exercise and kept them healthy."

"I like exercise," Tabitha murmured, then flushed when she realized she'd said that out loud. Her eyes locked with TJ's, and from the smoldering gaze he was giving her, she knew he'd heard her comment.

"I wish I had a sister," Abby said, and Tabitha was glad for her daughter's distraction.

"I know it's hard to be the only child. I always wished for a sister too."

"Guess what, TJ," Abby said, smiling. "Doris gave me a nickel."

"That was nice of her."

"I put it in my piggy bank."

"That's great. Saving money is smart. Do you have something special you're saving up for? Something you want to buy?"

Abby nodded. "A pony!"

TJ had to laugh. He'd never met a little girl who didn't want a pony.

"My mother told me you visited Doris on Tuesday also," Tabitha commented. "Is she related to you?"

"No. There's just something about that old lady that makes me want to look out for her."

Tabitha searched his face as her heart opened more to him. It was apparent he was kindhearted and generous, which were traits she appreciated in a person.

Standing up, she began gathering the dirty dishes.

TJ also pushed away from the table, "I'll help you with the cleanup."

Tabitha shook her head. "Why don't you and Abby go ahead and begin your game of Candy Land? I can manage this." She needed a few moments to herself, anyway. To compose herself and possibly place a cold, wet cloth on the back of her neck.

She was so horny she was going to combust. If not for Abby, Tabitha knew she would have ripped TJ's clothes off in a heartbeat.

* * *

TJ laughed, scooped Abby up from where she was sitting at the table and tickled her. "I know you cheated, you little rascal. I'm the Candy Land champion. No one has beaten me before!"

Abby wiggled and laughed as she tried to get away. "I didn't cheat! I promise!" She sucked in air.

He set her gently back down. "Are you telling me I lost to a three-year-old, and now you're the new champion?" He tried to make his face look stern but failed miserably.

"I'm almost four!" she declared.

"Oh yeah? When's your birthday?"

"October five."

TJ made a mental note of the date.

"The popcorn is ready," Tabitha said as she carried a large bowl of hot buttered freshly popped corn into the room. "Alf will come on in about five minutes." She looked at her daughter, "When it's over, it's time for you to have a bath, brush your teeth, then bedtime."

Abby shook her head no.

Tabitha nodded her head. "It's Wednesday night. I have an early day tomorrow, so I have to drop you off at grandma and grandpas by six-thirty in the morning, so yes, bedtime."

TJ kept his mouth shut. It was not his place to interfere between mother and daughter.

He had vowed never to fall in love again, but every moment he spent with Tabitha and Abby, that pledge felt as though it was slowly being forgotten. There was a tangible pull, a magnetic force that seemed to draw him closer to them. He knew it was ridiculous. Having only known them for such a short time and yet, as much as he tried to resist, he found himself unable to deny the growing feelings inside of him.

"But mommy!" Abby strung the word out on a whine, "I want to stay up with TJ!"

He held up his hands, "Don't bring me into this. I have to work in the morning too. That house next to your grandparents isn't going to fix itself, and I want to stay on schedule so I can get it on the market in the fall."

Abby's bottom lip moved into a pout.

"Oh boy, Scooby-Doo. That lip sure looks awful. Do you want me to get some ice for it? You can lie in bed while TJ and I watch Alf and enjoy this yummy popcorn ourselves." She lifted the popcorn to her nose and sniffed. "Mmm, delicious. Obviously, it would be better with a lip like that if you didn't have any."

TJ almost laughed at how quickly Abby's lip when back in.

"I want popcorn," Abby said.

"All right then," Tabitha moved to the couch, sat down as she picked up the remote and switched on the television. "Will you take your bath and go to bed after the show without complaining?"

Abby made a face, but she nodded her head yes.

"Good," Tabitha glanced at TJ. "Were you going to watch Alf with us?"

"Of course," he said, and moved to sit next to her.

As he settled in beside Tabitha, Abby promptly jumped onto his lap.

His hiss alerted Tabitha that her daughter may have accidentally hit a vital part of his anatomy. "Hey, Scooby. I think you should sit with me." Setting the popcorn bowl down, she eased Abby onto her lap as she slid her eyes to glance at TJ. She mouthed, are you okay?

Nodding, he tried to discreetly readjust himself. "I'll wear a damn cup next time."

She stared at him. Then burst out laughing.

He scowled. "Babe, do you have any idea how much that hurt?"

Neither of them could say who was the most surprised by his use of an endearment.

"I love Alf," Abby said, oblivious to the sexual tension in the air between the adults as she laughed at the smart-mouthed creature on the television.

Tabitha kissed the top of her daughter's head. "Me too, Scooby," she said, trying to focus on the television rather than the man sitting beside her. It was an impossible task, and when she felt his arm go around her shoulder, she leaned into him.

What was it about this man that caused her to feel so at peace when she was with him? Was it his deep, soulful eyes that seemed to hold a universe of emotions? Or was it his kindness and giving nature?

She couldn't quite put her finger on it, but there was a sense of familiarity in his presence. As if they had known each other in a past life and were now reuniting once again. It was a feeling she couldn't shake off, and it both exhilarated and scared her.

When the show ended, TJ got up, stretched. "Enjoy your bath, munchkin. I'm going to head home. I'm sure I'll see you tomorrow during my break."

She nodded.

"Go get the toys you want with you in the tub tonight, "Tabitha told her daughter. "I'll be there in a minute to run the bathwater for you."

"Okay, mommy."

After she scampered off, Tabitha walked TJ to the door. As she opened it and he stepped out into the cold night, he turned back to her and said, "I don't suppose your bedroom has a lock on it?"

She blinked. "What?" She could not have possibly heard him correctly.

He leaned in, kissed her. Long and hard. "Sorry. Male anatomy talking. Goodnight, Tabitha."

When he would have turned away, she reached for his shirt, pulled him back. Wrapping her arms around his neck, she locked her mouth to his.

They both groaned.

Coming up for air, Tabitha told him, "You have no idea how difficult this is to tell you goodnight and not invite you back in. But I have to think of Abby." She pulled back.

Mischievously, she smiled at him. "However, if you do not have plans for Friday, since she'll be with the Turners, I'll be home all night." She caressed his cheek. "Alone."

His nostrils flared. He was well aware that he shouldn't let his emotional barriers down, but he could feel them crumbling. However, an image of Heather came to mind, and he used it as a support to steady himself. He didn't want Tabitha to misinterpret what he wanted from her, and he told her, "Just so we're clear," he spoke softly with a hint of gruffness in his voice, "I'm not seeking a long-term commitment with anyone."

Her eyes met his and there was a seductive glimmer in them, a hint of mischief that could not be ignored. She smiled at him, her lips parting ever so slightly, as if inviting him to kiss her. The smirk she gave him belonged to a seductress. "I wasn't attaching strings," she purred, her voice sending shivers down his spine and blood rushing to this groin.

Then she closed the door in his face. leaving him standing outside, trying to process the fact she'd given him an erection that wasn't going to be eased anytime soon.

Chapter Twelve

Thankfully, by the time TJ arrived home, he no longer had an erection.

He risked getting another one each time he thought about what would happen between himself and Tabitha on Friday night.

When he eased his Porsche onto the street he lived on, he could see lights on in his house. He considered he was being robbed for one split second, but then he saw the Corvette parked in the double car driveway and realized it was a welcome intruder.

He grinned.

He knew who that Vette belonged to, though how Mason had gotten into the house, TJ wasn't sure. Mason hadn't visited him here in the past, so TJ knew he didn't have a key to the front door or the security system code.

Parking the Porsche in the garage, TJ closed the garage door then walked around to the back of the house, where he heard music rolling out from the outdoor speakers.

At least Mason had the volume down to a reasonable decibel, and the neighbors wouldn't be complaining about the noise.

TJ opened the gate cut in the tall security privacy fence. When he rounded the corner, he found Mason sitting in the hot tub with a drink in his hand.

"Well, Mason. Welcome to my humble home. It's great to see you!" he walked forward to stand next to the tub. Reaching out, he placed a hand on top of Mason's head and gave his scalp a quick rub.

Mason grinned, flicked water at him. "Hey, Uncle TJ. Were you on a date?"

Tabitha's image formed in his mind, but he pushed it aside, not needing part of his anatomy to rise again. "No. I was having dinner with a friend and her daughter."

Mason saluted him with the glass in his hand. "A date, then. Was it a double?"

His surrogate nephew would probably always have a one-track mind when it came to women. However, TJ knew he'd finally matured enough to be choosier in taking bed partners. When he'd been sixteen, he'd probably slept with half the women tourists who came to Colten's ranch south of Medora, North Dakota.

An exaggeration, but Mason had spent a lot of time looking for sex in his early teens. And with those Greek god looks, finding a woman willing had never been a problem for him.

"No. The friend's daughter is three years old." TJ moved back, eased himself into a lounge chair. "What do I owe the honor of this visit?"

Mason smiled. "The agency has given me a few days' vacation, so I came here." He shrugged. "I have not seen your new home." His eyes glanced at the two and a half story house. "I am surprised you live in a shack."

The chuckle rolled out, and TJ shook his head. The house was over 3,352 square feet, but it was 5,000 square feet smaller than his penthouse had been. "It suits me, and I love it."

Mason wrinkled his nose.

"When did you become a snob, Mason? Sure, your childhood home is practically a palace. But you've spent your fair share of time in smaller places, sleeping in tents and going on horseback trips into the Badlands."

Mason shuttered. "Do not remind me." He glanced at the house once again. "How old is it?"

TJ smiled. "It was built in 1840."

"Putain," Mason swore in French. "Why do you like old things?"

TJ shrugged. When he'd moved from The Big Apple to here, this house, with its hardwood floors, porches and balconies beckoned him. The place was a testimony to true workmanship and artistry. The hardwood floors throughout, though original, had needed some tender care. Once he'd finished with them and polished them up, the high shine added elegance to the place. It had a massive basement that was a perfect workshop in the winter when he enjoyed building curio cabinets during the cold months, and there was plenty of room on the second floor for his business office.

The house had four bedrooms, three bathrooms, and now that the backyard's landscaping was complete, every time he arrived home and walked through the gate, it felt as though he was entering paradise.

"Enough about my choice of houses," TJ told him. "I'd like to know how you got into my house and disarmed the security system."

Now Mason grinned. "It is an old system."

"Bullshit. It's top of the line."

Pointing a finger toward the double patio glass doors, Mason said, "Actually, I brought an expert with me. He is responsible for breaking and entering when we discovered you were not home, and I did not have a key."

TJ glanced up. "Oh. My. God," he said in awe when he saw his nephew Hunter step onto the deck. It had probably been at least four years since he'd last seen him.

Standing up, TJ walked to him, then stopped a few feet away when he saw the crutches and cast. "What happened to you?"

"Got my leg broke. Isn't it obvious?" Hunter balanced himself on one crutch, stuck out his hand. "Good to see you, Uncle TJ."

TJ took the hand, leaned in to give him a quick hug, mindful not to off-balance him. "I can't believe you're here."

Hunter shrugged. "Uncle Cadman gave me time off while this thing heals up. I went to Mason's agency and hooked up with him, and since he was coming here to see you, I tagged along. I told him I'll spend some time with him, then I'm heading to North Dakota to see mom and dad."

"Don't bother. They're on their way here."

Hunter stared at him. "What do you mean, on the way here?"

"Well, actually, they're driving from North Dakota up to Clarion, Pennsylvania, to visit the Davidson's, then they're coming here."

"My parents do not leave North Dakota," Hunter stated.

TJ shrugged. "I guess Cadman told them they could and feels it's safe enough."

Hunter glanced over TJ's shoulder, met Mason's eyes with his. "Interesting."

"What is?" TJ asked.

"Cadman pulled security detail from Mason, too."

"Do you think that means he found out something about Pierre?" TJ glanced at Mason, who'd stood up from the hot tub and reached for a towel. He wrapped it around his naked loins and stepped out from the water.

Hunter shook his head. "If Cadman knew something, he would tell me." And he was a little peeved that Cadman hadn't mentioned he was allowing his parents to travel.

Mason joined them on the deck. "Perhaps Uncle Cadman is having a-" he frowned, flipping through English words in his head as he tried to remember what it was called here in America. "An old person's minute."

TJ raised a brow. "A what?"

Hunter sighed. "Translation; senior moment. Mason's English has improved considerably, but he still gets hung up on American slang sometimes."

"I am standing right here," Mason gripped, feeling as though he was being graded on his learning capabilities.

"And so you are," Hunter laughed, and Mason scowled.

"Cadman's too young to have memory loss," TJ pointed out. "He's only turning 60 this year."

"Well, I'm going to call him tomorrow and ask him what he's up to."

"In the meantime," TJ said, "You still haven't told me how you broke your leg."

"He allowed a bad guy to kick him," Mason explained, grinning at the scowl Hunter now had on his face.

"Yep. Four men trained in martial arts, angry that my team and I were there to shut down their drug operation, and I let one break my leg just for the hell of it."

"You had a team with you? How many in your group?"

"Three."

"And they didn't help you?"

"They were busy rescuing some villagers the cartel locked up for refusing to work for them. I kept the cartel's soldiers busy while my team was freeing the people and getting them to safety. Contrarily to what everyone believes, I'm not superman. The guy found an opening, and bam, my leg bone snapped. I took the bastard out before I felt the pain, though. That gave me great satisfaction." And knowing his team had gotten those people out made the whole thing worth it.

"Anyway," Hunter used his hand to gesture that conversation closed, "I believe you asked about your security system. It's easy to disarm it if you know the code."

"Say what? I've never given you the code."

Laughing, Hunter moved toward a nearby chair. Sat down. "When I was ten years old, you told me a string of numbers you liked to use to secure things."

"That was at least eleven years ago!"

Hunter tapped his forefinger to the side of his head. "Eidetic memory, remember? You know that shit sticks with me."

TJ sighed. "You guys want a beer?" he asked them, moving onto something else.

After they said yes, and TJ returned with the beers, they sat together at the small table on the deck to enjoy the quiet and still night, reminiscing about the past and catching up on family news.

After about an hour, Mason asked, "Who was the woman you were with tonight?"

In the process of taking a pull from his second beer of the evening, TJ almost choked. He had not expected the conversation of Tabitha to come up, but he should have known better. Mason's favorite subject was the opposite sex.

Clearing his throat, TJ said, "It's kind of a crazy story. I'm working on a house north of here," he began. And told them about Abby, and how he'd met Tabitha, and discovering she was Abby's mom.

Mason's eyes bulged. "How is it you are here and not in the woman's bed?"

Hunter rolled his eyes. "Seriously, Lafayette. Can't you think about anything other than sex?"

"You are so boring, Hunter. When was the last time you got laid?"

With a careless shrug, Hunter answered, "Probably three or four months ago."

Hand flying to his heart, Mason exclaimed, "No wonder you are cranky all the time."

"For the love of-." Hunter cursed the fact he couldn't just leap up and hit his best friend. "I'm usually kept too busy to even think about it. Maybe if you'd get a real job, instead of prancing all over the place for a camera, you'd know what it was like to be too exhausted to have it on your mind all the time!"

Undaunted, Mason looked at TJ. "We will need to find a woman for him soon, I am afraid."

Hunter threw his empty beer can in his direction, purposely missing only because deep down, he didn't want to hurt Mason. Kill him perhaps, but not cause injury.

"I'm fairly certain you don't need to know about my sex life when you have one of your own," Hunter claimed.

"Perhaps I am concerned that you have issues? After what happened to you during basic training, and what caused your phobia of spiders, I am only hoping you can still function." Mason said.

Hunter's face turned livid. "You can shut your pie hole, Lafayette, or I'll do it for you. And don't think my broken leg will stop me from climbing over this table to get to you. Just because I'm not trying to fuck every woman I lay eyes on doesn't mean I'm impotent! Why the hell would you bring that up?"

Hunter had used a portable toilet during his Navy basic training, unaware a poisonous spider was there with him until it was too late. The venomous spider bit him on his penis and put him in the hospital for a week. He'd been in severe pain, accompanied by sweating and nausea with an erection that lasted for hours.

There had been a concern because, yes, the incident could have led to impotency. But he'd fully recovered. He just wasn't the type of man to feel the need for sex constantly.

He and Mason had always teased each other throughout the years. Good-natured ribbing. But that had been a horrible nightmare for Hunter, and yes, he now had a phobia about spiders.

"All right, children," TJ said.

To Mason's credit, he looked ashamed of having taken the joking too far. "I apologize," he told Hunter. "I promise to never bring it up again. I was out of line."

Hunter's answer was a quick acknowledgment of his chin, but that was all he would say on the subject.

Wanting to turn the conversation elsewhere, Mason placed an elbow on the table, put his chin in his hand. "So, about Abby's mom. You like her, oui. What is the lady's name?"

"Her name is Tabitha, but as I said, we are not lovers." Going to be, but he refused to mention that to Mason for fear, there would be another round of sex talk.

Mason blinked and found it strangely coincidental for it to be the same first name of the veterinarian who'd written to him. "Turner?" he asked casually and watched TJ's eyes flare hot.

"How in the hell do you know that?!" TJ exclaimed. He had to wonder if this young stud had bedded Tabitha at some time while in a rut.

He would kill him if he had.

Mason stood up, oblivious to potential danger. "Give me a moment. I have something in my car I want to show you." He jogged off, returning within minutes with the envelope containing the letter from Tabitha in his hand. Handing it to TJ, he said, "Are you able to verify she is not a nut job? If so, I may consider what she is asking only because I like dogs."

Confused, TJ took the envelope. When he saw More Than Little Paws Veterinary Clinic's return address, he wasn't sure what his reaction should be.

"She wants me for a date," Mason tried to explain, but TJ leaped from the chair.

"The hell you say!" TJ exclaimed, taking an aggressive stance. He could not believe for a minute that Tabitha would do such a thing. Was she, like every woman in America, enthralled with Mason and his God-given looks? Impossible.

Hunter opened another beer, sat back with a grin on his face. "Finally, some entertainment."

"What?!" Mason asked, confused by TJ's sudden anger.

"As much as I would love to watch the two of you come to blows," Hunter said, "I think you should read the letter before you kill my best friend."

TJ tore the letter from the envelope, scanned the message. When he was through, he sat down and read it one more time. Yes, Tabitha wanted Mason for a date, but as a fundraiser event, not an evening with her.

Putting the letter back into the envelope, TJ told Mason, "Sorry. I had no idea she is interested in building a dog sanctuary."

"To be fair," Hunter said, "it doesn't sound as though you have known her long enough to know everything about her."

"So," Mason once again sat, "You are not going to hit me?"

"Not tonight, at least."

"Then I should meet her. Perhaps give her a chance to tell me about the shelter and what her idea of a date with me would include."

TJ looked him in the eyes. "As long as you understand that if you try to entice her into sharing a bed with you, I'll cut off your balls and shove them down your throat."

Mason raised his hands as though surrendering. "Uncle TJ, I would never do such a thing to you."

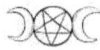

"Maybe I'll introduce you to her tomorrow." TJ stood up. "Good night."

Hunter and Mason watched him walk into the house, closing the patio doors behind him.

"Man, he's still thinking about what Heather did to him," Hunter said. "I hope her life sucks for the rest of her existence."

Mason sat back down, "I only hope this Tabitha is worthy of him."

Chapter Thirteen

"So," Grace singsonged when Tabitha walked into the clinic Thursday morning, "How was your date?"

Tabitha walked past the desk, placed her purse under the counter in her personal cubby. "It wasn't a date."

"Call it what you want. You cooked dinner for him, right?"

"Yes…"

"Yep, it was a date."

"Abby was there, Grace. Nothing happened."

Grace tisked. "Tabitha, dear. I know you've been out of the game for a few years, but nothing has to happen for a night with a man to be considered a date."

Tabitha sat down. "Confession time. I had to take a cold shower after Abby was asleep."

"Girl, you need to take care of that sooner rather than later."

"What if I told you Abby is spending Friday night with Greg and Peggy again?"

Grace took a large breath of air, let it out slowly. "I'm surprised they're still here. Normally they spend an hour with your daughter so they can feel good about themselves, then head on back down the road."

Tabitha sighed. "Oh, I find that extremely odd, but I've said this before- I will allow them to see Abby when they ask-"

"Yeah, yeah." Grace waved a hand. "So, Abby can never say you kept her from them." Grace rolled her eyes.

"Anyway," Tabitha said, not wishing to talk about the Turners more than necessary, "since I'm going to be free Friday night-"

"Oh, I'm sorry," Grace said, "My husband and I are having friends over Friday night. I can't go to Mindy's Over Yonder with you. Maybe Greta is free?"

Tabitha stared at her. "Don't be daft."

Grace laughed. "I'm pulling your leg. But tell me… Does this Friday night include seeing TJ again?"

Tabitha bit her bottom lip to keep her grin from splitting her face and nodded.

Grace squealed, stomped her feet in her excitement. "Oh, God. Greta and I are going to want details Monday morning."

"No details."

"You're such a party pooper."

Greta walked through the front door. "Who pooped? I didn't realize we had a patient bright and early this morning."

Tabitha and Grace laughed, then Grace explained about Tabitha's up-coming Friday night.

"Oh, you had better be giving us the details," Greta told her friend and boss.

"Nope," Tabitha picked up the clipboard with the list of today's appointments; pleased to note that, once again, Bubbles name was not listed. Hopefully, the cat's owner had finally stopped stressing over the pet.

The first patient of the day walked through the door with its owner in tow. Scout was a beautiful husky, here for its annual visit.

"Good morning, Scout," Tabitha greeted the animal, then the owner. "And good morning to you, Mr. Severson."

"Right back at cha, doc. Ol' Scout here has been eager to see you."

Tabitha stepped out from behind the desk, held her hand out for Scout to sniff. "You're such a handsome boy," she told the dog as it wagged its tail and then began a happy dance when it recognized Tabitha's scent.

Greta called to the dog. "Come on, Scout. Let's get you into a room so we can take a look at you."

Owner and beast followed the veterinarian assistant into one of the examination rooms.

When the door closed, Grace told Tabitha, "And we're off to a great start. Scout is the perfect patient."

"He's one of my favorites too," Tabitha confessed with fondness. She remembered the day she and Owen found the poor thing abandoned and neglected on the north side of town. The then five-year-old dog had been living in an alley and barely surviving. He had bald spots and was so thin they could see his bones.

She and Owen were able to get a leash on him and into their car. They'd taken him to their home, the house Tabitha still lived in, and carefully nursed the husky back to health. It wasn't a quick process. But over time, with grooming, plenty of nutritious food, and a whole lot of love, Scout's transformation from being close to death to the strong and healthy animal he was now was nothing short of a miracle. His makeover had indeed been astonishing.

Mr. Severson adopted the husky within days of Owen posting it in the newspaper. One stipulation of the adoption was that Mr. Severson had to bring Scout to this clinic at least once a year so the Turners could keep up on his progress.

It did Tabitha's heart good to see that Scout continued to flourish and knew Owen would have been pleased.

She stepped into the exam room, closed the door behind her, and began her day.

At noon, TJ walked into the clinic. Grace looked up from her place behind the desk and smiled.

"Hello, handsome," she said. "Was Tabitha expecting you? I don't re-call her mentioning she needed her noon free. Unfortunately, I sched-uled a few appointments for her over the lunch hour to accommodate a few pet owners. She won't be free until later." She glanced down at the scheduling book. "Correction, she won't be free until we close at five."

"No, I wasn't expected. But I could use five minutes of her time. I'll make it quick," TJ promised.

Grace glanced at the few appointments already sitting in the reception area, waiting for their turn. She supposed five minutes wouldn't hurt. "Okay, but only five minutes, or we'll have a mutiny on our hands."

TJ grinned. "Thanks, beautiful."

Grace felt a blush rise up. "Compliments won't get you any more time."

He was laughing when the exam room door opened and out walked a woman with a beagle on a leash.

"And you'll want to schedule that appointment to have his teeth cleaned as soon as possible," Tabitha was saying to the owner as she too stepped out.

"We'll do that," the owner assured her.

Tabitha noticed TJ standing by the desk. "Hi," she smiled as she walked up to him.

"Hi back. Grace has allotted me five minutes of your time. Is there somewhere we can talk?"

"Sure." She motioned him to follow her into the room she moments ago vacated.

The moment the door was closed, he suddenly turned her around. "I have to get this out of the way first," TJ told her and kissed her. It was intended to be a brief kiss, but it didn't work out that way.

She wound her hands into his hair, anchoring him.

There was a knock on the door. "Three minutes," they heard Grace's warning and stepped apart.

"Wow," Tabitha said, stepping back as she met TJ's eyes. "I did not expect that."

TJ shook his head. "Me either. I didn't think she was serious about only allotting me five minutes with you."

She laughed at his comment, knowing he was not talking about Grace. "Although Grace keeps a tight schedule, that wasn't what I meant." TJ Fisher was an excellent kisser.

He gave her a lopsided smile. "I know, and I'm running out of time; otherwise, I'd do it again."

"What did you need to see me about that couldn't wait until I picked up Abby from my parent's house?"

"Well, I was wondering if you and Abby would like to join me at my house tonight for supper? I could bring Abby with me, pick you up, and head to my home. My nephews are in town, and I really think you would like to meet one of them."

Tabitha frowned. "That seems odd?"

He chuckled. "I know. But trust me, you want to talk to him if you're serious about wanting to raise money for the dog sanctuary you want to build."

She was now more confused than ever. "How did you know about that?" Had she mentioned it to him?

"After you meet my nephew, you'll understand."

"One minute!" Grace's voice warned from the other side of the door.

"Give it a rest already!" Tabitha called back.

"I suppose I should let you go before you get into trouble," TJ told her.

"What is she going to do? Fire me?"

Considering Tabitha owned the place and was the boss, "I suppose not." He chuckled. "What do you say? Would you be okay with me bringing Abby with me to pick you up? Or would you rather follow me from your folks' house?"

"You can get her car seat from my folks. I'll call them and let them know I gave you permission to take her. I'm sure she'll be ecstatic, seeing how you've become her new hero. We close tonight at five unless an emergency comes up." Tabitha opened the door leading back into the reception area and wondered why she trusted this man completely with her daughter's safety. "If your nephews don't care that I'll still be in my scrubs, I'm in."

TJ glanced down at the bright blue uniform top with its print of cartoon cats and dogs. "You look adorable in scrubs," he told her.

Surprising them both, he leaned down and gave her a quick kiss before realizing they had an audience now that they'd stepped into the reception area.

"Gee, I guess I should have given you more time," Grace said, which caused the people waiting for their pets to be seen to erupt into laughter.

Tabitha flushed scarlet.

Laughing, TJ moved toward the exit.

"I'll see you later, Tommy Jack," Tabitha called after him.

"Still not it," TJ told her as he walked out the door.

Grace looked at her in question.

"It's a game. I'm trying to figure out what his initials stand for," Tabitha explained.

"Girl, that's obvious," Grace moved back to her chair behind the desk. "He's Totally Jacked."

"Who's next," Tabitha laughed, shaking her head at Grace's observation regardless of agreeing wholeheartedly.

Grace handed her a chart. "Prancer Walker. He's here for his shots."

Tabitha greeted the owner and her cat, brought them into the exam room, and closed the door as she forced herself to concentrate on the business at hand, and not on the upcoming evening.

She wondered, though, how TJ had known about the dog sanctuary, and why he thought it was important for her to meet his nephew.

* * *

TJ supposed he should have looked at the owner's manual of his extended cab before trying to install Abby's car seat in the backseat. But with a little finagling and moving the passenger seat all the way forward, he'd been able to tether it down.

The next time he offered to pick Tabitha up at work with Abby in tow, he'd drive his Porsche. It had been easier to place the safety device in the smaller vehicle than the truck.

Go figure that one out.

But driving home to exchange vehicles would have been a waste of time.

Maybe he should buy a Lamborghini LM002 to add to his two-vehicle collection. It was a four-wheel-drive off-road truck that would have plenty of room for Abby's car seat.

He found it odd that he was thinking long-term when he had no idea where this relationship with Tabitha would be after tomorrow night or even next week.

Angela Stevens stood in the driveway of the remodeling project with Abby next to her. "I think you secured it down well enough," Angela told TJ.

He grunted, pulling himself back out from the cab. It felt like he'd been wrestling with a hippo.

"I can't believe you guys transfer this contraption to each other's car every day. It would be a hell of a lot more convenient to have one for each vehicle."

Angela chuckled. "It would, but obviously you do not understand how much those cost. And they get more and more complicated every year. I can't imagine what they'll look like ten years from now. But since the government passed the law last year requiring them, we abide. Besides, it's a good idea."

"I agree," TJ told her, then looked at Abby. "All right, munchkin. Are you ready to climb in so we can pick up your mom?"

Abby nodded. "I want to see your house!"

"You'll have plenty of space to explore, I promise you that." And he remembered the pool and hot tub. "Hey, Angela, you wouldn't have a swimsuit for her here, would you?"

"I do."

"Could you send it along with us? I have a hot tub and pool. Maybe we'll go swimming later." He shrugged.

Angela rushed off to grab the swimsuit, returned with it. She passed the small suit to him, along with something else. "I have one of Tabitha's older suits. I'm sending it too."

TJ glanced down at the pieces of cloth she handed him and swallowed. He wasn't sure if he could live if he saw Tabitha in a bikini, and he sure as hell would not let Mason and Hunter see her in it either. Especially Mason.

He passed the two barely-there items back to Angela. "I think you can keep those here. If she decides she wants to go swimming, I've got something she can use."

Like, one of his long T-shirts that wouldn't reveal so much.

After that, he loaded up Abby, and they were heading toward Tabitha's clinic.

He parked the truck next to the exit and only had to wait fifteen minutes before she walked out of the clinic with Greta and Grace.

"Mommy!" Abby exclaimed from the back of the truck's cab when Tabitha opened the passenger door.

"Hi, Scooby. Did you have a good day with grandma?"

Abby nodded. "And with TJ. He let me hammer a nail."

Tabitha glanced at TJ.

"Everyone should know how to hammer a nail properly," he told her. "Besides, it's one of those wooden tool kits for kids with round dowels to hammer through pre-drilled holes. I picked it up for her after I stopped by here this afternoon."

"Oh," Tabitha relaxed. "Well then, cool, Scooby."

TJ put the truck in gear once Tabitha was strapped in. They headed toward his house located minutes away from downtown Binghamton.

When they arrived, Tabitha couldn't help but stare at the charming historic two-story. "You live in this big house by yourself? It's lovely!"

He nodded. "Yep. I live alone, but I have plenty of room for guests. Come on in. Hopefully, my nephews remembered to pick something up for supper."

"Interesting," Tabitha said. Obviously, his nephews didn't cook.

"Let's just hope they didn't pick up McDonald's. I hate cold fries," TJ told her as he slid from the cab.

"I like McDonald's!" Abby confessed.

"And what kid doesn't?" TJ commented, coming around to the passenger side to help Tabitha get Abby out from the cab's back seat.

They entered the house through the stunning kitchen. It had a center island with bar stools, white wooden cabinetry broken up by a faint yellow shade of paint between the countertop and upper cabinets. The farthest wall was brick, also painted white, and another doorway leading outside to a deck with patio furniture, giving the option to eat outside if the weather was pleasant. The appliances were black, and frying pans hung from hooks near the brick wall.

"TJ," Tabitha whispered, feeling as though the house was welcoming her. "My stars, it's lovely."

TJ smiled. "I like it too. It's kind of peaceful. But you haven't seen the rest of the house." His eyes glanced at the counter, noted there wasn't any food sitting there.

He'd kill Mason and Hunter if they forgot to pick something up.

Mason's Vette was sitting in the driveway, so TJ knew they were here.

"Come on, I'll give you a tour of the place. Maybe we'll run into one, or both, of my nephews in the process."

From the kitchen, they moved through a small nook with two openings. One room was the dining room, and the other led to a narrow hallway that shared space with a staircase leading to the second floor. Past the staircase was a living room, and from this room, there was another door leading to another deck with outdoor furniture.

"I love your house," Tabitha told him.

"Me too," he told her.

They were about to go up the stairs when Hunter hobbled in from the room across from the main living room. He took one look at Tabitha and grinned. "Hi," he said. "I'm Hunter. I'll take a wild guess and assume you're Tabitha. And this young lady," he glanced at the child, "is Abby."

"You assume correctly," Tabitha told him, holding out her hand to shake his as he used one crutch to balance himself with.

"What happened to your leg?" Abby wanted to know.

"I broke it playing ball," he lied. Besides, there was no explaining to a three-year-old exactly how it had really gotten broken.

"How bad was the break?" Tabitha asked, eyeing the full leg cast.

Hunter shrugged. "It took the surgeon a couple of hours to repair it, and I've got some temporary pins and rods in there, but it's healing. The worst part will be getting it back in shape. That's probably going to be more painful than this was."

He meant physically because he had spent a lifetime conditioning himself for combat. Now he would need to work hard to get the leg muscles back.

"By the way, Hunter," TJ spoke up. "Did the two of you forget to pick up something to eat?"

Hunter smiled. "We wouldn't let you down. Mason's out-front paying for the pizza now."

The front door opened on cue, and Mason stood there, holding four boxes containing large pizzas from a local pizzeria.

Tabitha stared. How could she not when the Touch My Bod jeans model just walked off the page of a magazine?

"Bonjour, Belle," his smile was sensual. Until he saw TJ's scowl, which wiped the look off his face quickly.

"My nephews, Hunter Fisher and Mason Lafayette," TJ said.

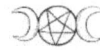

Chapter Fourteen

The tour of the house caused Tabitha to fall in love with the older home, and Abby squealed with delight upon discovering a few areas that would make excellent hiding places.

After the walk though was complete all of them sat on the balcony overlooking the swimming pool and hot tub while devouring pizza.

TJ's German beer was added to the party, though they offered Abby her choice of water, milk, or a can of pop.

Given permission, Abby opted for the pop. Of course. She was like every other child in America who liked carbonated beverages.

"I'm still in shock," Tabitha said after she finished her last slice of pizza. She also realized she was developing a taste for TJ's imported beer. "At least now I know how TJ knew about my dream to build a dog sanctuary. I never talked to him about it."

"It is only by chance I received your letter," Mason told her. "All mail that comes to me at the agency goes to my publicist or is shredded. Rarely do I see it."

Tabitha reached up, gently grasped her pendant. Her habit of thanking her goddess for intervening.

"I find it more amazing you're TJ's nephew."

"We are not blood-related," Mason confessed. "However, I have always considered him my uncle. My family is good friends with Hunter's parents."

"Well," Tabitha told him. "I'm glad he and I met, and it has nothing to do with you. Sorry, and no offense." She reached out to TJ, sitting on her right, and took his hand in hers.

TJ grasped her hand and smiled at her. He had been honest the other night when he told her he was not looking for a permanent relationship. However, he admitted he enjoyed having Tabitha and Abby in his life.

Mason laughed. "I will no be a fence."

Hunter shook his head, rolled his eyes. "Offence. Not a fence," he corrected. "Geez's, Lafayette. By now, you should speak perfect English." Getting that dig in after Mason's bringing up his misfortune during basic training last night gave him great satisfaction.

Mason's unique cat-like green eyes met Hunter's dark as chocolate ones. He asked, "Do you speak all the languages you know perfectly?"

Because of Hunter's eidetic memory and his ability to learn languages quickly, Mason shouldn't have had to ask the ridiculous question. "Yep."

"Trou du cul," Mason told him.

Laughing, as Mason had called him an asshole in French, Hunter said, "At least you didn't say that in English so someone little would learn a new word." His eyes discreetly moved toward Abby, who was drinking her soda as she watched the adults. He could tell she was listening to the adult conversation.

"How many languages do you speak?" Tabitha asked.

"Nine."

"Holy cr-" Tabitha's eyes slid toward her daughter and amended, "crab cakes. Holy crab cakes."

"What's a crab cake, mommy?" Abby wanted to know.

"A type of food. Maybe one day we'll make some," Tabitha answered.

"They are not as good as pizza," Mason said, taking another slice from the box.

"Keep eating those carbs, Lafayette, and women aren't going to be impressed by you anymore," Hunter warned.

Mason grinned. "I will go for a jog later and burn off the calories. If anyone should be careful, it should be you, my friend. With that leg in a cast, you will balloon up by the time you are allowed to report back for duty. Uncle Cadman will not allow you to fly on a helicopter for fear it will not be able to get off the ground with you in it."

"Who's the trou du cul now?" Hunter wanted to know.

Before a fight could ensure, TJ interjected with, "Who wants to go for a swim?"

Abby's hand shot up.

"Me too," TJ answered, standing up.

Tabitha's eyes slid to Hunter as a thought occurred to her. "I assume you know your uncle's name."

"Huh?" Hunter asked with surprise. What kind of fool question was that?

"Oh, no, you don't," TJ chuckled, sitting back down. "That's cheating." He explained to Hunter and Mason the game he and Tabitha had going on regarding his actual name.

Hunter raised his hands, palms out. "Sorry. We can't help you. He swore us to secrecy when we accidentally found out what it was. He threatened us with death if we ever repeated it."

Tabitha threw her head back and laughed. "Oh, come on! This is ridiculous. It cannot possibly be all that bad."

Hunter and Mason glanced at each other. "Yes, it can," Hunter confirmed. "Our family seems to have brain malfunctions now and again with giving names out to their children. My middle name, for example. My dad named me for the place where I was conceived. Sundance, Wyoming. I'll warn you, though, not to tell another living soul that. I detest it." He shook his head, marveling at the fact he had told her at all. He was not naturally someone to talk about himself.

It must be the German beer TJ kept serving him. It was loosening his tongue.

"Your middle name is Sundance?" Okay, Tabitha had to admit that was not a common name.

Mason chuckled. "Stop complaining. Your father gave you a short name. Mine gave me a mouthful."

"Which is?" Tabitha asked. He could not leave her hanging like this.

"Richard Fernando Antoine Albert."

Tabitha's mouth made an O.

"So," Mason leaned back in his chair and tried not to flirt with the pretty lady. Habits were hard to break, but for TJ, he would be on his best behavior. "You have not told me about this sanctuary for dogs you are interested in building, and how you thought I could help."

Tabitha shrugged. "Honestly, I wrote you that letter before I found out the land I've had my eye on for years was sold out from underneath me."

"Sacré bleu!" Mason bellowed. "That is not right."

"Do you know who purchased the land?" Hunter wanted to know.

"A construction company named Badland Builders!" Tabitha exclaimed with disgust. "I'd like to give them a piece of my mind, that's for sure."

TJ, in the process of taking a pull from his beer, almost choked.

"Are you alright?" Tabitha asked, concerned.

TJ managed to nod as the coughing subsided, and he felt Hunter and Mason's eyes on him. And he knew it was not out of concern for his wellbeing.

"Fascinating," Hunter said, sitting back in his chair.

Mason threw his head back and laughed. "Perhaps you can write them a letter and ask them to donate it to you."

TJ's scowl had both of his nephews laughing.

Tabitha wasn't sure what the joke was, but she said, "I doubt anyone would want to donate land that's worth over a hundred thousand dollars."

"You never know," Hunter said. "Would you like me to find the address for the construction company for you?"

He grinned like a Cheshire cat toward his uncle.

"I'll think about it and let you know. I just couldn't imagine them taking me seriously and my stars, why would they want to donate property they just purchased?"

TJ wanted this conversation to end. He'd had no idea anyone else was interested in those ten acres. The bank hadn't cared to inform him anyone else had an offer on the table, and at the time, he had not met Tabitha.

He wasn't sure if that would have swayed him from purchasing the property or not, but he felt uncomfortable right now. And he wanted to kick Hunter in the leg. He would have chosen the broken one just on principle, offering to give Tabitha his company's address. Which was this very house.

"Abby!" TJ said with enthusiasm as he stood up and refused to touch this subject for the time being, "You wanted to go swimming."

Abby's eyes turned to her mother. "Mommy, can I go swimming? Grandma gave TJ my swimsuit."

"The pool is heated," TJ added.

Tabitha looked at him and wondered, once again, how he could possibly afford the luxuries he had by only purchasing houses, refurbishing them, and reselling.

"Did grandma send my suit too?"

"I'm sure I have something around here you can wear," TJ told her confidently.

"I think a swim with the beautiful lady and pretty little girl would be fun," Mason said, standing up and stretching. "I'll put on a pair of shorts and join you in the pool."

Tabitha could hardly believe she was about to go swimming with Mason Lafayette. The same Mason Lafayette women all over the world drooled over. However, as impressive as that was, she was more excited to see what TJ looked like in swimming trunks."

She would consider it a preview of what she hoped to see tomorrow night.

Hunter sighed. "I suppose I can find something to entertain myself with."

"Would you like a magazine to look at?" TJ offered.

Hunter scowled. Being idle was killing him. He was used to being on the move, but he still had six months of being in this cast before physical therapy would come into play once the doctor removed the cast, rods and pins.

He probably would have pulled all his hair out by then.

"Sure. Why not? I can amuse myself by tearing out the pages and making paper airplanes to aim at all of you while you're splashing around down there."

Abby sat down on the chair next to him. "I can stay with you. Maybe we can play go fish?"

Despite his ill humor, Hunter laughed. "Kid, as much fun as that might be, I think you would have more fun swimming."

Abby shrugged. "Okay," she said and slid off the chair. She'd rather go swimming anyway.

"After I get Abby into her bathing suit, I could keep you company," Tabitha offered.

"Nah. That's okay," Hunter told her. "I need to call my boss." He pushed himself out of the chair, reached for his crutches.

"What type of work do you do?" Tabitha asked. "I hope you have insurance to get you through these months of healing."

"I get paid during this downtime but thank you for your concern."

"Hunter works for the government," TJ informed Tabitha.

"Wow. Really?"

Hunter shrugged. "We'll leave it at that," he told her. Setting his crutches in place under his arms, he began maneuvering his way into the house.

TJ watched his nephew disappear through the door, feeling the pride he had for him rise. Hunter had been eighteen when he'd graduated as a SEAL.

A while later, TJ found a couple of old t-shirts and a pair of shorts that would work for Tabitha to use as swimwear. The two T-shirts worn as layers would help conceal part of her anatomy when wet from Mason's wondering eyes.

The shorts proved to be the most difficult item to supply since she was nowhere near his size, but, using twine as a belt, she could tighten an old pair around her waist.

"I feel ridiculous," she said, stepping onto the deck. "If I do this again, I'm bringing my bikini."

TJ handed her a towel. Hell, to the no to that idea if Mason was anywhere near. "I think you look adorable."

She snorted. "That's a big lie. These are way too big for me."

"They'll work for now," TJ told her. "Give me a moment to change into a pair of trunks, and I'll join you in the pool."

"If I hear one snicker from your nephews-"

"They won't laugh," he promised.

Mason stepped out onto the back porch in a pair of shorts with Abby holding his hand. After Tabitha helped her daughter into her swimsuit earlier, Mason offered to watch her while Tabitha changed into the clothing TJ gathered up for her.

When Mason saw the ridiculous way his uncle had dressed Tabitha, his eyes filled with humor. He opened his mouth to say something, but the look TJ shot him had him clamping it shut. "Excuse me one moment," he said, letting go of Abby's hand before walking back into the house and closing the patio door.

Rich laughter, although muffled, could be heard coming from within the house.

"I'm mortified!" Tabitha exclaimed.

"Mommy, can we go swimming now?" Abby asked, not seeming to notice her mother's embarrassment.

Perhaps he should have brought Tabitha's suit with him when her mother offered it, TJ mused. But he also knew he would never have survived seeing her in that two-piece. "Come on, once you're in the water, it won't matter what you have on."

"Then maybe I should just go in my bra and under-wear!"

TJ swallowed audibly, envisioning that scenario. "Maybe I could find something else?"

"Mommy!" Abby tugged on her hand. "I want to go swimming."

Taking a deep breath and blowing it out, Tabitha closed her eyes for a moment. She supposed the damage was already done. "All right," she sighed, picking up one of the towels TJ brought outside earlier for their use. "Let's go, Scooby."

As mother and daughter began walking toward the pool, Tabitha looked over her shoulder. She told him, "I'll get you for this, Tyrone Joshua."

"Good guess, but still no!" TJ laughed as he called after her. "I'll be back in a moment after I change."

He met Mason on his way into the house as the young model was coming back out. "Thanks a lot for laughing," he griped.

Mason shrugged. "She is a beautiful woman. Why would you wish to cover her up?"

"To keep your lustful eyes from looking at her any more than you have."

"Uncle TJ. I have no interest in her in the way you suggest. I may flirt with a woman, but it is harmless. This one has eyes only for you. She is not Heather, and I am not Rick. It's time to move on."

Ignoring TJ's glower, Mason moved past him to join Tabitha and Abby in the pool.

TJ debated about shouting out, "I've been over Heather for a long time!" But stopped himself as he considered that perhaps Mason was right. Maybe the reason he was leery of Mason being around Tabitha was born from fear of being betrayed once again.

Mason wouldn't do that, TJ assured himself as he ascended the stairs leading to his bedroom. But neither had he expected Rick to sleep with Heather behind his back.

He glanced out his bedroom window, which overlooked the pool, watching the three in the water interacting with one another. For the most part, Mason stayed on the opposite side of the two-year-old twenty by forty-foot pool. At the same time, Tabitha and Abby splashed together at the shallow end.

TJ felt a little guilty over that, knowing Mason was good with children. Abby would have the time of her life if the famous man wasn't purposely trying to avoid being close to Tabitha.

Quickly changing into his swim trunks, TJ vowed to be less suspicious of the person he'd bounced on his lap as a baby and went downstairs to join the others.

Tabitha was reaching for Abby as the girl laughed and splashed, enjoying the evening swim, when she saw TJ nearing the pool.

Her mouth watered, seeing him in those boxer swimming trunks. He did not have six-pack abs like Mason. Obviously, the model worked out to keep his body toned, but TJ's body was muscular from the physical labor he did. His tapered waist and broad chest caused her breath to catch and anticipation built.

And when he turned his back to her briefly, to toss his own towel on a chair sitting along the edge of the pool, her eyes widened upon seeing the six symbols tattooed onto his back. The symbols all connected at the tips of three lines which crossed each other at a center point to form a circle. She did not know their meaning, but she recognized them as Runes. Symbols that were sometimes used as mystical tools to protect and connect to psychic insights, and the emblem on his back was called a Bindrune.

She wanted to ask him about them, but the questions would have to wait until they could be alone. Right now, Abby was tapping her shoulder and saying, "Mommy! You said you would show me how to float on my back!"

Reluctantly she moved her eyes away from TJ and looked at her daughter. "Yes, I did, Scooby. Come here, and I'll help you."

Distracted by her daughter, she was unaware of TJ slipping into the pool, but she felt his arms come around her just as Abby caught on to laying on top of the water.

"Hi," TJ said, and it was a caress in her ear. His breath caused her knees to go weak.

"Hi back," she told him and allowed him to turn her around to face him.

Abby exclaimed on a giggle when he leaned in and kissed her mother, "TJ gave you a Scooby kiss, mommy!"

Tabitha felt a blush creep up her face as she laughed, "Yes, he did. Come on, Scooby. Let's see if he knows how to swim."

"Mason!" TJ called, "Come over here and join us!"

"As long as you promise not to punch me in the nose," he called back.

"I promise," TJ told him, then shrugged when he saw Tabitha's questioning look. He was not about to admit to her the struggle he was having with jealousy. "It's an old joke," he smoothly lied.

The group played in the water for half an hour. At one point, Mason was carrying Abby on his shoulders, then was lifting her up and throwing her into the water as she giggled and kept coming back for more of the same.

"He is very good with children," Tabitha observed.

"Growing up, he spent time during the summers at my brother's horse ranch in North Dakota. The ranch has a tourist business, giving guided tours into the Badlands. And my niece Donna runs a horse camp for children with special needs. He helped with both when he was younger, so he is accustomed to being around children."

"Wow," Tabitha said as she watched her daughter splashing and laughing with the famous model.

When she leaned into TJ, he wrapped his arms around her. Relishing the feel of his flesh against her cheek, Tabitha closed her eyes and marveled at how well they seemed to mold to each other.

"You know," TJ's voice was husky, and his hand crept up and down her back, "since Mason has Abby occupied-"

Tabitha looked up at him, saw the want in his eyes, and knew it reflected what she felt.

Wrapping her arms around his neck, she moved up on tiptoes as he lowered his mouth to hers.

"Look, Mason!" they heard Abby exclaim, "TJ's giving mommy another Scooby kiss!"

Reluctantly the couple pulled apart, knowing neither of them had swimming on their minds.

"I can give you ten minutes!" Mason called out, laughter in his voice.

Taking Tabitha's hand, TJ led her out of the pool. As much as he wanted to take Mason up on the offer to watch Abby while he took Tabitha to his bedroom, he wouldn't do it. When the hour arrived to spend time in the woman's bed, he did not want to be rushed.

"If that's all you give your women Mason, it would surprise me to discover any of them claim your any good at-" his eyes moved to Abby and stopped himself from saying the word sex.

"Wrinkling sheets?" Mason suggested an alternative, then grinned. "Believe me when I tell you, women very much enjoy that activity with me."

TJ shook his head as a smile curved his lips. Mason was hopeless, and he knew it.

Later, once everyone was back in their street clothes, TJ reluctantly drove Abby and Tabitha to the clinic.

"How about I follow you home?" TJ suggested once he'd gotten the child car seat out of his truck and transferred it into Tabitha's vehicle.

"You don't have to do that," Tabitha told him. "We had a lovely evening, and I've been getting myself home by myself for the past four years." She placed her hand on his cheek. She liked the feel of his beards stubble's under her palm.

"I know, but-" But what? -he asked himself. Of course, she was right, and he did not understand where this desire to keep her safe came from when they had not known each other long.

"I'll be fine, mom," Tabitha teased, giving him a quick kiss on the cheek. "I'll see you tomorrow night if you still wanted to-"

"Oh yes," he told her, pulling her in for more than a quick peck on the cheek. "What time?"

"I should be home by five-thirty, as long as an emergency at the clinic doesn't happen." She held out her hand to Abby, "Come on, Scooby. You still need your bath and need to pick out what you want to bring with you tomorrow for your sleepover with grandma and grandpa Turner."

Abby shook her head. "I don't want to go!" she ex-claimed and stomped her foot for emphasis.

Tabitha bent down, stroked her daughter's hair. "I know, Scooby. Normally they don't stay this long, and they want to have another sleepover with you." She plastered a bright smile on her face. "I'm sure you'll have fun."

Abby shook her head. "All they want to do is read me stories. Boring, boring, boring!"

"I promise this will be the last time, Scooby. We'll pick out some books you like and send them with you. Okay?"

Abby stuck out her bottom lip.

Tabitha sighed. Perhaps forcing Abby to spend time with the Turners wasn't wise. But she agreed to another sleepover, and she would not go back on her word.

TJ helped get Abby into the car, kissed her cheek, and told her, "Sleep well tonight, munchkin."

Still in a pout, Abby turned and looked the other way.

Straightening, TJ pulled Tabitha in for one more kiss before telling her goodnight. "I know I'm going to have some really great dreams tonight, thinking about tomorrow." He wiggled his brows.

Tabitha swatted his broad chest. "Dream about a meadow in a forest, and I'll come to join you," she teased, thinking about the vivid dreams she'd had herself regarding making love to this man.

"What? Don't you like the beach?" TJ teased back.

Her body jerked. "What?"

"Babe, I've been dreaming of you since the night we met and the things we've done on a beach in my dreams-"

"Holy stars," Tabitha whispered, staring at him.

"What?"

"TJ. I've had the same dreams."

It was his turn to stare.

Chapter Fifteen

Friday at noon, when there was a break in the day's appointments, Tabitha told Greta and Grace, "I have someone bringing us lunch today."

Grace put her paper bag containing her lunch back in her drawer. "Had I known; I wouldn't have brought anything. But I will not look a gift horse in the mouth. What's on the menu?"

"Actually, I don't know."

Greta sat down in the extra chair next to Grace behind the desk. Fridays were usually their slowest day in the summer months. Many pet owners wanted to get an early start to their weekend and tried to bring their animals earlier in the week because of travel plans.

"Maybe we should think about closing early on Fridays," Greta suggested.

"Not a bad idea," Grace agreed. "At least during the summer months."

"I'll think about it," Tabitha told them, thinking she would probably do as they suggested. No point staying open in case one person came through the door. They had booked this morning with appointments, but there were only a dozen slated for the afternoon.

"Well, while we wait for our mystery meal to arrive, what time were your former in-laws picking Abby up from your folks today?"

Tabitha sighed. "That's why my mother called earlier. They picked her up at ten, which was way before the agreed-upon time. They told me they would get her later this afternoon, but my mom said they showed up and said they were eager to start their day with her." She leaned against the counter and frowned. "I think this is the last time I'll allow them to see her without me being there or one of my parents. For Owen's sake, I've tried to help Abby get to know them, but they aren't exactly loving toward her."

"Have they hit her?!" Greta exclaimed, leaping from her chair.

"What?! No!" Tabitha was firm. "How could you even consider I would allow them within five miles of her if I suspected something like that?!"

Chastised, Greta sat down. "I'm sorry. I know you wouldn't allow that."

"What I meant was," Tabitha explained, "is that their visit this time feels more like they are trying to convince Abby that my parents and I are evil." She stood up and paced. "You know the type. Radical religious group who believes they are the only ones who know the true path to God, and everyone else's beliefs are wrong." When she stopped her pacing, she told them, "I almost called them this morning and told them Abby was sick."

"Why didn't you?" Grace asked.

"Because I'm selfish!" Tabitha cried out. "TJ's coming over tonight-"

"Say no more," Grace held up her hand. "Listen, wanting to have some time with a hot guy isn't being selfish. My god, Tabitha, you hardly ever take time out for yourself, and you should not feel guilty! Besides, it's only for one night. Abby will forget about them as soon as they drop her off tomorrow."

The front door of the clinic opened, putting an end to that conversation.

Greta glanced up, saw the guy on crutches coming through the door, and said under her breath, "Talk about hot guys." She fanned herself. "Hubba, Hubba."

Tabitha swatted Greta's shoulder.

"What?" Greta asked with innocence as though she didn't know Tabitha was telling her to keep her voice down.

"Hi, Hunter," Tabitha said, going around the desk to greet him. "Does this mean the food is here?"

He nodded. "They sent me to scout ahead. Do you have a table in your break room?" At Tabitha's nod, he continued, "Cool. Now, if you ladies wouldn't mind going into one of the exam rooms while they set your meal up, we would appreciate it."

Grace stared at him. "That's crazy. And besides. Who's going to watch for anyone coming through the door who might decide they want to rob us?"

Hunter touched his chest with his fingertips. "I'm on guard duty. Both to make sure you ladies don't peek, and to ensure your safety."

Greta's eyes raked him from head to toe. "No offense, sugar, but you're in a full leg cast. What'cha going to do? Throw your crutches at them?"

Had she known how lethal Hunter was, even with the cast and crutches, she would have swallowed the snide remark.

Hunter returned her stare. "Do you always insult the person bringing you a free meal?" Gee. You'd think someone who was, he estimated, in their late forties, would have better manners than that.

Greta's face flushed with shame.

"Come on," Tabitha told her friends. "Let's do what he asks. I'm starved and anxious to see what they brought."

"Who are they," Grace asked, having no clue who was bringing their meal.

"TJ and his nephews. He called me this morning before I left the house and asked if I thought the two of you would like a surprise. Knowing the answer would be yes, that's what I told him." Tabitha glanced at Grace. "Promise me you won't swoon."

Grace's face scrunched up with confusion. "Over food? I have never fainted in my life, and certainly not over food." But she followed Tabitha, along with Greta, into one of the exam rooms to wait. Fifteen

minutes later, Hunter opened the door and told them they could now go into the break room.

When the women walked into the associate lounge, which only had enough room for a small table, two of the women stopped dead in their tracks. They could hardly comprehend who was standing in the corner, presenting the feast spread out on white linen cloth.

"Bonjour," Mason said, opening his arms to indicate the table. "Please, have a seat."

"Oh. My. God," Grace squealed like a teenage girl and sounded nothing like the fifty-five-year-old she was.

"How?" Greta asked, turning to Tabitha for an explanation of how it was possible that Mason Lafayette, the popular guy of Touch My Bod fame, could be standing in their small break room.

Tabitha walked to TJ as he entered the room after them as she explained that Mason was TJ's nephew.

"Oh. My. God," Grace said again.

Mason gave Grace his best smile of seduction, which almost caused the woman to faint. "Please, have a seat, ladies. Eat before your steak grows cold." He held out a chair and nodded toward Grace, who looked as though she needed to sit soon before passing out onto the floor.

As Grace and Greta moved toward the table, Tabitha pulled TJ into the dispensary.

TJ grinned. "Anxious to be alone with me?" he asked, reaching for her.

He had no idea how true that was, but that was not why she separated them from the others.

"Steak?!" she exclaimed. "Are you out of your mind?!"

TJ blinked. That sounded as though she were mad. "Umm, I thought they would like it. I ordered it from the steakhouse on Leroy Street. They have the best in town, in my opinion."

"And expensive! Holy stars, TJ! When you offered lunch, I thought you meant McDonald's, not a three-course meal with all the trimmings!"

He stared at her. Why was she mad? He wanted to do something nice for the women who'd helped and supported her during Owen's death. Why was she angry about it?

"Well-" he began, but she cut him off.

"You do not need to spend tons of money to impress me, TJ. In fact. If you were a billionaire, which obviously you're not, even if you do own a Porsche, I wouldn't want you spending your money so lavishly on me. The fact you do all the physical labor on fixing up that old dump of a house Doris lived in, instead of paying someone to do it, indicates your need to conserve your money." Considering the house he lived in, with the pool and hot tub, the man obviously had bills to pay. He shouldn't throw away his money foolishly on expensive meals.

"Dump?" he got a little heated over that statement. "I have you know that house has a sound foundation and is going to look killer when I'm done with it."

She threw her hands in the air. "Typical man. You're missing my point."

"Okay," he did his own hand gesture, "what is the point?"

Tabitha took a deep breath, blew it out slowly. "We do not know where this relationship is going. You have already told me you are not looking for a permanent deal, and I can except that since I'm not sure I'm looking for one either. If down the road, whatever we are building between us right now doesn't work out, I do not want you regretting draining your bank account because you purchased expensive things for me."

"Maybe I can drain it a little and not miss it," he suggested.

"That's ridiculous."

"Now I'm ridiculous. How wonderful."

Mason poked his head through the door. "You are both being absurd and much too loud. You will spoil their appetite." He motioned toward the other room to indicate the women sitting at the table, trying to enjoy the lavish meal.

"Then close the damn door!" TJ snapped.

"Merde," Mason muttered, then closed the door on the two of them.

Tabitha poked TJ in the chest. "Ha! I just figured out what your initials stand for!"

"Want to share?" he asked snidely.

"Total Jerk!"

He opened his mouth. Closed it. Opened it again. "Seriously?" He'd wasted half the day setting up this surprise for her two employees. Using time he could have spent working on the project house. Instead, he put himself behind schedule regardless of the fact she had not asked him to bring the expensive feast. It was his idea to provide lunch for them, so he wouldn't blame her for his time loss. However, as far as he was concerned at the moment, if ungrateful had a picture attached to it, her image would be the poster for its meaning. "What exactly did I do to deserve that?"

Those enormous eyes of hers stared at him, reminding him of an animal wondering if it should run.

Reaching out, TJ gently clasped her right arm. "I would appreciate it if you would clarify what has you so upset."

Her head fell forward, her shoulders slumped. "I'm sorry," she whispered. "No. You did not deserve being called a jerk."

"All right," he said, keeping his voice calm because Mason was right; everyone did not need to hear a shouting match going on in here. "Could we back up? Why are you so mad over steak?"

She shook her head as she swallowed the lump that formed in her throat. "I don't want you to spend that kind of money on me," she whispered.

"Maybe I can afford to. Maybe I wanted to because I'm a nice person."

"And you'll be able to throw it in my face if our relationship sours."

TJ stared at her. "Did Owen do that?" he asked gently.

Once again, Tabitha shook her head.

Heaving a sigh, she pulled back, wrapped her arms around herself. "Not Owen. His parents have money. When he and I got engaged, before they understood I was not of their faith and on the opposite side of their belief spectrum, they wanted us to have an outlandish wedding. I didn't want a church and a fancy dress. I wanted a handfasting like my parents had when they were wed. But Owen wanted us to remain silent regarding my spiritual path because he knew his parents wouldn't approve."

TJ did not understand what a handfasting was and filed that information away to look up later.

"I wanted to make Owen happy," she continued to explain. "I wanted his parents to like me. So, I kept my faith to myself. I allowed them to plan the wedding, buy my dress and throw their outlandish party." Her eyes met his. "The entire time, my skin kept wanting to reject that damn dress. I hated it. But I plastered a smile on my face for Owen's sake and made it through the ridiculously long ceremony in their church."

She wiped at the moisture pooling in her eyes. "Then they sent us to Hawaii for a honeymoon. After we returned, at some point, they discovered I was raised Wiccan. Boy," she gave a shaky laugh, "you should have heard them! I'd bewitched their son, you see, and would take him to hell with me. And they reminded me every chance they got that it had been their God-given money that allowed me to marry their son properly."

"And Owen didn't tell his folks to knock it off?" TJ asked. Had it been his parents, as much as he loved them, he would not have allowed them to twist what should have been a gift into something to make a person feel guilty if they did not comply with their wishes.

Tabitha shook her head. "He would tell me it was the way they are and not let it get to me."

He was going to keep his opinion of Owen to himself if it was the last thing he did.

"The Turners told me when Owen passed away, and they found out I was pregnant, that I could expect nothing from them. As far as they were concerned, they'd spent a fortune on a wedding they hadn't wanted their son to have in the first place."

TJ moved to her; wrapped her in his arms and pressed her cheek to his chest. "I'm sorry you have the misfortune of knowing them."

"Abby is going to be four, and they have only seen her a handful of times since she was born. I have made excuses to myself for them. They retired, sold their home, and can afford to travel. And why shouldn't they enjoy life? This is the longest they have stayed in town. They have been here for two weeks, and this is only the second time they asked to see Abby and have another sleepover."

She threw her hands in the air. "Maybe I shouldn't have let her go with them."

"They do not deserve her, nor you." TJ stroked her hair. "Are you sure you don't want to pick her up from the campground, and we'll call tonight off?"

And he would cut out his tongue for having asked. He'd been anticipating being alone with Tabitha tonight. But if her mind were anxious over Abby being with the freaky ex-in-laws, she would be too distracted to enjoy their time together.

Tabitha sighed. "No. I already told Abby this will be the last time, and it will be the Turner's loss. So, they better enjoy tonight because, after this, they can no longer see her without my parents or me with her the next time they visit."

Her arms came up and went around his waist. "I'm sorry I called you a jerk."

He stroked her hair. "Well, I suppose sometimes I can be one," he amended.

"But you weren't today, and you have been nothing but kind to us." She pulled back, looked up at him. "Thank you for providing Greta and Grace with a lunch they will never forget. And for talking Mason into tagging along. I know Grace is going to talk about meeting him for a long, long time."

"You're welcome. Now, do you think you're ready to eat? I hope Mason kept your portion in the container we used to transport everything here; otherwise, I'm afraid, your steak is ice cold by now."

"I could probably eat a salad if it was included."

He eyed her. "You need more than a salad." Her figure did not give away the fact she once carried a child inside of her.

She shook her head. "Now you sound like my mother. She's always harping on me to eat, and she should know by now I have a high metabolism. I've always been thin."

Placing his hand on the small of her back, he guided her from the room, but as he did, he leaned down and whispered in her ear, "Well, I do like your curves. They're just right."

Her face was flushed when they entered the break room.

Mason smiled when he noticed it. "Good. You made up." He glanced at TJ. "I thought you told me you took your time with your women."

Tabitha choked.

TJ shook his head. "You are probably the only one in this room who assumed anything happened in there other than pleasant conversation."

"Well, it didn't sound like good conversation in the beginning," Greta pointed out.

"Are you enjoying the steak?" TJ asked, choosing to ignore her observation.

"Oh god yes!" she exclaimed. "And we thank you. It was a wonderful surprise."

"So was the hot waiter," Grace claimed and winked at Mason.

"The pleasure, madame, is all mine," Mason told her as he reached for her hand and kissed the top of it.

"Did you have to do that?" Tabitha asked. "She'll probably never wash that hand again."

"You might be right about that," Grace sighed.

"You're hopeless," Tabitha told her.

TJ held out a chair for Tabitha, but Hunter appeared in the doorway when she would have slid into it.

"Hey," he said, leaning on his crutches. "There's a woman out there who's demanding to see the doc. She's got a cat with her and let me tell you. It's one of the ugliest things I've seen."

Tabitha's eyes collided with Greta's. In unison, they exclaimed, "Bubbles!"

"It can't be Mrs. McGillicutty," Grace denied. "She doesn't have an appointment!"

Tabitha stood up. "That's never stopped her before," she sighed. "Good Kris Kringle, what could she want now?"

"Who's Mrs. McGillicutty?" TJ asked.

"Crazy cat lady," Greta explained.

"Greta!" Tabitha abolished her in a half-laugh.

The veterinarian assistant shrugged.

Walking to the reception area, Tabitha confirmed that yes, indeed, it was Mrs. McGillicutty, with Bubbles in tow.

"Good afternoon, Mrs.-" Tabitha began, only to be cut off.

"Bubbles needs a distemper shot!" the eccentric woman exclaimed. "Her behavior this past week has been horrible, and I want her to calm down!"

Tabitha shook her head. "The distemper shot has nothing to do with a cat's behavior," she told the woman. "And I recall Bubbles had her vaccination less than six months ago."

Mrs. McGilligutty stared at her. "Dis temper," she said the word as though Tabitha was an imbecile. "Temper is part of the shots name, so obviously it is for behavior issues."

Tabitha wanted to smack her. "The Distemper shot protects against three diseases: feline viral rhinotracheitis, calicivirus, and panleukopenia."

"Then why is it call distemper?!" Mrs. McGilligutty wanted to know.

Rather than trying to explain, Tabitha told her, "That's a good question. Maybe one day you can look it up and let me know what you find out. That way, you can educate me."

Mrs. McGilligutty seemed to like that idea. She straightened and allowed a small smile to curve her lips. "I knew you didn't know everything!" she exclaimed in a superior tone.

A little research would do the woman good. "I bet if you pick Bubbles up a new toy with some catnip, she'll enjoy it, and you won't have to worry about her behavior for a while."

"Bubbles has never been around catnip," the woman claimed.

"Oh, she'll love it," Tabitha smiled. "She might even meow or growl at the same time, so don't be alarmed. It's her way of expressing how happy she is."

"Really? Meow and growl at the same time?" Mrs. McGilligutty repeated, intrigued.

"Yes. I've seen it happen before."

"Well then," the cat's owner decreed as she picked up the crate and began walking to the door. "I'll do that!"

The door closed, and Tabitha sighed with relief.

"Did you just tell that woman to get her cat high?" Hunter asked with a hint of laughter in the tone of his voice.

"Well, there's only a fifty percent chance Bubbles will be affected by the catnip."

"Or become hyperactive or downright aggressive," he said.

Tabitha blinked. "How did you know that?"

He shrugged. "I read about catnip once. In a magazine, someone brought with them on a mission I was on. I was board at the time."

"Mission?" she asked.

Shaking his head, he told her, "Never mind. It isn't important."

TJ and Mason came into the waiting area, carrying the container that had housed the meal during transportation.

"We need to get going," TJ told Tabitha.

"So soon?"

"I need to work a few more hours on that old dump before tonight," TJ explained.

Tabitha grimaced. "I'm sorry about that statement."

"It's alright. One day you'll eat those words," TJ handed the container over to Mason to carry the rest of the way out to the work truck, and Hunter followed his friend.

"Just be sure to eat at least half that steak," TJ reached out, pulled Tabitha to him. "If you're serious about me coming over tonight to do more than watch a movie, you'll need the protein to help keep your endurance up." The smile he gave her caused her body to hum with anticipation.

In return, the smile she gave him reminded TJ of an imp about to do mischief as she fisted his T-shirt, pulled him to her. Standing up on her tiptoes, she pulled his head down and whispered in his ear, "I haven't had sex in four years. I suggest you eat your own source of protein, TJ Fisher. It's going to be a long night."

Chapter Sixteen

Four years without sex? Good god. Even he hadn't lasted more than a month after Heather's betrayal before finding someone willing enough to share a bed with him, and he hadn't paid for.

Earlier in the day, after dropping Mason and Hunter off at his house, not caring what the two of them did for the rest of the day, TJ went straight to the project house. He threw himself into finishing the flooring in the bathroom to take his mind off of tonight.

Hearing Tabitha's whisper, "It's going to be a long night," in his head on constant repeat, made the job of concentrating on the ceramic tile next to impossible.

When five o'clock arrived, he drove home at a speed that would have guaranteed him a sizable fine had law enforcement been aware of his behavior.

Arriving back at his house, he ignored Mason and Hunter's good-natured ribbing about what they knew he would do later. He rushed up the stairs to the master bedroom, took a quick shower, and changed into clean clothes.

On his way back down the stairs, he saw his nephews waiting for him at the bottom of the steps. TJ asked, "What's up?" as he stopped on the landing while finishing buttoning his shirt.

Mason's hand came out from behind his back with a can of whipped cream clasped in it. "I have found this to be a useful tool," he wiggled his eyebrows, "when making love to a woman."

Despite being thirty-six years old, TJ felt his face flush.

Laughing, Hunter commented, "I never realized your cheekbones did the same thing as my dad's when he's embarrassed."

"I'm not embarrassed," TJ tried to claim, but the knowing looks on the faces before him caused the shade to deepen.

"Sure," Hunter said in a voice that sounded as though he were saying, "Yes you are."

"Give me that damn thing," TJ told Mason as he grabbed the can of whipped cream from his hand and began walking toward the kitchen.

"That isn't the only thing we got you," Hunter told him.

TJ stopped walking, looked over his shoulder. "I'm afraid to ask."

Hunter, leaning on one crutch, brought his free hand out from behind his back to reveal the box of condoms he'd been hiding.

TJ shook his head, not understanding why he was mortified by this teasing of theirs. He was a grown man for god's sake. This wasn't the first time he'd had sex with a woman.

He reversed direction, grabbed the box from Hunter, and turned back toward the kitchen.

"They're cherry-flavored," Hunter claimed.

TJ's laugh came out with a half snort. "I hope the two of you are enjoying this," he said as he reached for his Porsche keys from their place on the wall.

"Immensely," Mason grinned.

Opening the backdoor, TJ stopped, glanced at them. "At least I have a date tonight that suggests I'll be spending the night in her bed."

Mason grinned. "Do you imply I do not?"

TJ rolled his eyes. Chances were, Mason had at least five women lined up to keep him company tonight. "I thought you had matured enough to realize it's not wise to sleep with every woman you meet."

"I will have you know I am no longer as promiscuous as I was as a teenager. And I have a woman I am seeing in New York City. It is an exclusive relationship. I am driving back there after you leave to be with

your lady. Once I arrive, she and I are going to a club for a little dancing. Afterword," he smiled, "A different kind of dance."

"You're leaving?" TJ asked, surprised by the revelation. He knew Mason and Hunter hadn't seen each other in over a year. They had been best friends from the cradle, and TJ would have thought they would spend more than a few days together unless- "Are you leaving too?" he asked Hunter.

"No. I'm staying with you regardless of the fact it might cramp your lifestyle after tonight," Hunter grinned.

"And," Mason interjected, "Hunter isn't able to do much-"

"Thanks for being a true friend," Hunter griped.

Ignoring Hunter's complaint, Mason continued. "I wish to celebrate my new career." He flexed his muscles and laughed, "Hero of romance novels."

"Barf," Hunter commented. "I seriously do not understand what women see in you."

Before an argument could begin, TJ asked Hunter, "I'm glad to have you here. I'm just wondering if there is any particular reason you're going to remain behind and grace me with your presence."

Hunter shrugged. "I was going to head to North Dakota in a few days to visit my folks, but since they're going to be here next week, I might as well save myself the trip."

"Did you talk with them?" TJ inquired.

He nodded. "This afternoon. After we got back from impressing your girlfriend."

"She's not my girlfriend," TJ denied.

"Whatever." Hunter shook his head, wondering why his uncle was bothering to deny it. "Anyway, they told me we can expect them on

Monday, or Tuesday of next week, so," he shrugged, "I might as well stay here."

"I won't mind that," TJ told him. "I haven't seen you since the day you graduated from BUD's." TJ knew for a fact that he would never have lasted the 24-week training course SEAL candidates went through. The Basic Underwater Demolition programs were intense. Not everyone entering the program made it through to the end of the drill. "And now you're working for Cadman Benson, although I don't know everything that entails."

Hunter grinned. "More adventure than I ever had on mom and dad's horse ranch, that's for sure."

"Uncle TJ," Mason said, "When are you planning on telling Tabitha you are the one who stole her land from her."

TJ's jaw dropped. "Now, just one minute! I didn't steal it! It was for sale. I bought it. I hadn't even met her before I signed the deal."

"But," Mason continued, "you know now. Will you tell her?"

Running a hand through his hair, TJ answered, "I haven't decided how I want to broach the subject yet."

"I like her sanctuary for dogs idea. I will participate in her fundraiser. I only have to work the details out with my agency and lawyer."

"For what it's worth, Uncle TJ," Hunter spoke up, "I like Tabitha. I like her a lot better than I ever did Heather."

"Agreed," Mason said. "I hope you will keep this woman around for a long time."

TJ shook his head. "You both know how I feel about marriage."

"Brother," Hunter told him. "We aren't expecting you to put a ring on Tabitha's finger anytime soon."

"And you should not compare Tabitha to Heather," Mason voiced Hunter's own thoughts. "I do not perceive Tabitha as a money hungry-

" he paused, searching his mind for the correct English expression. "Gold miner."

"Digger, Lafayette." Hunter rolled his eyes. "Gold digger."

Mason shrugged.

"Personally, I prefer the term bitch." TJ claimed.

"That works, too," Hunter laughed. "Regardless, though. Tabitha does not fall into the same category."

No, TJ admitted to himself. Tabitha was nothing like Heather, but that did not mean he was ready to let his guard down.

He decided this line of conversation was over. Looking to Mason, he told him, "Drive safely back to the Big Apple. And don't be a stranger. Come back and visit sooner."

"I will," Mason promised.
With that, TJ walked out of the kitchen door and got into his Porsche.

* * *

Tabitha opened the front door of her house on his third knock.

Her smile was sensual, and the sexy black mini dress she had on, with its plunging neckline, had TJ swallowing his tongue and slowing his thought process down. Her marvelous hair was full and wild. She'd out-lined her eyes with black liner and smudged it into the smokey tone eyeshadow she favored. The shade of lipstick was a dark pink, and, in his mind, she looked like a goddess come to life.

He wanted to devour her.

And then she said, in a purr, "Hello, Thaddeus."

Staring at her, he wondered if he somehow imagined it. His dreams of her, where they were entwined in bed, or on a beach, gave her that exact inflection when she would call out his name in the heat of passion.

"What?" he asked, trying to dislodge the fog from his brain.

"I said, hello, Thaddeus, though I suppose I'm wrong with that guess too." She frowned, disappointed. Trying to figure out his name was hard. She would really like to know the actual name of the man who was about to become her lover, not just his initials.

Reaching for her, he grasped her shoulders and pulled her to him until she was pressed up against him. "Say it again," he demanded.

Confused, she said, "What?"

"My name. I don't know how you figured it out, but I like the way you said it."

Her eyes widened. "Holy stars TJ, I was only guessing. I had no idea-" She smiled provocatively as she raised her arms and encircled his neck. "Your first name is Thaddeus? I cannot believe you don't like it. It's a great name!"

"Only when you say it," he told her as his mouth hovered over hers.

"Are you going to kiss me? -or are you waiting for an invitation?"

He crushed his mouth to hers as he advanced her backward into the small foyer and kicked the front door closed behind him.

"Bedroom," TJ demanded, breaking contact only long enough to say the word.

She pulled back, placed her hand on his chest to ward him off. "Are you sure you don't want to have supper first? Watch a movie?"

His growl almost caused her to laugh.

"Maybe if you hadn't answered the door in that dress, we might have made it to your dining table." he told her. "Though I won't rule it out as a place to lay you on."

She shivered at the image his words caused to form in her mind. "I set the plates and silverware on it earlier-"

"Easy enough to remove," he claimed. "So, if you don't want broken glassware on your floor-"

Untangling herself from him and stepping away, Tabitha turned her back on him without a word and began walking toward the hallway, knowing TJ's eyes watched her hips sway.

His nostrils flared. "If you're playing games with me-" his tone warned.

Pausing for one moment, she looked over her shoulder coyly and said, "I'm not opposed to games of a certain nature, Thaddeus. However, my bedroom is this way, and, for your information, I'm not wearing any underwear."

* * *

TJ did not discover Tabitha's bedroom was a sanctuary of lavender and purple until much later.

Oh, he'd made it into the room without a hitch. However, he'd been too consumed with lust to care what the place looked like. It had a bed. That was all that mattered, although he would have been more than willing to couple with her on the floor if a bed had not been available immediately.

Now, as his breathing became regular, laying entwined with her on her queen-size bed, his eyes roamed his surroundings. He lazily ran his hand up and down Tabitha's arm as she lay pressed against him with her cheek resting on his chest.

He wanted to comment about the color but doubted he had enough strength to do so just yet.

Mind-blowing. He had experienced nothing like it.

Often, he'd heard the phrase two become one during Christian wedding ceremonies. Until this moment, he never believed something like that was possible. It had felt as though Tabitha's pleasure was his during their heated joining. Before reaching the bed, they were practically tearing off each other's clothes in their haste to feel flesh against flesh.

When he entered her, it had been swift, and she'd matched his rhythm and met his every thrust, as hungry for him as he was for her. And when she orgasmed, he'd been right there with her.

Oh. God. Had he used a condom?

He tensed. It was not like him to be so foolish. As much as he loved and had wanted children, he never wanted to father one unintentionally.

Unfortunately, he had not used a condom this time, and there was no excuse for it. It wasn't as though he didn't have an entire box of them sitting in the Porsche parked in the driveway, and a couple more tucked in his wallet in the back pocket of his jeans. Which were on the floor of her bedroom, and sure as hell, he knew his wallet was still in the back pocket, undisturbed.

"Shit," he sighed. Hopefully, he hadn't gotten Tabitha pregnant and he was not going to ask now if she was on birth control.

He felt her move away from him and watched as she slowly sat up, tugging the sheet around her to cover those glorious breasts.

They stared at each other.

"Umm," Tabitha began, then paused as she cocked her head to one side: contemplating her words. "I guess I'm not sure how to decipher what you just said."

Running his hands through his hair, he lay back onto the pillow, looked up at her. "I'll begin by saying that was the most amazing sex I've ever had." Which was not a lie. The sex he'd shared in the past, including with Heather, could not compare to what he'd experienced moments ago with Tabitha.

She continued staring at him. "I can honestly say the same thing; however, I feel a but, coming."

TJ sat up, reached a hand out to touch her cheek. "No. No buts. It was amazing." He would not tarnish what they'd shared because of his mistake. What was done was done. If he'd gotten her pregnant, he'd make

it right. But that was something he would worry about when and if the time came. Moving forward for the rest of the evening, he would make sure he used a condom.

He leaned toward her, cupped her face with both hands. "Honestly, Tabitha. I have never had a woman enthrall me as much as you can. I have no idea how you do it, but ever since I've met you and Abby, I can't get you out of my head."

Tabitha placed both of her hands on his as she leaned in and kissed him. "I feel the same way about you, but I don't want to analyze it. Let's just enjoy tonight and let tomorrow come. Alright, Thaddeus?"

He groaned. "You don't know how much I wish you hadn't figured out my first name."

Now she smiled at him. "I told you. It was a lucky guess. You could have lied and denied it."

"I could have, but I am not a liar. I told you I would let you know when you hit the bullseye."

"Are you going to tell me your middle name?"

"No." Absolutely not, and he hoped to heaven she never came up with it as a guess because yes, if she did, he would be hard-pressed not to lie to her about it.

"In that case," she moved off the bed, "I'm getting hungry, and I don't want the dinner I made to go to waste. It's keeping warm in the crock-pot." She brought the sheet with her and wrapped it around her slender body as she walked to the bedroom door. "I made chicken and gravy."

As she began moving away from him, the tattoo on her shoulder caught his eye.

"Hold it," he told her.

His tone startled her. She couldn't fathom if he was angry or didn't want her to leave the bedroom. "What's wrong?" she asked him.

He beckoned her back by wiggling his index finger toward himself.

She complied only because his face didn't appear angry. But there was curiosity in his expression as he continued watching her.

Stopping beside the bed, she asked, "What?" Then yelped when he grabbed her hand and off-balanced her enough to have her falling onto him.

"TJ, for goodness sakes, I-"

He flipped her onto her back and rose above her as he angled her so he could get a better view of the tattoo. "What the hell?" he whispered in a voice full of shock upon reading the initials embedded in her skin with black ink.

TJS.

She winced because she knew how he was probably deciphering it in his mind. If one put an apostrophe between the J and the S, it would mark her as his.

"I've had this since I was sixteen years old, TJ. It was the first tat I ever got. My name. Tabitha June Stevens."

He stared into her eyes. "You know what it looks like," he told her.

She nodded. "Yes, and I've kept it covered up since meeting you."

"Why?"

"I don't know. Maybe because I was afraid you'd think I did it on purpose."

He leaned back but kept his eyes on the letters. "I can tell it's not a fresh tat," he told her, "But, geez, Tabitha, since meeting you, I've had some extraordinary experiences. Seeing my own initials like that on you just raised the hairs on my neck."

It was her turn to stare. "Does that mean you're going to leave?"

His smile came slowly. Leaning down until his lips were almost touching hers, he told her, "No, because I'm willing to risk experiencing a few more unexpected events with you."

She cupped his face with her hands, smiled back at him. "Apparently you're a daredevil."

He chuckled.

"My turn to ask about tattoos," she told him as her hands slid over the one on his back. "I saw yours when we went swimming the other night. The symbol. It's a combination of Runes, isn't it?"

"Like you, I got it a long time ago. As I mentioned before, I enjoy history. I came across a photo of this Bindrune one day when reading about ancient languages and Runes. I liked it enough to have it tattooed onto my back."

"What does it mean?"

TJ ran his finger down her cheek, along her neck, and over her collarbone bone before he answered. "It's a symbol to bring me energy for success."

Tabitha smiled up at him. "Is it working?"

Whether or not the symbol had anything to do with his ability to create wealth for himself, no one could deny it might have helped. But he was not at the point to tell her that, so he said instead, "I guess if I make a profit from Doris's old house, you'll know the answer to that."

She searched his eyes. "And you drive a Porsche. I suppose that speaks for itself."

With a grin, he agreed as his hand wandered down to one of her breasts and began kneading it, "Do you think that crockpot will continue to keep the food warm? I'm interested in something else right now."

After four years of going without sex, Tabitha was more than willing to feed the hunger he had in mind.

Chapter Seventeen

Tabitha sensed the sun coming through her bedroom window. At the same time, she felt something touch her cheek. Batting away whatever the offensive object was, she rolled away from it and tried to go back to sleep.

Her cheek was assaulted again.

She whacked at it once more.

Then she heard the male chuckle.

"Wake up, sleepyhead."

"Go away."

Another chuckle. Another brush of something tickling her cheek.

Now she did roll over, opened her eyes, and glared at him. "You cannot possibly want to have sex again."

TJ's laugh was a roar. "I probably could rise to the occasion if that was what I wanted at the moment." He leaned down, kissed her cheek. "But that isn't what's on my mind, babe."

The endearment rolled off his tongue with ease.

"Would you like to know what's on my mind?" she asked as she plucked the peacock feather he'd undoubtedly gotten from the plume and feather arrangement she kept in a vase on the desk of her office from his hand.

"Well-"

"Sleep," she told him, setting the feather down on the nightstand next to the bed before fluffing her pillow and putting her head back on it as she closed her eyes.

He moved down, snuggled her. "You're the one who told me you hadn't had sex for four years. I felt obligated to help you make up for it last night. Obviously, I did a good job." His stubbled cheek rubbed against hers.

"Do you ever shave that?" she asked, trying to push him away.

"Apparently, I do since I don't have a full beard. I like a little facial hair." He brushed her cheek with a fingertip. "Are you grumpy? You shouldn't be grumpy after last night."

"Are you always bright-eyed and bushy-tailed in the morning when you've spent most of the night having sex?"

He rubbed his nose against her cheek in a quick motion. "It was great sex. Admit it." He grinned.

"Ugh," she pulled the pillow out from under her head, swatted him with it, then placed it over her face. "Yes. Amazing. I'm well satisfied. Thank you for that. Trust me when I say I can probably hold out for another four years after our marathon last night."

"Bite your tongue."

Apparently, he would not take the hint and allow her to sleep. "Thaddeus," she removed the pillow from her face and looked at him. "If you're not looking for sex-"

"I think I'll always be looking for sex with you, and please promise me you will never use my name outside of this house."

She rolled her eyes. He had a wonderful name, and she could not understand why he hated it. "All right, TJ. Could you kindly tell me why you woke me up?"

"Well, I was thinking of Abby. It's only a little after nine. Maybe you and I could drive out to the campground where the wicked Turners are staying, rescue her, and the three of us could go out and eat breakfast together."

188

Slowly, a smile formed on Tabitha's lips as she raised her arms to encircle his neck. "How can you possibly know how to make me happy? It would be a wonderful surprise for her, and it is sweet of you to think of her."

TJ kissed her. "Abby's a great kid." He moved off the bed. "Come on, lazybones. Let's shower, dress, and rescue your daughter from the Turners."

The shower delayed their plans to drive to the campground by an half hour. Once the water was running, and the couple stepped under the warm spray, Tabitha discovered TJ could easily entice her into sex while surrounded by steam as water cascaded over them.

Later, they transferred Abby's car seat from Tabitha's car into TJ's Porsche, then headed to the campground.

"Which site is theirs?" TJ asked as he slowed the Porsche down upon entering the campground.

"I'm not sure," Tabitha told him. "But I'll recognize their Winnebago when I see it. It's top of the line. When they sold their house, they purchased it with the idea they would live in it year-round." She shrugged. "Like I said. They've got the money to squander."

TJ glanced at her sideways. "Do you have something against people who have wealth?" If so, this relationship was set up for failure. He couldn't keep pretending he didn't have a sizable bank account if whatever was between them lasted more than a month.

He hoped it would, but would not question why it was important to have Tabitha in his life for a long time to come.

"No," Tabitha sighed. "I know that sounded as though I have a problem with rich people. I don't. It's just Owen's folks that bring out the disdain."

Well, that was good to know, TJ thought.

They drove slowly through the campground, but Tabitha did not see the Turner's RV.

"Maybe it isn't as remarkable as you remember," TJ told her.

She shook her head. "It has a gigantic mural of a scenic view of the Rocky Mountains painted on the back of it. No one could miss it."

The frown on her face had him saying, "Let's take one more pass through. Then we'll stop at the camp office and see what time they pulled out. They probably took Abby out for breakfast themselves."

"Maybe," Tabitha whispered but felt a sense of foreboding.

"Or," TJ tried to reassure her, "they dropped Abby off at your parents' house this morning."

Tabitha shook her head. "That doesn't make sense. If anything, they should have brought her to me. Besides, my mother would have called if they'd shown up at her door."

TJ drove the Porsche once more around the weaving roads of the campground. When they still did not find the camper, TJ stopped the vehicle in front of the camp's office and cut the engine. "I'll be right back," he told Tabitha and stepped out from the car.

Tabitha watched him walk up the steps as she began nervously chewing on her bottom lip. This wasn't right. They should be here.

When she saw TJ coming back to the car, his expression was grim. Her heart began a rapid beat as her anxiety tripled.

The driver's side door opened, and TJ slid in behind the wheel. "They left yesterday morning," he told her, hating to be the one to deliver the news.

"What?!" Tabitha's heart threatened to stop. "What do you mean, they left?"

TJ turned the key in the ignition, slammed the Porsche in gear, and pressed the accelerator down. At this moment, he couldn't care less what the speed limit in this campground was.

"Thaddeus?"

He dared a glance at her as he pointed the vehicle toward the exit. Her eyes were huge, and he could see his own fear reflected on her face. "The Turners. They packed up early yesterday and told the office they wouldn't be back."

Her apprehension was almost crippling. "They took my baby!" she cried, terrified.

"We'll get her back," TJ made it a vow. "They can't hide for long. Especially not with a custom-painted camper."

"We need to call the police!" Tabitha made a fist, pressed it against her mouth as she suppressed the urge to scream out her anguish. Never in her life would she have thought Owen's parents were capable of doing such a thing.

"We're not going to the police," he told her. "Not yet. Not when I have someone staying at my house who is an expert at tracking people."

"What are you talking about?! Of course, we need to let the police know! My god, TJ! They have kidnapped my daughter!"

"Hunter," TJ made a sharp right, continued at high speed toward his house. "Hunter works for a special task force. He'll have more resources than our local police department." Another sharp right. "Trust me, Tabitha. We'll get Abby back."

"I thought you said he worked for the government."

"He does. It's complicated. Nor does it matter right now."

The Porsche screeched to a halt in the driveway of TJ's home. Getting out, TJ rushed around to the passenger side and helped Tabitha out. Taking her hand in his, he felt her trembles and wished he could take them away.

They found Hunter in TJ's weight room doing one-arm pull-ups.

"I didn't expect you home so early-" he began. But when he saw the expression on their faces, he knew something was wrong. "What happened?" He eased himself down from the rigging, reached for his crutches.

"Abby's been kidnapped." His uncle said.

"Fuck," Hunter hissed as he placed his crutches under his arms and began moving out of the room. "Fill me in as we head to your office. I'll call Cadman."

TJ explained what they discovered earlier when they'd gone to the campground, hoping to pick Abby up.

While he was relaying what they believed happened, Tabitha burst into tears. "Oh god, I should have known! She didn't want to go with them! And yet I made her because I was selfish! All I could think about was spending the night with you. And now she's gone!" She collapsed into a nearby chair, raised her hands to her face, and sobbed into them.

TJ went to her, squatted down before her on the balls of his shoes. More than anything, he wanted to take her in his arms to comfort, but he was at a loss. She was blaming herself for allowing this to happen. "It's not your fault," he tried to soothe.

"Isn't it?!" she cried out, dropping her hands and looking at him. "I should have paid more attention to their behavior this time. I found it odd they wanted to spend another night with her when they'd been in town for almost two weeks before contacting me again for a sleepover with her. But I pushed it aside because I hoped they finally wanted to know her! When Abby told me they were reading her books about evil witches, I should have stopped their nonsense in its tracks."

Hunter, having eased himself into the chair behind TJ's desk, glanced at her. "Witches?" he inquired.

"Tabitha was raised Wiccan. The Turners are from a radical religious group claiming to be Christian."

"Ah," Hunter said. "That explains their motive."

"What does?"

"They are on a mission to save," he used his fingers to put quotation marks around the word, "her from witches." He reached for the phone, punched in a telephone number. "Ignorance from others is one of the reasons people who once considered themselves witches felt the need to drop the term and refer to themselves as Wiccans. But they still get a bad rap."

"Tabitha," TJ turned to the woman before him, who seemed to wrap guilt around her like a shield. "This is not your fault," he repeated, then gently pulled her up from the chair and into his arms.

She groaned but accepted the comfort he offered.

"Do you know the places they like to frequent? You said they tour the country."

She shook her head. "The only contact I have with them is when they show up out of the blue."

"Family members, they talk to?" TJ continued his questioning while Hunter spoke on the phone.

"I have names and phone numbers at my house, but Owen's family are only a handful of relations, and they have no contact with me either. I tried several times after Owen's funeral, but all of them have shunned me."

She wiped the tears from her eyes as she stood up. "I need to call my parents. Let them know what happened."

"Do you want me to take you there?" TJ offered.

Tabitha was about to answer TJ's question when Hunter looked up from the phone and said, "I've already got the local police bringing your parents here."

Tabitha stared at him. "How?" Her own question had her mind wondering how he would have the authority to do that. He looked as though he was somewhere between the ages of twenty to twenty-five.

Hunter hung up the phone, grabbed his crutches, and stood up. "I contacted my boss. He's putting a team together, and they are starting to track the Turner's credit cards for where they've been used. We'll do everything we can to find Abby. I only regret I'm not much use in the field because of my leg." He looked at his uncle. "I assume you will not mind your house becoming the main headquarters for this operation."

"Of course not," TJ turned to Tabitha. "You can trust Hunter. If anyone can find her quickly, he can."

"I don't understand."

TJ shrugged. "To be honest, I'm not sure what the government organization he works for does. It's kind of like the FBI-"

"Hey," his nephew said, "You don't need to insult me. It's nothing like the FBI." He moved away from the desk to stand beside them. "I track down terrorists and drug traffickers around the world, to name a few things Task Force Ghost does." He looked at Tabitha. "The bottom line is, I have a lot of resources at my disposal."

When the phone on TJ's desk rang a half-hour later, Hunter answered it. Whatever was said on the other end of the line caused Hunter's face to harden. "All right, keep me posted." When he hung up, his eyes met TJ's, then Tabitha's. "Apparently, your ex-in-laws put some thought into their scheme. They sold that Winnebago of theirs for cash at a local RV place. Along with the car they pulled behind it, a few days ago. However, they had a deal with the business they sold it to not to expect it to be dropped off until yesterday at noon. They put their belongings in a storage unit and paid in advance for three months. They also withdrew a sizable amount of cash from their bank and have not used their credit cards since Friday morning. They dropped off the radar after that."

"What does that mean?!" TJ questioned.

"It means it complicates things. They're using cash, which cannot be traced, and we have no idea what type of vehicle they have now."

Tabitha cried out, wrapped her arms around TJ. "God, oh god," she sobbed, understanding getting Abby back would be next to impossible.

The doorbell rang, and Hunter moved away to answer it, leaving his uncle alone to soothe and comfort.

"He'll do everything in his power to find her, Tabitha," TJ promised, stroking her hair as she wept into his chest.

"I'm devastated," she sobbed. Pulling away from him, she wrapped her arms around herself. "All because, in their eyes, I'm evil! They're the ignorant ones! My religion predates theirs, but they chose to believe the lies their leaders tell them, and now they have taken my daughter!"

"I wish people weren't prejudice against another's faith," TJ told her. "I don't know what else to say."

She quickly wiped at her tears, then looked at him. "How is it you accept the way I was raised?"

He shrugged. "I told you before. I was raised to be open-minded to people and their faith. My parents believe everyone's spirituality is a personal choice. Mason's parents have the goddess Aphrodite as their guide. For myself," he shrugged. "I won't tolerate violence in the name of anyone's religion or someone's cause, although, in this case, I might make an exception and punch Owen's dad in the nose once they're found."

His declaration almost caused her to smile.

"Tabitha!" She heard her mother's frantic voice and looked over to watch as her parents rushed into the room. "What in the name of Asherah is going on?! The police came to our door and told us the Turners have taken Abby! Then they brought us here."

"It's true, mom," Tabitha said, surprised by how steady her voice sounded.

"A curse on them!" her mother spat, "And protection for Abby."

"So mote it be," John Stevens agreed.

"Mr. and Mrs. Stevens," Hunter said, coming into the room. "I need to ask you some questions."

"Are you with the police?" Angela asked.

To keep things simple, Hunter said, "Yes," as much as it galled him to say so. "Did the Turners say anything when they picked Abby up yesterday?"

"No. Only that they wanted an early start to their day with her," John explained.

"Were they in their RV, or in their car at the time?"

"They picked her up in their car. Why? What difference does it make?"

"I'm trying to put together a timeline regarding when they would have left town and when they changed vehicles. I've got someone heading to the RV place now to question the employees. Maybe we'll get lucky, and someone from the lot might know what type of vehicle the Turners are driving now."

"I cannot believe this is happening!" Angela exclaimed.

"Can you think of any conversations you had with Ab-by over this past week that suggested where they might have taken her?" Hunter questioned.

"No. When they dropped her off the first time, she didn't say much except she didn't like the books and bible verses they read to her. After that, she didn't mention them again. As far as she was concerned, they didn't exist after that day."

"If you remember anything, no matter how small a detail, call me at this number." Hunter reached for a notepad on TJ's desk and wrote his uncle's phone number down for the older couple.

"Maybe I should go home," Tabitha said. "What if they reconsider and try to call me?"

"Yes. I believe that would be wise," Hunter agreed. "And I'll have the officers who brought your parents here take them back to their home on the off chance the Turners try to call them."

TJ stepped to Tabitha. "I'll pack a few things, then take you home. I don't want you to be alone."

Tabitha nodded; glad he would be there. She wanted his strength because she did not know if she had it in her to endure this alone.

While TJ was upstairs gathering the items he wanted, Hunter spoke with the officer who brought the Stevens here. After the conversation ended, he went back to TJ's desk to write the information down he'd already learned. As they gathered other information, he would add that to it. From there, he could put together a visual board that would assist in tracking the Turners down.

Coming down the stairs, TJ motioned for Hunter to join him in the kitchen. Keeping his voice low, he asked, "Can you find her?"

Hunter stared at him. "I'll give it my best shot, Uncle TJ. But they obviously knew what they were doing. By using cash, it's going to be like fishing for a needle in the haystack. But Cadman is deploying people to all their relatives to question them. And the task force is digging into all their records to see if there's a pattern. I wish I could say we'll have her back by tonight, but realistically I don't know how long it's going to take. On the upside, Cadman is more than willing to help with this regardless of it being outside the task force's usual missions. We have at our disposal task force members around the country, and technology the regular police don't have."

"Maybe I should get a cell phone," TJ suggested.

"A cell phone?" Tabitha asked, coming into the kitchen. "Those things cost around four thousand dollars."

"But it would be handy to have. Especially since I'll be staying with you. Your line might be tied up when someone's trying to reach me."

"Four thousand," she emphasized the word, "dollars." Had he not heard the outrageous amount the newest technology cost?

Hunter shook his head, chuckled. Apparently, his uncle hadn't told Tabitha what his bank account looked like.

"I'm just saying," TJ told her, "that it could be useful to have."

"Four Thousand-" she began to reiterate, but he cut her off.

"I heard you the first time. Christ, Tabitha. It was only a suggestion."

"It would be cheaper to have another line installed in my house!"

Hunter began moving out of the kitchen. "I'll just be in your office, TJ." He knew when to retreat to safety when obviously there was a fight brewing.

"Do you want me to call the phone company and have them do that?" he asked, his voice beginning to rise.

"It's the weekend! You can't just ask them to do it without scheduling an appointment!" She snapped.

"Would you like to make a bet on that?!"

"For the love of Peter, Paul, and Mary! Why would you even suggest such a thing?!"

"Because I'm staying with you until they find Abby! And because I might need access to a phone at the same time you do. And why in the hell are we arguing about this?"

"I don't know!" she cried, throwing her hands in the air. "I'm so lost right now I can't think straight! I need to call Grace and Greta and let them know-" her voice hitched. "There is no way I can think about opening the clinic on Monday morning if Abby isn't found before then and-" Her eyes met his. "I'm devastated, Thaddeus!"

Three steps took TJ to her. Wrapping his arms around her, he kissed her forehead then gently pressed her face into his chest. "I know, babe." He stroked her hair, trying to comfort. "I'll take you home. You are probably exhausted, both mentally and physically, and need to lie down for a bit."

She sniffed, nodded her head, but didn't speak. No words would bring Abby back. And nothing could ease the guilt she felt over sending her daughter to spend the night with her kidnapers, all because she, Tabitha, had wanted one night of pleasure with this man.

Hunter peeked his head around the corner of the kitchen. "Hey, Tabitha. Can you come to TJ's office? I want to ask you a few questions."

Tabitha looked at him, nodded.

TJ slipped his hand into hers and walked with her through the house to the area where Hunter waited.

Hunter had a notepad in front of him when they entered the room. Motioning for Tabitha to sit down, he told her, "I need you to tell me everyone you can think of that Abby has been around lately. Maybe she said something to one of them."

Tabitha shook her head. "The only time she's with anyone other than my parents or myself is on Wednesday mornings when she goes to daycare for half the day."

"That's a starting point," he told her. "I can deploy a few people to question the daycare and the kids. One never knows when a minor detail will lead to a break-through."

Chapter Eighteen

On Sunday morning, Jacqueline Fisher opened the front door on the Davidson's home as she said to the woman behind her, "Linda, thank you for everything. Once your husband and mine come back from wherever they drove off to this morning, we'll be out of your hair. Colten and I had a lovely time visiting with you and Gary. And of course, the rest of your family."

"Gary and I were thrilled to have you!" Linda assured her. "And we are both pleased to know the two of you have been cleared to travel. I'm sure you and your husband are enjoying the pleasure of having something other than the Badlands to look after," her brows lowered as she thought a moment, "twenty-five years of basically being under lock and key."

Jacqueline chuckled. "Colten and I never felt locked up. We did what we thought was best for ourselves and our family. And Colten's former boss isn't loosening up enough to give us the green light to travel overseas together. I'll still be doing it alone whenever I want to visit France, and Cadman and his wife Kasey will continue to escort me. And force me to wear disguises the whole time." She made a face, hating the wigs and make-up that altered her appearance from anyone who might report back to Pierre that she was alive and well. "However, being able to travel around the United States with my husband is exhilarating. But we have discovered that, although the states we have passed through are lovely, they do not call to us as the Badlands do."

"Well, as they say. There is no place like home," Linda quoted the line popularized by the 1939 film The Wizard of Oz.

"Very true. Besides, I have a new grandson I miss spoiling waiting for me when we get back."

Linda chuckled. "Grandbabies are the best. I know I adore mine."

Jacqueline stepped from the Davidson's home onto the front porch. Once there, she closed her eyes for a moment as she took in a deep breath, allowing memories to come flooding back.

"I remember the first day I arrived here from France as a foreign exchange student. You and Gary welcomed me with open arms and made me feel like a part of your family."

"You'll always be our family," Linda told her.

Jacqueline leaned in to hug the woman. "I wish I could have come back sooner before Digger passed away."

"He would have liked that." With a smile on her face, Linda confessed, "I think he was half in love with you."

With a laugh, Jacqueline shook her head. "Your husband's brother was a wonderful man."

"That he was," Linda agreed as she moved to a nearby chair. Sitting down, she motioned for her visitor to do the same. "He pretended to be scatterbrained whenever you were around so he could get extra attention from you. How long did it take for you to figure out he was only pretending to forget things?"

"I'm not sure. He was so good at the pretense. But I know for certain it wasn't long after the day Pierre tracked Colten and me to Digger's cabin, intending to kill us, that I realized Digger sometimes slipped from scatter-brained to normal." She shook her head, brushed tears from her eyes. "I wish Digger were here now, still playacting his absentmindedness."

"Me too," Linda agreed.

Jacqueline sighed. "All of that is behind us now. Old history. We have had children since then, and now our families are growing even more."

Linda nodded. "Two of mine have gotten married and are expecting babies. And I hardly believe your oldest daughter is married! Good lord, where does the time go?"

"I know what you mean. Colten and I talk about it all the time. Especially now that the youngest ones, the twins, turned ten this year. Next thing I know, they'll be off to college. Melissa already has plans to find a college that teaches computer technology when she turns seventeen next year. Slowly my children are leaving the nest. I am so grateful Donna and her husband love the ranch. They have no intention of moving away, and it will allow me to have little ones around for a while longer."

"And both of us have boys- men," Linda amended, "who will be with us as long as we live. How is Clinton doing these days?"

At the mention of Jacqueline's stepson, who was on the autism spectrum, she laughed. "Clinton is doing very well. And although he loves the ranch, he took a leap this summer and took a job in Medora helping with the musical. He enjoys selling popcorn at the concession stands and talking with the tourists."

"Good for him! Gary and I are hoping to come out that way next year, and of course, the musical is on our list to attend. It gets better every year!"

"There has been talk about the possibility of one-day installing escalators."

"I hope that happens! As much as I love the Musical, that walk back up that hill after the entertainment about kills a person!"

Both women laughed, knowing the statement was close to the truth.

"And your son Grant," Jacqueline said after the laughter subsided, "is a successful artist. I'm so proud of him!"

"We owe you for showing us that just because he has Down syndrome, it didn't have to be a handicap. People are truly impressed with his art."

"And they should be. He is extremely talented."

Linda hit her own forehead with her palm. "I forgot to tell you! I can't believe it slipped my mind! President Reagan recently commissioned Grant to do a portrait of Nancy!"

Jacqueline's eyes widened. "Oh, my gosh! When did that happen?"

Linda squared her shoulders as only a proud mother could do. "Actually, it happened just before you got here. You and Colten were already on the road driving, so we couldn't call you. I meant to tell you both the moment you arrived."

"It is exciting news!" Jacqueline exclaimed.

The front door opened, and Grant Davidson stepped out to join his mother and Jacqueline on the front porch.

"Grant!" Jacqueline stood up quickly and rushed to the now thirty-two-year-old artist. "Your mother just told me the news about President Reagan calling you! That is so exciting!"

Grant Davidson blushed and ducked his head. "Thank…you, Miss…Jackie," the young man said in his broken speech pattern.

Jacqueline gave him a quick hug. "I hope you will send me a photo of the finished work so I can see it."

"I will," Grant promised, then stepped back. "If you…promise to…take this with you…and give it to…this person." He held up a thick manila envelope he brought outside with him.

Jacqueline looked down at the envelope, then reached out to take the item. "What is it?" she asked, looking at the envelope and the address of whomever it was addressed to.

Tabitha Turner
c/o Little Paws and More Veterinary Clinic
Binghamton, NY.

"Did you want me to mail it for you?" She was confused and surprised to note the person lived in the same town as TJ did.

"No," Grant shook his head. "She wanted a…donation."

At Jacqueline's raised brow, Linda told her son, "Grant, why don't you get the letter Tabitha sent you. I believe Jacqueline will enjoy reading it."

Grant disappeared quickly into the house and returned a short time later carrying an envelope. Handing it to Jacqueline, he waited for his friend to read the contents.

Jacqueline scanned the neatly handwritten letter, then reread it a second time. Looking up, she met Linda's eyes. "I cannot believe this!" she exclaimed on a laugh. "Little Tabitha Stevens, the little girl who, all those years ago, was trying to convince us to take the stray cat she found is now a veterinarian and living in Binghamton!"

"It's a small world," Linda commented, then explained, "And because Grant loved that kitten so much, he wanted to help support her cause to build a dog sanctuary."

Jacqueline looked down at the larger envelope. "What is it?" she asked, assuming Grant had rendered a drawing for the raffle that would be held at a later date.

Rather than tell her, Grant carefully opened the package. Pulling out something with cardboard protecting it on both sides, he withdrew a framed drawing.

"Oh!" Jacqueline had no other words as she took the enclosed black and white pencil drawing into her hands and stared at it. The image was a portrait of a photograph Linda had taken on the day Colten brought the cat to Grant.

In the photo, Colten sat on the front porch with Grant as the kitten nuzzled the boy's neck. This was a closeup rendering of Colten and Grant's faces as they looked down at the animal. The image's detail closely resembled an actual photograph and showcased Grant's ability to draw lifelike replicas.

Linda explained, "Grant chose that photo because of its connection between himself and one animal Tabitha has saved over the years."

"It's the perfect choice," Jacqueline whispered, remembering that day. The day before Colten lost an eye because of Pierre. "I might have to buy this from Tabitha before she allows it to go into the raffle." And she meant to offer the woman almost any price for the image because she wanted it that badly.

If Jacqueline wasn't a woman of honor, she would never deliver Grant's donation. But her integrity would not allow her to keep it without buying it from the person Grant gifted it to.

A car door slammed, and those on the porch looked up to see that Gary and Colten were back from the drive they had taken together.

"It's about time the two of you showed up," Linda called out to the pair. "I was wondering if the two of you got lost."

"Nah," Gary, Linda's husband, answered, "we were hoping you'd have the Fisher's bags all packed and their car loaded by now so we wouldn't have to carry the luggage down the stairs."

"Ha, ha," Linda told him. "The bags are packed, but we left them upstairs for the two of you to load up."

"Darn," Gary sighed.

Colten moved to his wife, kissed her on the cheek. "I suppose we should head on down the road if we expect to be in Binghamton before the sun sets."

"Yes," Jacqueline agreed. "And I'm eager to see Hunter. I need to see for myself he's all right."

Colten shook his head, chuckled. "You know he won't want you to baby him."

"What he wants and what will happen are two different things," Jacqueline vowed. "I haven't seen him in almost two years. So, while I'm home having to worry about him getting hurt, what does he do? He gets hurt! He'll just have to deal with me nursing him back to health."

Colten clamped his lips together, knowing there was no point arguing with his wife, but also knowing their son. Hunter was not the type of person who liked to be waited on hand and foot.

"I'll just run upstairs and get our bags," he said, escaping before his wife said anything more about their child who had more enthusiasm for danger than anyone they knew.

Jacqueline put the sketch back into the envelope. "We'll be glad to deliver this for you," she told Grant. "I'm eager to see what she looks like all grown up."

Linda turned toward her husband. "Where did the two of you go off to so early this morning?" she asked him.

"We just drove around town. Colten wanted to drive by the hospital he'd spent a month in back in the day." Gary shrugged. "And it gave the two of you a little more time together before they headed out."

Colten came out from the house carrying their luggage. "I'm ready to leave whenever you are," he told his wife, then walked down the few steps from the porch and placed the suitcases into the trunk of the car.

Jacqueline gave Linda and Gary one last hug, and Grant a kiss on the cheek as she said her goodbyes. As she made her way to where Colten stood holding the passenger door open for her, he asked, "Have you talked to TJ to let him know we'll arrive tonight instead of tomorrow?"

She shook her head. "I thought we would surprise him."

Once she was seated inside, Colten closed the car door then walked around to the driver's side. He gave one last wave to the Davidson's before climbing behind the wheel and starting the engine. "Are you sure you don't want to call Thaddeus to let him know to expect us tonight?"

"For heaven's sake, Colten. I'm not sure why you seem insistent we call him. He'll be happy to see us whenever we show up." She buckled the seatbelt as her husband put the car in gear and pulled away from the curb. "Besides, if I'm lucky, the girl Hunter told us TJ is dating when we spoke to him on Friday, will be there."

"Ah," Colten said.

She gave him a sharp look. "What's that supposed to mean?"

"I knew there was an ulterior motive."

With a gasp, Jacqueline folded her arms across her chest, leaned back in the seat. "I have no idea what you are talking about."

Colten made a left turn as he laughed. "Admit it. When Hunter told you my baby brother had a date, your curiosity got the better of you."

"I'm not going to talk about it," she told him.

"All right. If you want to change the subject, I'll let you."

"Are you patronizing me?"

He risked a glance in her direction. The look on her face had him suppressing the urge to smile. "I would never dream of it," he said.

Jacqueline stared at him long enough; it caused him to squirm.

"I just want him to be happy," she told him after a while.

"Well, I understand that. What Heather and Rick did to him messed him up. It was one reason he sold his business and got the hell out of New York City."

"Do you blame him?"

"No. Especially when they moved into the same building where TJ's penthouse was."

"I heard they got kicked out of there."

Colten chuckled. "Well, my brother purchased the building after they moved in. Then he kicked them out before he resold the place."

"Serves them right."

"Anyway, what's in that envelope you've been holding onto since we got in the car?"

"Oh!" Jacqueline exclaimed. She told her husband about the commissioned work Grant would do for President Reagan. And she explained Grant had also received a request for a donation from Tabitha Turner. "She was Tabitha Stevens at the time she convinced you to take that cat. Do you remember her?"

Colten chuckled. "How can I forget? She was determined to make sure that cat had a home." He shook his head. "I remember thinking at the time, with those big eyes of hers, she could wrap any man around her finger once she was older. I'm looking forward to meeting her husband. Obviously, she's married now since she has a different last name than back then."

They headed out-of-town north on highway 66 toward Allegheny National Forest. As the miles rolled away, each of them remembered back almost twenty-five years ago when they had taken this same route. At that time, they were on their way to a ranger station. From there, they went by horseback into the forest to seek Digger Davidson out at his cabin.

Colten almost lost his life in that forest.

As they passed the turn for the ranger station, where they had gotten the horses to use for their trek to Digger's place, Jacqueline reached out and took Colten's hand with hers.

"It seems like a lifetime ago," Jacqueline spoke out loud as she observed the thick trees as they drove over the road that cut through them.

Colten raised their joined hands to his lips, kissed her knuckles. "It was a lifetime ago, but I wouldn't have changed a thing. It brought us together, and we have a good life. I love you now as much as I did back then."

Jacqueline pulled her hand away to wipe at the moisture his statement caused to leap into her eyes. "I love you, too," she told him, then sat back in the seat, settling in to view the scenery as they traveled the four-and-a-half-hours to Binghamton.

At three-thirty in the afternoon, they arrived at their destination. Colten pulled their vehicle into the double-wide driveway and cut the engine. Together he and Jacqueline stared at the house, admiring the structure.

"It's a lovely home," Jacqueline said, opening the car door.

"I can see why Thaddeus would be drawn to it." Colten stepped out of the vehicle, then waited for his wife to walk around the car and join him. "It has character. I wonder how much time he spent remodeling it."

Jacqueline slipped her hand into his. "However long it took, he would have loved every minute of it."

"Come on. We'll let him know we're here before bringing the suitcases in. Hopefully, he's home. I don't see that Porsche of his, though it could be in the garage."

"I think that truck parked next to the garage would be his work truck. It looks like something he would use for his construction business."

"At least we know he isn't working today then. And he might have a couple of guests since there are a few cars parked in the street."

"Maybe one belongs to the girlfriend," Jacqueline suggested hopefully.

With a shake of his head, he told her, "Try to not quiz her the second you meet her."

"Don't be silly. I'll do no such thing."

"Refrain?"

She swatted his arm. "You know what I meant."

Yes, he did. His wife would subtly size the woman up before asking twenty questions.

Together they mounted the steps leading to the front door, stepped onto the porch, and Colten rang the bell.

The door opened within moments, but it wasn't TJ standing there to welcome them to his home. Nor was it their son, Hunter.

"Cadman?" Colten all but sputtered, never in a million years expecting his former boss to be in Binghamton, and certainly not in TJ's house.

"Yep. It's me. We weren't expecting you until tomorrow, but come on in."

"I suppose that makes us even as we weren't expecting you at all." Colten told him as he guided Jacqueline over the threshold.

"Your son requested my assistance. Actually, he didn't ask me to come here. He just needed my go ahead to use my resources, but since my wife is busy painting our bathroom and shooed me out, I flew up here to get out of her hair." He chuckled.

Colten cocked a brow. "Assistance for?"

"A missing person."

"TJ's missing?!" Jacqueline gasped.

Cadman stared at her for a beat. "What?" He shook his head. "No. It's a little girl."

"I'm so confused," Jacqueline admitted.

Hunter moved into her line of vision. The moment Jacqueline saw the crutches and full leg cast on her son's leg, she forgot all about whatever reason Cadman was there for. Stepping toward her second oldest son, she said, "Oh, honey! Shouldn't you be sitting down with your leg propped up?"

He looked at her as though she had lost her mind.

When his mother moved in to hug him, he allowed it. He even returned the embrace because yes, he loved his mother to the moon and back but still, he was no longer a child. Besides, if she knew about half the bruises he'd suffered over the years because of what he did for a living, it would curl her hair.

"I'm fine, Mom," he told her.

She eyed the cast. "I see that," she told him in a voice laced with sarcasm.

Hunter sighed. "Why don't you and dad come on into the living room. I'll fill you in on why Cadman is here."

Chapter Nineteen

That same afternoon TJ found Tabitha outside on the back yard deck, seated at a small patio table. At some point on Friday night, Tabitha explained to him that this spot was her favorite area of her home. Each night, weather permitting, once Abby was in bed, she would come here to take in the night air, enjoy the quiet, and look up at the moon and let the stress from the day fall away.

They'd made love out here that night, under the stars and moonlight, while the crickets chirped, and the moon bathed them with its rays.

He would never forget the feel of the night on his skin and the touch of this woman's hands on his body.

Now, standing in the doorway that led from the kitchen to this spot, he watched her. Her head was bowed, but not in prayer. There was a notebook open on the table, and she was jotting in it as though possessed.

Reluctant to disturb her, yet curious to know what she was up to, he closed the distance between them and stopped behind the chair she was sitting on. Looking over her shoulder, his eyes followed her hand as it moved the purple pen across the page with quick angry strokes as though it were a sword.

Barbra Taylor. Andy. All the kids at daycare. Witches are devils, thus says the Lord. Chad and Mary-

"What are you doing?" he asked her, trying to make sense of the random words scrolling across the paper.

She jerked as a yelp escaped past her lips, and the pen went flying somewhere toward outer space.

He wanted to laugh but suppressed the urge as those beautiful amber eyes turned on him, and he could easily see he'd unintentionally frightened her.

"I'm sorry I scared you-"

"My stars, TJ! Why did you sneak up on me like that?!"

He pulled out the chair next to hers and sat down as he said, "I didn't mean to." He reached out, stroked her arm, trying to reassure her she was all right. "I came out here to see what you were doing."

Taking a deep breath, she closed her eyes and took a moment to settle her nerves.

"I'm making a list of every person I can think of who Abby might have mentioned anything cryptic. Anything regarding the Turners telling her they were going to take her, or where they were going." She took another deep breath as she tried not to give in to her urge to cry. She'd done a lot of that last night as the nightmare of not knowing where her daughter was kept her awake with fear the Turners would harm Abby.

Today she was determined to be strong. She would not allow the horror of Owen's parents betrayal to cripple her. Whatever she needed to do to get her daughter back, she would do.

"Didn't you go over all that with Hunter yesterday?"

"Yes. But maybe I missed someone? I'm writing the names all down because I want to make certain I didn't forget anyone."

TJ nodded. "That's a good idea." He reached a hand out to the page, pointed as he asked, "And the reason you wrote that?"

Tabitha glared at the words: Witches are devils, thus says the Lord, randomly placed on the paper in between the names. "It's one of the books Abby told me the Turner's read to her. I guess I just wrote it down in my anger."

"It's not true," he told her gently, reaching a hand up to brush a stray hair away from her face. "You're a kind person and a healer. I've seen how you interact with Abby and others. And that soft spot you have for animals, especially dogs, tells the true tale. You're an amazing woman. I'm sorry there are uninformed people in this world, Tabitha."

She grasped his hand as she met his eyes. Hers were filled with moisture when she said, "Thank you, Thaddeus. For caring enough to be with me. Especially now." She stood up, paced. "I feel so helpless! I just want Abby back! I wish there was something I could do to help find her!"

He went to her, wrapped her in his arms. "I know, babe. I can't believe no one at that RV dealership knows what kind of vehicle the Turner's have now! I'm about ready to drive down there myself and have a word or two with those people!"

TJ might have done just that had Tabitha's phone not rung at that moment.

"Can you answer that, TJ?" she asked. "I just need a moment to breathe."

"Sure, babe," he told her and moved into the house to take the call as he hoped it would be good news being delivered.

"Yeah?" he said, picking up the receiver.

"We've got a lead," Hunter's voice came through the receiver. "My dad's a badass when it comes to intimidation."

TJ grinned, elated at the news. "Tabitha and I are on our way so you can tell us about it in person-" His mind caught up with what else his nephew said. "Did you say something about your dad?"

"Yeah. Uncle Cadman put him to work the moment he and mom got here."

"Your parents are here? I thought they weren't coming until tomorrow."

A pause. "Uncle TJ. Does it matter? We'll see you when you get here."

The click sounding in his ear informed TJ his nephew ended the conversation.

Thirty minutes later, he and Tabitha arrived at TJ's house. There were people already gathered in the larger living room when they entered the space.

They recognized the police officer standing in the corner, speaking with Cadman Benson. Hunter was on the opposite side of the room talking with a man and woman Tabitha did not know but assumed were TJ's brother and sister-in-law and Hunter's parents. However, Tabitha could easily see TJ and the older man's resemblance to each other, even without an introduction. Their features were similar enough for anyone to understand they were related.

TJ took Tabitha's hand in his as he walked to where his relatives stood, bringing her along with him for introductions.

"I didn't expect you until tomorrow," TJ told his brother as he stepped forward and gave him a hug.

Returning the embrace, Colten said, "And we didn't expect to find Cadman here, and an investigation into a kidnapping case involving your girlfriend's daughter." He stepped back, turned to Tabitha. "My wife and I are very sorry this happened to you."

Tabitha nodded but could not speak because of the emotions that welled up in her. Here were two people who didn't know her but were willing to help find Abby.

Jacqueline moved to TJ, hugged him, then turned her attention on Tabitha. "With my son, husband, and Cadman in your corner, they will do everything that can be done to bring your daughter home." She stepped forward and embraced Tabitha. "You turned into a beautiful woman. We thought you were cute as a button the first time we met you. We wish with all our hearts this second meeting would have been under different circumstances."

Confused, to say the least, Tabitha looked inquisitively at Hunter's mother.

Smiling, Jacqueline said, "Years ago Colten and I were in your parent's diner in Clarion. You convinced him," she motioned to her husband, "to take a stray cat you'd found, and he gave it to Grant Davidson."

Having just walked into the living room with her husband, Angela Stevens gasped when she heard what Jacqueline said. "Oh, sweet goddess, Asherah," she exclaimed. "I knew TJ looked familiar!"

"Could someone explain?" TJ asked.

Angela retold the tale of the day a then eight-year-old Tabitha brought the stray cat into the diner in Clarion.

"The first time I saw TJ, I thought he looked like some-one I'd seen before," Angela said, looking between Colten and TJ. "I can easily see the two of you are brothers."

"I'm the better looking one," TJ grinned.

"Keep dreaming, brother," Colten laughed.

Jacqueline spoke to Tabitha. "I know it's a lot to take in. It's amazing that, after all these years, we meet you again and discover you're dating this brother-in-law of mine. I can hardly believe how small this world is. But as a mother, I know that at this moment, you probably don't care."

"I do," Tabitha assured her. "My head is spinning from all of this, but please," she turned toward Hunter, "TJ told me you have a lead. Do you know where Abby is?"

Hunter shook his head. "Not yet, but it's the break we were looking for. Because of it, we've been able to issue a BOLO to all law enforcement agencies in the country."

"A BOLO?"

"It's short for be on the look-out. It's also called an all-points bulletin. Law enforcement in all states will keep their eyes open for a white Ford E250 Falcon high top camper van."

"That's good news!" A spark of hope leaped into Tabitha's eyes.

TJ turned to Hunter. "I thought no one saw the Turners after they dropped that Winnebago off at the dealership and collected their cash."

"I did. And that was the story the investigator got from the three employees who work there." He raised a brow. "Didn't I mention my dad was a badass when I called you earlier?"

"Yeah, yeah. We all know my brother can be intimidating. He passed the trait onto you. Trust me, nephew. By the time you're his age, you'll strike fear into the hearts of men with just a look."

Hunter beamed.

"He already does that," Cadman said. "Team members report back to me that the people they've arrested want to be as far away from him as they can get."

"Anyway," Hunter continued. "Since I'm not able to head down to that used dealership myself, when dad got here he and Cadman went there. The two of them got answers no one else seemed to be able to."

Colten took up the story from there. "I couldn't believe not one person could remember seeing an older couple with a little girl in tow. I was more than willing to go down there with Cadman and have a chat with those fellows who purchased the Turners camper."

"By chat, do you mean bodily harm?" TJ wanted to know.

Colten shrugged. "I might have mentioned something about cutting off their nuts if they didn't tell me the truth. Even with only one eye, I could see they were lying about not knowing anything." He glanced at Tabitha, "I wasn't about to let those people get away with being accessories to kidnapping."

"So, after you threatened them, they came clean right off the bat?" TJ asked.

"Well, no. One of them took a swing at me. Ha. Just because I'm fifty-four and Cadman's almost sixty, they thought we'd be easy to get rid of."

Cadman spoke up. "We've still got what it takes to make people talk. It still pisses me off Colten retired from working for me, though."

Colten looked at his former boss. "Well, much to my wife's dismay, you've got our son working for you now."

Cadman smiled. "I always knew that boy was destined for greatness."

TJ shook his head. "Could we just move this along? Why wasn't the investigator who originally questioned them able to discover anything?"

Colten shrugged. "Possibly because he's too easily duped, and because he's got a baby face that shows his gullibility." He used his right hand to wave that information away as irrelevant. "As it turns out, the three employees who, by the way, are now unemployed and facing jail and a trial, took money from the Turners to keep quiet about what vehicle they switched to."

Tabitha asked, "What do we do now?"

"We wait for whatever authorities find them to call us," Cadman told her.

"How long will that take?!" Tabitha almost demanded and felt TJ's hand move to the small of her back.

"Babe, no one can predict when they'll be found. But at least now we have more to go on than we did before," TJ told her. "All it's going to take is for whoever is driving the van to break the law. You know? Speed. Hell, if they get a flat tire, it will bring notice to them."

She crossed her fingers for luck as she hoped someone would spot her ex-in-laws soon.

"Well," Cadman said, "I'm not needed here. I'm heading back to Washington. Kasey should be done painting the bathroom by now and be glad to see me."

"Or throw a roller at you for ditching her," Hunter grinned.

Cadman shook his head. "She's the one who told me to get lost, claiming I have no flair for painting walls." He snorted.

Tabitha looked up at TJ. "This not knowing is driving me insane. Isn't there something we can do now?"

Hunter answered her, "Not at this time. Sorry."

"How about you come into the kitchen with me," Jacqueline suggested to Tabitha. "It's nearing dinner time, and you can help me cook something to feed everyone."

Knowing it would keep her mind occupied for a moment, Tabitha agreed to help Jacqueline.

"I'll help too," Angela told them, following them through the house. Walking into TJ's kitchen, she ex-claimed, "Oh, my goddess! I love this kitchen!" She looked around the wide-open space, approving the skillets hanging from the ceiling for convenience and saving space.

"It is lovely," Jacqueline agreed as she looked in the refrigerator and freezer for some ideas of what to put on the menu tonight. Pulling out hamburger meat from the freezer, she handed the packages of frozen meat to Tabitha. "If you could put these in the microwave and start thawing them?"

Nodding, Tabitha took the packages and moved to the microwave to begin the task.

Together the women made a spaghetti and meatball dish with garlic bread and a side salad of plain lettuce.

Once the meal was eaten, Tabitha asked TJ to take her home. "I need to call Grace and Greta. I can't open the clinic tomorrow."

TJ could understand her reasons behind wanting to keep the clinic closed for a little while. It would be hard for her to concentrate on anything other than Abby's whereabouts. "All right," he told her, deciding he wouldn't work on the project house tomorrow and knew that by doing so, his timetable for completion would be shot but did not care. "Let me say goodbye to my brother first."

She nodded. "Of course, but once you take me home, you don't have to stay. I know you would probably rather be with your family since you haven't seen them in a while."

"I'm staying with you, Tabitha." He reached out, touched her left shoulder, where her tattoo was covered by her sleeve. "I know you told me those initials are for the name you were born with, but seeing them the other night, knowing they entwine with my name, did something to me. I don't want you to be alone, and Abby means a lot to me too."

She leaned into him, accepted his embrace, and tried to absorb some of his strength into herself.

Jacqueline approached them, cleared her throat to gain their attention. Once she had it, she said, "I wish there was something more we could do. We will keep Abby in our thoughts and hope she's back in your arms safe and sound soon."

"Thank you," Tabitha told her.

The drive back to Tabitha's home was done in companionable silence. Once there, Tabitha set about calling each of her employees to let them know she was closing the clinic until they found Abby.

"You don't have to do that," Grace told her over the phone. "Greta and I kept this place running after Owen passed away, and we'll do it again," she promised. "It might take a few days to get a few volunteers, but we're going to get through this! Greta and I don't want you to worry," she broke off on a sob. "You'll get Abby back!" she cried.

Tabitha wiped at the tears in her eyes. "Yes," she agreed and swallowed the lump in her throat.

"Do you need me to come over there? Keep you company?"

"No. TJ's here."

"He's a good man, Tabitha."

Tabitha glanced toward where TJ sat on the sofa, looking through the newspaper he brought with him from his house. "Yes, he is," she whispered.

When she hung up the phone, she took a deep, cleansing breath. Then another as she determined not to let grief rule her. As far as anyone knew, Abby hadn't been harmed. She needed to believe that or allow anxiety to cripple her.

Once she felt she had her emotions under control enough, she turned to TJ and tried to find something normal to occupy her mind. With that thought, she asked him, "So, Thaddeus Jackie, would you like to watch a movie with me?"

TJ stared at her. "Jackie?"

She shrugged. "I thought maybe the reason you hate your middle name so much is because it's girly?"

He thought that over a moment and was glad she was still trying to play the name guessing game. "I suppose that would make it worse than what it is, so that's something to be thankful for." He set the newspaper down and moved off the couch. "But no, it's not Jackie." Walking to her, he caressed her cheek. "What movie would you like to watch?"

She shrugged. "I have a VHS player, but my selection of movies is limited."

"We could drive to the video store and rent one," he suggested.

"All right," she nodded, welcoming another opportunity to get out of the house. Being here, the quiet of the rooms were loud reminders of Abby's absence.

Once they arrived at the video rental store, they browsed the racks together. Tabitha gravitated toward the comedy section, wanting something lighthearted to view. When she saw the movie, The Money Pit, she snatched the box up and showed it to TJ. "Oh, look. Here's a movie about Doris's old house."

He shook his finger at her as he suppressed a laugh. "You'll eat those words when I'm done with the remodel, and her house isn't nearly as bad as the one the characters in that movie purchased."

"If you say so," she teased, putting the movie back on the shelf.

TJ reached for her hand as they continued to browse the large selection of comedy movies on display. He could have chosen to be insulted by her little dig about the job he was doing on the house next to her folks. However, he was glad she was attempting, at least, to remain upbeat tonight.

It took almost a half-hour before they found two movies they thought they would enjoy. And with Ferris Bueller's Day Off and Crocodile Dundee riding in the backseat of the Porsche, they drove back to Tabitha's home.

When they walked into the house, he noticed her eyes slide toward the answering machine. Then he watched her shoulders slump slightly when she saw no messages were waiting to be heard.

He couldn't blame her for her disappointment. He felt it too. No blinking light meant there was still no word on Abby's location.

Wishing he knew what to say to help ease her stress and worry, he did the one thing he could do. Stepping to her, he wrapped her in his arms, kissed her forehead. "Someone will find her soon, babe," he told her and tried to believe it himself. He could only guess at the turmoil going through her. He felt the burden of worry as well.

Abby had gained a place in his heart. And her mother was taking up residence there right along with her.

"Let's make some popcorn," she told him, trying to remain optimistic although her voice was a little more monotone than it had been a little while ago.

"With lots of butter," TJ commented as he followed her into the kitchen to help her with the task. He knew there was nothing he could say to help bring comfort to her, but that did not stop him from trying.

They watched Crocodile Dundee while sitting on the couch, eating the popped corn, and drinking Coca-Cola only because Tabitha had no beer stocked in the house.

During the movie, Tabitha stretched out on the couch, using TJ's leg as a pillow while he gently massaged her shoulder and stroked her hair.

Tabitha had longed for a scenario like this, but now that she had it, the not knowing where Abby was did not allow her to truly enjoy the moment.

The movie brought out a few laughs from her, but she sat up and looked at TJ when it was through.

"Will you do something with me?" she asked him, and her serious tone let him know she wasn't talking about sex.

"Whatever you need, Tabitha," he told her, reaching up to remove a few strands of her hair caught on her eyelashes.

She stood up as she told him she'd be right back, and when she returned, she held a white tapered candle, a holder, and a box of wooden matches in her hands. Setting the items onto the coffee table in front of the sofa, she slid out a drawer and removed a black-handled knife, a small notebook, and a pen.

TJ watched silently as she used the knife to carve Abby's name into the wax before placing the candle in the holder. After that, she opened the notebook and closed her eyes for a moment as though she were silently saying a prayer before writing something onto a small section and tearing it off.

Tabitha folded the paper, then looked at TJ. "I'm going to say a spell. Will you repeat it with me?"

He'd learned enough about Wicca in the short time he'd known the Stevens to understand what they called a spell was the same as a prayer.

"All right," he said, and tried not to feel ridiculous.

Tabitha closed her eyes and said, "Goddess of all, on this night, and in this hour, we seek your power. Abby waits in a hidden place. Open the veil, let justice prevail."

She repeated it, and on her third time through, TJ reeated the words along with her.

After the fifth time through the prayer, spell, incantation, or whatever she called this ritual, Tabitha reached for the matches, lit the candle, and said, "So, mote it be."

"So, mote it be," TJ whispered, watching her place the paper she'd written on earlier into the flame. Once it caught fire, she set the burning paper onto a small dish resting on the table.

When the paper was consumed and the fire burned out, Tabitha blew out the white candle, stood up, and reached for TJ's hand. "Make love to me tonight, Thaddeus."

Chapter Twenty

That night, TJ took his time making love to Tabitha, using his body to express the depth of his feelings for her. He did not understand when the fear of being betrayed again left him, and his heart opened to this woman. It was as if he suddenly realized that his previous feelings for Heather were shallow and based solely on her external appearance.

Which didn't say much for the person he'd been back then. Confusing love for lust was foolish. He knew that now. Love should be based on a person's soul because beauty can disappear in a heartbeat, and if it was only that person's beauty that attracted you to them, you were left with nothing when it faded over time, or some tragedy distorted it.

Heather had always been superficial. That aspect of her personality he ignored because he liked the looks of envy he'd gotten from other men when they were in public together.

He could no longer hate Heather. He'd looked past her shallowness, and that was his own damn fault.If he had truly taken the time to see what was in her heart, he would have realized that they were not meant for a long-term relationship.

Rick, on the other hand, would never receive his forgiveness. They had been best friends while growing up in Bismarck. Moving to New York City together, they'd had dreams of building up a construction business. But the company had only been the success it was because of TJ's hard work, intuition, and personal finances. Rick had done nothing to earn the money he'd gotten because of their partnership in Badland Builders.

It was after TJ caught Rick in bed with Heather that the truth came out. The rental properties they had co-ownership in were Rick's responsibility. TJ's mistake had been trusting Rick to handle all maintenance tasks on the units without checking up on him. TJ himself was busy working with crews, who worked with him side-by-side to construct buildings

on time and within budget, leaving little time for worrying about their three apartment buildings in Manhattan.

Having put that much trust in Rick was a mistake. One he learned his lesson from. He would never again give someone that much responsibility without following up. Once his engagement to Heather was called off, TJ heard the rumors. There were unhappy tenants who'd paid their rent but had leaky plumbing and heating and cooling systems that did not function properly.

TJ sued Rick, breaking the partnership, and retained all rights to use the business name and kept three-fourths of its assets. Soon after the final verdict, TJ sold all his properties in the Big Apple and moved out of the city.

The last he'd heard, Rick and Heather had blown through the money the court awarded Rick in less than two years. Which gave TJ the satisfaction of revenge without having lifted a finger.

But the betrayal wounded him. Opening his heart again wasn't easy. There was always the possibility of another flawed relationship, but this time he knew Tabitha was worthy of trust. She wasn't a woman who wanted to take but earn. And she'd earned his trust in spades.

Now his heart was broken for a different reason. It ached for Tabitha's own experience with betrayal, and he longed to see Abby's smile again.

Where was she? Where had her ignorant grandparents taken her, and for what purpose? Was it only because they believed Tabitha and her parents were evil? If so, they were sorely mistaken.

TJ kissed Tabitha's throat as his fingers slid along her collarbone, stopping at the place where her initials were tattooed on her upper arm. People would think he was crazy if they knew what he believed the real reason those letters were there.

TJS.

TJ's.

She was meant to be his.

And when he entered her, he vowed to himself that when Abby was found, he'd spend a lifetime making both of them happy.

Now they only needed someone to find that van the Turners were driving sooner rather than later.

When the couple was spent and resting in the aftermath of love making, Tabitha curled into his side. His last thought was of Abby and wished with all of his heart there would be news of her whereabouts in the morning.

* * *

"Hi! I'm Abby Nicole!"

TJ watched the three-year-old riding her trike in large circles in her grandparent's driveway. She was going way too fast, and he feared she would tip over and harm herself.

"Abby!" he called out, trying to get to her before the unthinkable happened, and she hit her head on the pavement if the tricycle toppled over.

Why hadn't he gotten her a helmet?

"I'm Abby Nicole!" she cried out again, laughing as her speed increased.

"Abby! Slow down! You're going to get hurt!"

He felt someone come up beside him and link their arm through his.

"She can't hear you, Thaddeus. She's not here."

TJ glanced at the person beside him and scowled. "Tabitha, she's right there!" he motioned toward the driveway where Abby continued to make circles around the pavement.

"We don't know where she is," Tabitha told him.

He shook his head to clear it. Was the woman crazy? "Look!" he exclaimed, "She's right in plain sight! She's going to get hurt if she doesn't slow down."

"Mommy doesn't know where I am," Abby told him. "But you do. That's why you can see me."

"What are you talking about?" He was surely going insane.

"My ex-in-laws took her, Thaddeus. Don't you remember?"

He frowned at Tabitha and motioned once again toward her parents' driveway. "Tabitha, she's right-"

His words cut off as he watched with fascination as the trike slowly transformed into a pony.

"Abby," his voice came out as a whisper. "What's happening?"

"You know where I am," the little girl claimed as she patted the pony's neck. "I told you. I told you where grandma and grandpa wanted to take me."

She began to fade before his eyes, and he cried out for her, knowing Tabitha would be heartbroken if her daughter disappeared again.

But the child vanished despite his wish, and he heard Tabitha's voice sooth, "It's all right, TJ. Settle now. It's all right."

* * *

TJ came awake on a gasp as though he'd stopped breathing. Above him, he could make out Tabitha's face. It was full of concern and unease.

"It's all right," she soothed as though he were a child. "Did you have a nightmare?"

He would have laughed if he'd been able to. He was thirty-six years old and hadn't needed someone to talk him down from a goddamn dream for over twenty-four years.

Laying back on the pillow, he swiped a hand over his face.

"Do you want to talk about it?" she asked, continuing in her calming voice.

Hell no, he thought, but the words came out. "Abby," he shook his head to clear it. "Abby was on her trike, and it turned into a pony."

Tabitha's lips curved into a slight smile. "She'd like that."

"She told me I know where she is-"

Northdah Koda. Abby's voice echoed in his ear as though brought to him on the air.

"TJ-?" Tabitha began, but he sat up as he shushed her.

"Wait!" He told her, trying to think as he attempted to bring back the memory the words stirred in him.

He felt her eyes on him and knew she probably thought he'd gone crazy. "Did you just shush me?" she asked him, indignant.

"Please," he whispered on a plea as he closed his eyes and desperately held onto the memory before he lost it.

"She read me a story about witches being evil. Dumb book."

"What else does she read to you?"

"About Badlands. She said they were going there and would take me with them."

"Did she mention where they were?"

"Northdah Koda."

"Oh, my god!" TJ exclaimed, throwing the sheet off from him as he bolted from the bed.

"TJ?" Tabitha's eyes were larger than ever as she stared up at him from where she was kneeling on the bed.

His laughter did not convince her he hadn't lost his mind.

"I think I know where she is!" he exclaimed as he picked up the receiver on the telephone next to Tabitha's bed and dialed his home number.

"What?!" He could tell she was beyond shocked. "How do you-?"

"I think Abby's in North Dakota!" he shouted on a giddy laugh.

"Umm," was all Tabitha managed to get out.

"Pick up the damn phone, Hunter!" TJ exclaimed into the receiver as it continued to ring.

Abruptly a voice on the other line said, "Fuck me. It's three o'clock in the freaking morning."

"Hunter! I know where she is!"

"What?" His nephew was no longer hostile because of being woken up in the early morning hour.

"Abby! I think I know where she is!"

"How?"

And TJ rapidly explained the conversation he'd had with Abby the first time the Turners' dropped her off at Tabitha's parent's house. "I think they're in Medora, or on their way there!"

"Unbelievable," Hunter said, and laughter came over the wire.

"I'm going to call my pilot and have him get the jet ready," TJ informed his nephew.

"Don't bother. Uncle Cadman is still here. He decided to spend the night so he could visit with mom and dad. His Cessna is at the airport, and as you know, he pilots it. I'll wake him up and tell him he's got passengers to take to North Dakota." Hunter laughed again. "It's got four seats, so I'll tag along. I'm sure mom and dad won't mind staying at your house while you're gone. Besides, if you used your jet, you couldn't land at the ranch. The airstrip isn't big enough for larger planes.

You'd only make it as far as Dickinson and have to arrange for transportation from there to the ranch."

"I'll have Tabitha pack a bag, then we'll head to my house to gather a few things for myself. I'm too wired now to try to go back to sleep."

"Dawn should break by the time everyone's ready, and the plane fueled up." Hunter paused. "I still can't believe it! I'll give Donna and Jake a call, too. Let them know to be on the lookout for the Turner's in case they've got plans of doing a trail ride if the authorities haven't located them beforehand."

TJ hung up the phone and had the most enormous grin he'd ever had on his face as he turned to face Tabitha.

The look on her face was somewhere between excitement, confusion and shock.

"Babe, is something wrong?"

"I don't know where to begin!" Tabitha exclaimed. "I just overheard a conversation that implies Abby's location quite possibly is known and-" she raised her fingers to her temples as though she had a headache. "You have a jet? How in the hell do you own a jet?"

TJ grimaced. "Can I give you the short version now? And tell you the rest later?"

Tabitha was a mass of conflicting emotions. Knowing she might see her daughter soon had her racing to the closet to pull out a suitcase as she told him, "All right. Short version while I pack a few things and gather some items for Abby too."

TJ watched her throw the bag onto her bed and begin gathering underwear and tossing them inside.

It was at that moment he realized they were both naked. He reached for the jeans he'd shucked out of earlier and put them on as he said, "I'm a billionaire."

Her hands were in the middle of folding a T-shirt to put in the suitcase when he said that. She froze. And when she looked at him, her eyes were those huge ambers he adored.

Then she laughed. "Sure. Why not?"

Her tone implied she didn't believe him.

"I told you the truth. I wasn't going to lie."

With a shake of her head, she gathered the last of the things she wanted to bring along, although not knowing how long she'd be gone made the decision making difficult. "I expect you'll explain once we're in the air?"

"I'd rather do it while we're alone but sure." He motioned to her. "Maybe you want to put some clothes on?"

She looked down at herself. "Oh, for the love of Peter, Paul, and Mary!" she exclaimed the moment she realized her state of undress.

"I don't know about them, but I like the view."

He caught the shoe she threw at him for that comment and laughed. "Are you through packing? I'll take the bag into Abby's room while you get dressed."

At her nod, he closed the bag and walked it into Abby's room, set it on the bed. If he had any idea what a little girl might need, he would have added them to the suitcase to save time, but as it was, he was clueless. Except, he saw Eddy the teddy sitting on her pillow. Picking it up, he put it into the suitcase on top of her mother's jeans.

Staring at the bear, he felt moisture gathering in his eyes.

When Tabitha walked in, it was in time to witness him wipe them away. Until that moment, it hadn't really struck her that, quite possibly, she would see her little girl by tomorrow afternoon.

Her own tears surfaced. Walking to TJ, she wrapped her arms around him, and he encircled her with his.

"I hope you're right," Tabitha whispered, resting her forehead against his chest. "I hope with all my heart she's there."

"Me too," he told her, stroking her hair. "Finish packing. The sooner we can get to my house than Cadman's plane, we'll be that much closer to discovering if I'm right. It will take a little over eight hours to get there. Sunrise is about three hours from now. If we can leave by six-thirty, we'll be there by two in the afternoon."

"If they've hurt her-" Tabitha began.

"Even if they haven't, they'll wish to their god they hadn't taken her," TJ vowed, picking up the suitcase from the bed. "We'll make sure they're locked up for a very long time."

With his free hand, he reached for hers, and together they headed for the front door.

Chapter Twenty-one

The F&L Horse Ranch
20 miles south of Medora, North Dakota

Donna Harper stepped out from the house she'd grown up in, onto the wide wraparound porch with her six-month-old baby cradled in her arms. Scanning the activity going on around her, she smiled as she watched one of the trail riding tours begin its trek into the Badlands surrounding this place.

She'd given enough tours in her lifetime to know that trail would take the group of tourists an hour to complete.

Looking down at her son resting in the crook of her arm, Donna snuggled him as she said, "And one day, you'll be out there, too."

Baby Steven yawned, and his mother laughed.

Her twelve-year-old adopted son Randy was walking toward the mess hall with Donna's youngest brother, Wyatt. There was only a year difference in their ages, Randy being the oldest, but that didn't stop the two from being best friends.

Wyatt didn't seem to care that Randy had cerebral palsy and needed leg braces and arm crutches to help him walk and balance. Randy would never be able to run and play the way other kids did, but regardless, Wyatt stuck to him like glue. The two of them were inseparable.

Wyatt's twin sister Rebecca was in the house reading a book. Something she'd rather do than be outside with the horses and tourists.

Melissa, five years younger than their brother Hunter, wasn't at the ranch. She'd driven to Medora to visit their oldest sibling and half-brother, Clinton.

Although now thirty-one years old, Clinton decided to get a job in Medora. The decision had taken the entire family by surprise. Clinton's autism had always caused him to obsess over horses, and no one thought he'd ever want to leave the ranch. However, it appeared as though his choice to help with the Musical, put on nightly during the summer in the historic town, was helping him grow and accept changes in his routine.

Donna often wondered if Clinton's success at slowly overcoming some of his obstacles was because her mother came into his life early enough to teach him coping techniques.

Whatever the reason for Clinton's choosing to try something different, it elated his family. Although one of them usually made the twenty-mile trip to Medora once a week to check in on him, wanting to assure themselves he was doing all right.

Glancing up at the almost cloudless sky, Donna calculated the time. The early morning phone call she and her husband Jake received from Hunter let them know they could expect company this afternoon. Possibly in a little more than a half-hour Uncle Cadman's plane's engine would be heard approaching from the east.

She was excited about seeing her uncle TJ and begrudgingly admitted to herself she couldn't wait to lay eyes on her ornery brother. Four years was a long time to go without seeing him. At least Uncle Cadman kept her parents informed about Hunter's health. Otherwise, Donna knew her mother would worry herself sick about him; knowing her son was out in the world seeking and arresting some of the worst criminals most of the earth's population didn't have a clue about.

But the reason for this visit from TJ broke Donna's heart. A child had been kidnaped from its mother.

Now that Donna was a mother herself, she could only imagine the woman's heartache and turmoil.

She hoped her Uncle TJ was correct in knowing the little girl's whereabouts, and this visit did not add more stress to the woman her uncle was dating.

It surprised Donna when Hunter told her in his early morning call that TJ was finally seeing someone. But it was also bittersweet to know she would meet this woman under circumstances that were not ideal. The woman would be anxious to discover her child's whereabouts and not be interested in getting to know TJ's family.

And who could blame her?

Donna heard another group of tourists returning from their own adventure into the Badlands and she looked up to watch their approach. It wasn't the guests that held her attention, but the man leading the small party back to the ranch.

Sometimes she still marveled at the love she had for him.

Jake stopped his horse for a moment in front of the porch his wife stood on. His lopsided smile caused butterflies in his wife's belly.

Donna loved that smile.

"Hey, darlin'. How's your day goin'?" he asked her in that Texan drawl of his.

"It's going great."

Jake jerked his chin toward the baby in her arms. "Is he awake?"

She nodded.

"Then hand him over so he can help me finish takin' these folks to the dismount area."

It was a routine they'd done countless times since Steven's birth. Jake enjoyed having the baby in his arms when he road and Donna enjoyed watching him gently cradle their son while in the saddle.

Donna was about to do what he asked when she glanced toward the ranch entrance and witnessed a camper coming up the road.

"Jake," she whispered and used her chin to indicate he needed to look over his shoulder.

He turned his head and saw what his wife had seen. A white Ford Falcon high top camper was driving over the red scoria rock that made up the road. "Well, I'll be damned." He looked back at Donna and told her, "Maybe you should take Steven into the house and have Rebecca watch him for a while. And then you can join me down at the corral."

"Do you think it's them?"

A shrug was his only answer before he nudged the horse forward to continue his journey toward the area used for the tourists to dismount.

By the time Donna joined Jake at the corral, the tourists he'd led there were gone. Another group of people were standing in the shed that sold the fares for the trail rides, trying to decide if they wanted to begin their own adventure into the Badlands on horseback.

A young couple with two children and an older couple with a little girl in tow stood debating about which, if any, of the packages offered they wanted to participate in. The options ranged from half-hour guided tours to four-hour ones although the longer ones needed to be booked at least a day in advance.

The ranch also offered overnight campouts, where they would travel on horseback to a campsite, spend the night in tents, then be guided back to the ranch by noon the following day.

Donna tried not to single out the little girl standing with an older couple in the shade of the building. She might not be the one her uncle was searching for and if she was, Donna did not want to spook the grandparents.

"Hello!" she said to the group of seven. "Welcome to the F&L. I'm Donna Harper." She motioned toward Jake, who was near the back of the building talking in low tones to one of the ranch's temporary summer help. "And over there is my husband, Jake. While he's busy, I

would be happy to answer any questions you might have. Where are you all from?"

The young mother answered, "We're from Idaho."

Donna smiled, keeping her eyes on them although her attention was on the older couple. "Great state! My husband and I visited Coeur d'Alene last year."

"That's where we live," the couple's, Donna guessed at the age, ten-year-old boy said, and she could have kissed him on the cheek for giving him an excuse to ask, "And what's your name?"

"I'm Will, and that's my brother Ed. Do we really get to ride a horse?"

"That's up to your parents. But even if they decide not to have you go on a trail ride, there are lots of places to explore right here on the ranch, and plenty of walking trails with some stunning scenery."

Now she turned her attention to the older couple, "And where are you folks from?"

"We're from the eastern part of the country," the man answered vaguely.

Then Donna turned her attention to the little girl. "And what's your name, young lady?" she asked in a friendly tone.

"Her name is Amanda," the old woman answered, grasping the child's shoulder, but Donna saw the very slight shake of the child's head and the fear on her face.

"Well, it's nice to have you all here for a visit," Donna told the group and wished she knew what to do at this point because it was apparent the little girl was afraid to say anything. And she also could not jump to conclusions, regardless of the fact her every instinct was screaming at her that the little girl was Abby Turner.

She felt Jake come up alongside her, reached out, and took his hand in hers.

"You folks interested in doin' a trail ride?" He asked the newcomers.

"Well, it's kind of expensive," the mother of the two boys dared to say.

"Some people feel that way," Jake agreed. "But I'll tell you what. If all of you want to go, I'll make you a deal. Everyone can do the one-hour ride for half price. What do you say?"

Donna would have argued about cutting the fair price, except she trusted Jake. There must be a reason for making the offer, and she tried not to hold her breath as she watched the older couple discuss the matter between themselves.

"My husband and I have never been on a horse," the older woman said, seeming to hesitate.

"Nothing to worry about, ma'am," Jake assured her. "The horses we use for our guided tours are gentle, and we have a mounting block to assist you in getting in the saddle."

"Well-"

"I'm positive your granddaughter would enjoy it very much. She'd probably love you more than ever if you let her ride a horse today. Everyone knows how much little girls love horses."

"I think she's too little to ride," the older man claimed.

"Not at all," Donna interjected. "We have small saddles for children her age, and I would ride alongside her holding the reins of the horse she's on. It's something we often do." She glanced at the little girl she knew in her heart was Abby and said, "I'll keep her safe."

It took a few moments, but the older couple agreed at last, and the younger couple was game.

After all. Who wouldn't want to take advantage of a half-price sale?

Donna helped saddle horses and was surprised when four summer employees arrived at the corral with their own horses. It appeared as though

they were going to accompany this group along with Jake, which was three extra hands more than a group of this size needed.

Her eyes slid to her husband. She wondered what, and if, there was a plan of some sort going on in his mind and if that was why the extra hands were here. To assist with whatever scheme Jake had cooked up.

Once the horses were saddled, Donna casually reached for the little girl's hand. She smiled at the older woman and said, "I'll introduce your granddaughter to the horse, if that's all right with you, while my husband helps you into the saddle of the one you'll ride."

"Well-" the woman said, clearly anxious about being separated from the child.

"Children enjoy petting the horse before they're set on it."

The woman glanced at the child, then the horse, then back to Donna. "I suppose it's all right." And the woman's gaze hardened when she looked back at the child and said, "You mind your manners, Amanda. And remember what grandma and grandpa told you, and what happens to little girls who disobey."

The child hung her head, clearly afraid of the older woman, "Yes, ma'am," she whispered, stepping closer to Donna.

Donna wanted to wrap the poor thing in her arms and tell her this nightmare would end soon. But she couldn't. Not until she and Jake could separate her from the grandparents, and she still had not confirmed that this was the missing child TJ was coming for. She could not afford to assume anything and risk a lawsuit against the ranch if her instincts were wrong.

She reached out her hand to the little girl. "I'll introduce you to Maggie. She's a gentle horse, and she loves children. Would you like to pet her?"

Hesitantly, the girl looked up at her, and Donna could see the anxiety in them. But she gave a slight nod and grasped Donna's hand with a grip that felt as though she were about to be swept away on a current, and Donna was her only support.

Donna led the child to the Shetland horse, which appeared dwarfed by the full-grown Quarter horses everyone else would be riding but was the perfect match for the child. Donna was surprised Jake was using the Shetland. It was one of a handful they kept at the ranch for days the F&L offered pony rides on the weekends.

Donna squatted down so she could be at the girl's level as she gently took the girl's hand and raised it to the pony's nose. "My mom taught me when I was your age to talk to the horse, I was going to ride so it would learn my voice and know I meant it no harm."

The girl said nothing but stroked the horse's nose.

Glancing over her shoulder, Donna could see Jake and the other ranch hands currently occupying the child's grandparents. They were assisting them in mounting the horses they assigned them and were keeping them distracted.

Taking a deep breath, knowing she might not have another chance, she whispered to the child, "Are you Abby Turner?"

The child jerked, and when she looked at Donna, it was easy to see she was holding back tears in her huge amber eyes.

"Grandma said I can't say that name anymore," the child whispered back in a voice choked with emotion.

"Then you don't have to say it. You only have to say yes or no."

"Amanda!" the grandmother called out. "Are you being a good girl?"

"She's doing great!" Donna replied, wanting to do nothing more than walk to where that woman now sat on a horse and pull her off it just so she could punch the woman in the nose.

"Let's get you up on the pony," Donna told the child and lifted her up.

"Yes," she whispered. "Help me."

Donna's heart broke at the double meaning. "Soon, baby. Just be ready, okay?"

Their eyes met, and Donna could see hope spring into the girl's eyes.

And then, as though on cue, a plane's engine was heard approaching from the east.

Jake rode his horse to his wife's side and asked her, "Well, darlin', what do you know?"

"We need to separate them. It's her."

Jake looked toward the employee mounted up at the front of the line, waiting for his boss's orders. Jake raised his arm and yelled, "Move 'em out, Mark!"

"Hot damn!" Mark exclaimed, as three of the employees circled the horses the young couple, and their two boys were on. They would prevent those horses from moving forward once the ones the Turners were on were set in motion. The fourth employee moved up on the little girl's grandparents and grabbed the reins of the horse the older woman was on, while Mark did the same to the one the older man sat.

Without a word, Mark and the fourth hand took off at a fast pace with the horses the grandparents were on in tow, heading them onto a trail that would take an hour to complete.

"Stop!" the older woman shrieked as she bounced in the saddle and held onto the saddle horn with a death grip, but the employees paid no heed to the older couple's demands to abort the tour.

"What on earth?" the young mother said as she watched the older couple being taken away.

"Not to worry, ma'am," one of the employees who was assigned to them told her. "They paid for a different adventure than the one you did. You and your family are going on a different route, and we can assure you, you'll have a more enjoyable time."

The plane came into view, and Donna took off her cowboy hat and used it to wave to it.

Jake moved his horse close to the Shetland; reached down for the little girl. "Well now, Abby Turner, I believe there's someone in that plane that's eager to see you." He lifted the child with ease, set her in the saddle in front of him.

Donna reached out, touched the girl's hair as she attempted to soothe. Little Abby was currently speechless. She did not understand what was happening and probably thought her life had just taken on a different nightmare.

"You know my Uncle TJ," Donna told the child. "He's in that plane and is going to take you back home."

"TJ?" Abby asked, and her eyes filled with tears.

"Yep," Donna nodded. "And even better than that, he's got your mom with him."

And now Abby's tears overflowed, and she cried, "I want my mommy!"

"Then han' on tight," Jake told her as he used the heels of his boots to cause his horse to leap forward into a gallop. Donna's horse kept pace right along with him as they rode toward the airfield located a mile away from the ranch house.

By the time he and Donna arrived at the runway, the plane was on the ground, the engine cut, and the occupants were disembarked.

Jake rode his horse right up to the place where her mother stood with TJ.

"Abby!" Tabitha cried on a choked sob, reaching out her arms to take the child from Jake as he lowered her down from the saddle. "Oh, baby!" Wrapping her in her arms, holding her tight, they both wept tears of joy and relief.

TJ stepped toward Jake. His mouth set in a determined line as he demanded to know, "Where are they?"

Jake grinned down at his wife's uncle. "If you're meanin' the grandparents, they're being led around on an hour lon' trail. Once they're back, I expect the Sheriff will have arrived as I had someone call the authorities the moment we saw that camper of theirs pull into the yard."

"They better hope they're safe behind bars when I see them," TJ said, then turned to watch the reunion between Tabitha and her daughter. His own eyes filled with tears as he looked at the little girl, and his feet carried him forward to kneel on the blacktop to hug the child and see for himself she was all right.

"Abby," he whispered, touching her back.

"TJ!" the child cried, leaving her mother's arms long enough to wrap her small arms around his neck.

He had no words to give as he held both the child and mother close to him.

"So," Hunter said, looking up at his sister, "were you expecting me to walk to the ranch?" He glanced around the area, looking for a vehicle that was not there.

"You're such an ass," Donna told him, wiping at her own tears. "We had no idea those people would show up here, and we didn't think about switching out to a vehicle when we wanted to get Abby to her mom as soon as possible."

Her brother shrugged. "Maybe you could think about it now?" He leaned on his crutches. "I truly do not want to walk all the way to the house."

"Gee, why not?"

"Now, children," Cadman told them. He stepped away from where the reunion was going on, giving the mother room to reassure herself her child was safe without four pairs of eyes watching them. "I realize

Hunter hasn't been home in a while and probably hasn't noticed the garage your folks added last year. Even though it's sitting only a few feet away, but I'm disappointed you don't remember what's in it."

Donna shrugged. "I know. But why should I mention it to him when he seems hell-bent on insulting me for what he thinks is a lack of providing transportation on my part?"

Cadman rolled his eyes, shook his head. "Brother," he sighed and walked toward the garage and slid up the door. Within moments of entering the building, he was backing a vehicle out from it.

"Hey!" Hunter called out to him, "That's my jeep!"

"Like you use it," his sister told him.

"I do when I come home," her brother claimed.

"And that's so often," Donna told him. Then a grin split her face. "But I'm glad you're here. I'll see you back at the ranch." She turned her horse toward the homestead, and the horse took off like a rocked in that direction.

Jake tipped his hat toward his brother-in-law in a welcome home salute before turning his horse and following his wife.

Hunter watched as the two road away, then made his way to his jeep. Climbing into the front passenger seat he told Cadman, "You could have told me they're storing my vehicle at the airstrip."

Cadman laughed. "Why would I do that? All you'd do would bitch about it. But let me tell you, it sure makes things easier when Kasey and I come for a visit. Having transportation handy prevents us from having to wait for someone from the homestead to drive out here to pick us up."

"Yeah, yeah. I get it." He glanced toward the place where his uncle and Tabitha remained kneeling on the ground, hugging Abby and speaking comforting words to her.

"They got lucky," he said. "Can't believe the Turners came here, of all places. But for all of their sakes, I'm glad this is over."

"Me too," Cadman agreed. "It's a miracle. That's for damn sure."

Chapter Twenty-two

After speaking with Grace and Greta to assure them Abby was all right, TJ hung up the phone in Colten's office. He'd informed them they were going to take the week off with pay. He had not told Tabitha he was going to pay their wages during that time. He didn't want her arguing with him about it.

Before speaking to the two employees at Little Paws and More, he talked to Colten to deliver the news that Abby was safe and with her mother.

His brother told him to take his time getting back to Binghamton. He and Jacqueline were enjoying his house, hot tub, and pool and considered it the honeymoon they'd never had.

TJ did not want to know what those two were doing in the bedrooms or elsewhere in his house but was glad they were appreciating their extended vacation.

With the list of phone calls completed, he made his way through his brother's large house and stepped out onto the porch, where he found Tabitha and Abby snuggled together on the porch swing.

The sky was darkening. As the sun gradually sank behind the buttes, the sky slowly faded from blue into vivid colors of reds and oranges.

"Pretty," Abby whispered. She was wrapped around her mother like a squid holding on for dear life. No doubt, it would be a while before she felt safe.

"Yes, it is beautiful," Tabatha kissed the top of her daughter's head. "I've never seen a sunset like it." She looked up when she saw TJ walk onto the porch and smiled at him. "Hi," she said. "Your brother's ranch is lovely."

"It's a pleasant vacation spot. That's for sure." TJ answered and moved to sit on the swing next to mother and daughter.

Abby untwined herself from her mother's lap and moved onto his, giving him the same attention as she had her mother. She said nothing to him but seemed content wrapped in his arms with her ear pressed against his heart.

If she could read the message it was sending out, she would understand how much she meant to him.

He'd only known them for a couple of weeks, but it felt as though they had been in his life longer than that. There was a familiarity when he was with them, as though they had always belonged in his life.

They sat there a while, watching the activity happening around them. Employees unsaddled horses from the last trail ride of the day and put away the saddles and tack. TJ had seen the activity hundreds of times, but tonight he felt as though it was all new.

"I was wondering," TJ said after a time, "if you and Abby wouldn't mind staying for a week. I'd like to take you into the town of Medora that's north of here and show you the sites there." He cleared his throat, "And maybe you wouldn't mind driving to Bismarck with me in a few days. I'd, ah," he cleared his throat again. "I'd like my parents to meet the two of you."

He felt Tabitha's eyes studying him, and he knew his cheekbones were taking on that same damn blush Colten got when he was embarrassed.

"I'd like that," she told him at last.

Abby raised her face to him, her eyes were wide as she asked, "Your mom and dad live here?"

He shook his head. "They live about two hours away. In the town I grew up in. Maybe we could go to the zoo there?"

"The world's largest bear!" Abby quoted him from when he'd told everyone about the bears, Bonnie and Clyde.

"Darn right, munchkin" he laughed, pleased she'd remembered.

She nodded her head with enthusiasm. "I want to see the big bear!"

"Then we'll go," he promised her as the door to the house opened, and Cadman stepped out from it.

"Hey, Abby," Cadman greeted the child, as he sat down in one of the single patio chairs across from where TJ and Tabitha sat. "How are you doing?"

"Okay," she said, but kept her place on TJ's lap. "I'm glad you took grandma and grandpa Turner away. I never want to see them again!" Now she climbed back onto Tabitha's lap.

"And you won't, Scooby-Doo," her mother promised. "Never, ever again." It broke her heart when her daughter told them her grandparents warned her she'd never see her mother again if she told anyone who she was whenever they stopped somewhere.

Owen had been a kind and gentle man. How that had happened when his parents turned out to be lunatics, no one would probably ever know.

"They'll be locked up for a very long time, Abby girl," Cadman promised the child.

"And throw away the key!" Abby declared.

Cadman blinked at the child's wit, then threw his head back and laughed. "I can probably make that happen," he claimed.

"We have Donna and Jake to thank for smoothly separating them from her," Cadman continued, "And for Jake having an employee call the Sheriff the moment they were seen. It gave Sheriff Lareau enough time to get here before the hands brought back their reluctant guests." He laughed. "I doubt those two will fail to remember their unexpected adventure into the Badlands."

Cadman and his group arrived at the ranch house from the airstrip in time to witness the Turners being brought back and delivered to the law. It was a sight no one would forget soon.

Greg and Peggy both were screaming and hollering as they were returned to the ranch.

They threatened to ensure those employees would be fired and never work again.

They threatened retaliation.

They threatened to sue

And then they saw the Sheriff.

They shut their mouths right after that.

"Anyway," Cadman told them, "I would like to leave in the morning. I'm kind of missing my wife." He smiled. "I could detour back to Binghamton and drop the three of you off before continuing on to D.C."

Tabatha leaned into TJ, and he put his arm around her. "Actually, Abby and I are going to stay for a bit longer. I'm not at all ready to open my clinic right now. I just want time with my daughter."

"I can understand that," Cadman said, standing up. "Enjoy the rest of the sunset. It's the best thing about this place."

"It's lovely here," Tabitha said.

"Yeah, but it's got horses all over the place. Filthy things."

Tabitha stared after him well after he'd gone into the house. "How can he not like horses?"

TJ shrugged. "For as long as I've known him, he's never liked them."

The front door opened once again, and this time Donna stepped out. "I've got the guest house in the back ready for you, Uncle TJ. Whenever the three of you want to call it a night. You know the way."

"Thanks," TJ told her, and she went back into the main house.

It was another half hour before Abby nodded off, lulled to sleep by the safety of her mother's arms holding her. The peacefulness around her, and the sounds of night insects were relaxing and soothing to her ears.

TJ stood up, took Abby into his arms, and led Tabitha around the house and across the path leading to the one-bedroom guest house. It was a dwelling that had housed many famous people over the years; people who'd wanted privacy when they visited. Once a year during the week of the fourth of July, it was where Mason's parents stayed.

Entering the structure that had a living room, small kitchen, and full-size functioning bathroom with a walk-in shower, TJ moved into the bedroom and gently lay Abby on the king-sized bed. When he stood up, he noted their luggage was setting in one corner of the room.

"I'll take my suitcase out so as not to disturb you," he told her. "The couch is a pullout. I can sleep on it tonight."

Tabitha shook her head. "I think it would disappoint Abby if her hero wasn't here in the morning," Tabitha said.

"I'm not sure if the word hero applies," he said, feeling almost uncomfortable with the label. He'd always associated the word with surgeons, firefighters, police and military, and especially his nephew Hunter and Cadman Benson.

Abby lay sprawled on the bed, eyes closed, and appeared sound asleep. "You're my hero, Thaddeus Fisher, and I can guarantee you're Abby's too. You knew where to find her."

He laughed. "That was dumb luck because of a dream."

"The goddess reminded you in your sleep of what Abby told you, and you were brave enough to voice it even when you had your doubts. Accept it. You're our hero, and we would like to have you stay with us tonight."

Regardless of knowing his cheeks probably had that frickin' red hue, he reached out and pulled her to him. Bending his head, he touched his lips to hers when she offered hers up to him. And when he would have moved back, she placed her arms around his neck and anchored him in place.

A giggle came from the direction of the bed.

TJ pulled his face away from Tabitha and eyed the child watching them from the bed. "You should be sleeping, young lady."

Abby shook her head. "Not until you and mommy are sleeping, too," she told him.

The adults climbed onto the bed and snuggled Abby between them as though making a sandwich.

"I love you, mommy," Abby said, then added, "I love you, TJ."

"We love you too," her mother said, gazing into TJ's eyes and wondered what she had done to have the goddess bring this man into her life.

It also frightened her to know the money he had. He'd explained during the flight how he'd earned his finances over the years. Through stocks and growing a successful business in New York City. And he'd told her about his onetime friend Rick and his ex-fiancé who Tabitha could not feel the least bit sorry for. She could not understand how any woman would risk losing this man over an affair and not because of his wealth. His very heart was an open book, and Tabitha knew without a doubt that when he loved, it would be completely.

She could understand why he hadn't been looking for any commitment to another woman. A broken heart often pushed people away for fear of being wounded again.

Not that TJ had made a commitment to her, and she would not demand one from him. Their relationship was still in the early stages, and they needed time to understand they could trust one another.

And she vowed that if their relationship went beyond what they had now, moving to permanent, she would demand to sign a prenuptial agreement between them.

She loved him for the person he was.

Her body jerked upon the realization that she was very much in love with TJ Fisher.

"Are you all right, babe?" TJ asked as his eyes met hers over the top of Abby's head.

For just a moment, she stared at him, imprinting his handsome face upon her memory. His dark-colored eyes were chocolate pools she would gladly drown in.

"Yes," she told him, reaching for his hand over the top of Abby. "I have my daughter back, and a handsome man helping me keep her safe. I couldn't ask for anything more than that."

After breakfast the next morning, TJ used Hunter's jeep to drive Tabitha and Abby into the historic town of Medora.

Hunter, surprisingly, didn't grumble about his uncle using his vehicle.

As the jeep with its three occupants approached the small town, TJ explained how the town had come to be founded.

"A Frenchman named Antoine Amédée Marie Vincent Manca de Vallambrosa, who you'll hear people refer to more often than not by the title, the Marquis de Morès, arrived by train to the area in 1883. He claimed these six square miles, and founded this town and named it after his wife, Medora."

TJ slowed down as they entered the settlement. "My grandfather was seventeen years old back then and got hired on by de Morès. Grandpa passed away when I was fourteen at the ripe old age of 98, so I grew up listening to his tails about Antonine and President Teddy Roosevelt. Part of the land Colten owns was passed onto him by our grandfather in his will, which de Morès had given him as a bonus for work he'd done for him."

"That's amazing," Tabitha said as she glanced around the area, feeling as though she were stepping back in time with the rustic buildings that housed businesses.

TJ parked the jeep on a side street in front of the de Mores Memorial Park in downtown Medora where a bronze statue of de Mores, donated by the man's sons in 1926, stood on the .25-acre lot.

"Actually," TJ said, opened the driver's side door, stepped out, and lifted Abby from the back seat. "The amazing part is the fact Colten's wife is a descendant from the same family line as Medora. And Mason's family tree puts him as de Morès 5th or 6th great-nephew."

Tabitha stared at him, then shook her head. "The goddess has a way of bringing families back together." She got out of the jeep, walked around to take Abby's hand in hers. The fact she had her daughter back was proof of that.

"Come on, we'll walk around for a while, then take a tour of the Chateau de Mores," TJ motioned with his hand toward the historic home resting on a hill overlooking the town. "It might look like a house to you, but de Mores called it a hunting lodge."

"They lived there?"

"Well, the North Dakota winters surprised them, so they only occupied it seasonally from 1883 to 1886. But I'll let you learn the rest when we take the tour."

They spent a few hours browsing the various gift shops before driving to the Chateau to take the walking tour so Tabitha and Abby could learn its history. After that, they went to the South Unit Visitor Center of the Theodore Roosevelt National Park, which was only a short distance from the Chateau. They toured the museum, then Roosevelt's Maltese Cross Cabin, before going on the 36-mile scenic drive, which took an hour and a half to make around the stunning picturesque loop drive.

In the evening, they attended the musical production in the Burning Hills Amphitheatre. The show had a mix of singing and dancing along with skits and a patriotic salute to the military.

Abby's highlight of the evening was getting to be on stage for the kids' segment of the show, along with a dozen others, to interact with the cast members as they put on a children's song.

TJ also made it a point to say hello to Colten's oldest son, Clinton. TJ considered Clinton more of a brother than a nephew as they'd lived in the same house together until Clinton turned eight, and Colten married Jacqueline.

Clinton was at the window of one of the concessions stands selling popcorn and refreshments to the waiting crowd that stood in line during intermission. TJ waited patiently for his turn to order and watched as Clinton interacted with the guests and efficiently handled the financial transactions.

He'd come a long way since being diagnosed with autism, and TJ couldn't have been prouder of him.

They'd once spent a month together. It had been right after his breakup with Heather. Clinton had talked him into taking him on a tour of the country searching for the perfect horse he wanted to buy.

Stepping up to the window, TJ said, "Hi, Clinton."

Clinton shrieked in his excitement at seeing his uncle, causing his fellow employees, and the surrounding crowd, to make them the center of their attention. And when Clinton tried to climb through the window to hug TJ, one of the other employees gently reminded him to use the door.

He did. And came through it at lightning speed and practically tackled his uncle.

Thankfully, TJ had prepared himself. He'd had this greeting before.

"Hey, buddy," TJ said on a laugh as his nephew hugged him.

"I miss you!" Clinton announced in the high-pitched voice of a child he'd learned to control over time, but when stimulated with excitement, it poked its head out.

"I miss you too, buddy." TJ turned toward Tabitha and Abby, who'd accompanied him to the concessions and were now looking on with twin wide-eyed amber eyes.

"I want to introduce you to someone," TJ said in a soothing tone, hoping it would calm Clinton.

"Oh, boy! I would like that!"

"This is Tabitha, my-" he refused to put her in the friend category. She meant so much more to him than that, and although they hadn't talked about what their relationship was, exactly, he claimed her as his. "My girlfriend and this little one is her daughter, Abby."

Clinton jetted out his arm towards Tabitha, grabbing her hand for a firm shake. "Hi!" he said, "I like you!"

Tabitha laughed.

Then Clinton put his hand out to Abby and slowly shook her hand. "Hi, Abby. I'm Clinton. I like you too."

Abby smiled up at him. "You're silly," she told him.

"I'm going to Bismarck tomorrow to see my parents," TJ informed Clinton. "And I'll be back tomorrow night. If you have a day off, maybe you'll be able to come home to the ranch so we can visit. And Hunter's there."

The smile on Clinton's face radiated his joy upon hearing that news.

Intermission was ending, and TJ convinced Clinton to go back to work with a promise to see him again before he left North Dakota.

After TJ and Tabitha made it back to their seats, Abby crawled onto TJ's lap and rested her cheek on his chest.

"Are you getting tired, munchkin?"

She nodded.

"It's been a long day," he told her. "You can sit on my lap for the rest of the show."

"Okay," she said sleepily.

TJ felt someone poke him on the shoulder, and he twisted around to see the person.

The older woman sitting behind him said, "Your daughter is the cutest thing! She reminds me of one of those Precious Moments figurines."

"Thanks," he said, liking the idea of people thinking Abby was his daughter. He did not bother to correct the woman's assumption, even though he felt Tabitha's eyes on him.

To be fair. She didn't contradict the lady either.

He felt Tabitha lean into him, resting her head against his shoulder and felt as though he'd received a gift in the form of these two people.

He would introduce them to his parents tomorrow.

It was in that moment when TJ realized he didn't want Tabitha listed in the girlfriend category. In only a short time of knowing them he'd unexpectedly fallen in love.

Knowing his parents weren't getting any younger, TJ made up his mind then in there what he wanted to do when he introduced Tabitha and Abby to them. And he knew it would make his folks happy to know he'd at last found someone he wanted to spend the rest of his life with.

Chapter Twenty-three

"What a lovely house," Tabitha commented a few days later when she and TJ, along with Abby, arrived in Bismarck and drove to Donald and Barbra Fisher's home on the north side of town. "Is this the house you grew up in?"

TJ nodded. "My parents have no interest in moving. And because they're still fairly spry, for people in their eighties, we, their kids, don't see any reason to ask them to move into a nursing home. My sister Margret checks in on them once a week, and we hired a housekeeper who comes in every day to make them meals. But mostly, they're self-sufficient."

He stepped out from the jeep once he parked it in the driveway and, in what was fast becoming a habit, lifted Abby out from the back seat of the vehicle. For a moment, he stood there, looking south onto the city as he remembered that when he'd been growing up, this house was the only one this far north. But the capital city continued to grow, and a lot more structures were surrounding the Fisher's property now.

Taking Tabitha's hand in his, along with Abby's, they walked together up the sidewalk leading to the split-level house and rang the doorbell.

His mother opened it in a short amount of time, then just stood there looking at him as though she couldn't believe her eyes.

"Oh, my," she said. "Apparently, I need new glasses, young man. You look just like my son, Thaddeus."

"Ha, ha," he told her, kissing her on the cheek and knowing full well she was toying with him. "Your eye-sight's just fine."

Barbra stepped forward and wrapped him in her arms. "I don't know what I did to deserve an unexpected visit from you, but I'm happy to see you." When she moved back, she noticed Tabitha and the little girl standing beside him. "And who do we have here? Did you get yourself married, have a child, and not bother to tell us?"

"Why would you think I wouldn't tell you something like that?"

His mother smiled, and the twinkle in her eyes told him she was still teasing him.

"Well, don't just stand there, come in!" she stepped back and hollered over her shoulder, "Donald! You'll never guess who's come to see us!"

TJ's father appeared at the railing. Looking down at their guests, he said, "Holy smokes, Barbra. He looks just like Thaddeus." And Donald winked down at his son. He'd known he was coming but had kept silent about it. Sometimes he liked to surprise his wife and having one of their children, who lived out of town, drop by unexpectedly always gave her a thrill.

Tabitha burst out laughing, instantly liking the older couple.

Once up the stairs and standing in the living room area, Donald noticed Abby and told her, "Welcome to my home, young lady. If you would like toys to play with, there's an entire room full of them just down that hall, or you're more than welcome to sit with us and listen to boring conversation."

"I like boring conversation," Abby told him.

Donald blinked, then chuckled. "Apparently, you spend a lot of time around adults."

"She does," Tabitha informed him.

"Well, that's good. It develops their vocabulary." He motioned to the sofa. "Have a seat."

TJ sat down with Tabitha next to him while Abby wandered around the room, looking at the assortment of photos set on various shelves and hanging on the walls.

"Dad used to be one of the best surgeons in North Dakota," TJ told Tabitha proudly.

"Ticks me off that age caught up to me," Donald claimed. "I miss the excitement of the hospital."

"So," Barbra said, "Are you two friends? Dating?" she paused and then asked hopefully, "Engaged?"

Tabitha looked at TJ. She wondered how he was going to define their relationship to his parents.

"I haven't asked her yet," was TJ's response as he kept his eyes on his father.

Donald stood up, saying, "Hey, son. I need help with something."

"For heaven's sake, Donald, we have company."

"I'm aware of that, dear." He looked to TJ and said, "Son, could you give me a moment? Just down the hall."

"Of course," TJ stood and followed his father, suspecting his dad was going to give him the items he'd asked him for last night during a private phone call.

Barbra shook her head. "I apologize, dear. I do not understand what my husband is thinking."

"It's all right," Tabitha told the woman, but her heart drummed. She'd gone numb when TJ had said, I haven't asked her yet, and tried not to assume anything.

The men returned, and although Donald sat back down, looking as though he knew a secret, TJ remained standing.

Gazing at Tabitha, TJ cleared his throat and told her, "I don't know what a handfasting is, but if it means marriage, would you have one with me?"

Tabitha stared up at him, her eyes wider than they'd ever been before. "What?-" Dear goddess, she needed clarification.

TJ obliged her by getting on one knee in front of her and lifting his right hand up. She could clearly see he held an elegant 18K white gold ring with delicately engraved leaves circling the band between his thumb and index finger. "Will you marry me, Tabitha June?"

His mother gasped, but he ignored it.

Abby, having stopped looking at the photos when she'd heard the word handfasting, squealed with delight. She rushed forward, threw her arms around TJ's neck, and exclaimed, "I knew you were going to be my daddy!"

He hugged her to him. "Your mom hasn't said it was okay yet, munchkin."

She stepped back from him as her eyes slid to her mother, waiting for the answer.

Barbra was getting to her feet as tears of joy slid down her face. "Oh! I need to get my camera!" she exclaimed.

Donald rolled his eyes and shook his head. His wife took more photos than the photographer for the Bismarck Tribune.

"Tabitha," TJ prompted when she continued to sit on the couch, gaping at him. "Are you going to say yes, or no?"

She had been caught off guard by his unexpected proposal. For a moment her eyes shifted between him and the glittering ring in his hand.

"I…" she began and looked into his eyes. Those dark depths that could draw her in and in that moment, she knew if she said yes it would be the right decision. They had not known each other long but she knew deep down he was her soulmate and with him there would be happiness and fulfillment she'd never had with Owen.

She slid off the couch and joined him where he knelt on the floor as a smile spread across her lips and she laughed. Wrapping her arms around his neck she shouted out with joy, "It's a yes, Thaddeus Jim!"

This, Tabitha knew, would be the start of something truly special.

Barbra shook her head, shocked. "Is that what he told you his middle name was?" she asked, annoyed. She'd given him that name, and as far as she was concerned, it was a darn fine one.

"Mom!" TJ exclaimed, trying to stop her from saying it. "Shush. It's a game-"

"Thaddeus Julius, did you just shush me?!"

TJ sighed, put his forehead against Tabitha's and said, "Damn it."

Tabitha kissed him, then smiled against his mouth. "I would have found out, eventually."

"I would have preferred never."

"It isn't horrible."

"I detest it so much I've often considered having it legally changed."

"I promise never to say it," she swore to him on a whisper as she reached for his hand. Julius. She doubted she would have ever guessed it. "Are you going to put that ring on my finger? -or did you change your mind?"

"I won't change my mind," he told her, slipping the ring onto the ring finger of her left hand. "This was my grandmother's. It was willed to me, but I never gave it to anyone because it didn't seem good enough, but I think it's exactly the type of ring you'd want."

With tears in her eyes, Tabitha extended her hand as she looked at the simplicity of it. "It's perfect," she told him in a voice full of emotion, before wrapping her arms around him once more. "I love it, and you."

"I have something else," he said, turning his head to look at Abby. "Come here, munchkin."

There was no hesitation on Abby's part. She moved straight back into his arms and hugged him tightly.

From his pocket he produced the tiny 14k white gold ring his father picked up for him from one of the local jewelers that morning. The design was simple, a band of tiny beads that was perfect for an active little girl as it would not wear out quickly.

"I want to adopt you, and make you mine," he told her, reaching for her left hand, he asked, "Would that be okay?"

Too emotional to say anything, her little head bobbed up and down.

"This ring," TJ told her, "Is my promise to be the best dad you'd ever ask for."

There wasn't a dry eye in the room as he slipped the ring onto her finger.

"Oh, Donald, where is my camera!" Barbra cried once again, continuing to search for it.

"It's where you always put it," her husband told her. "Second shelf down on the bookcase."

"I can't believe this is real," Tabatha said. "I'm so in love with you. I could shout it to the world!"

"Hold that thought," he said, deciding he wanted a clean slate. He'd told her his financial status, but he had not told her everything. "If you still want to build that dog sanctuary-"

"Of course, I do! But I told you I have to find some other land. And I'll do it through donations and fund-raisers, TJ Fisher. I don't want you spending that kind of money on me. You know how I feel about extravagance."

He grinned. "Yes, ma'am. We'll live on the streets, so we won't squander a dime."

"Don't be ridiculous. Abby and I want to move into that beautiful house of yours, and you know what I meant. I'm no gold digger."

"We'll work the finances out later, but right now, I'm telling you; I'm donating the land to your cause."

"I don't want you buying property just because you can."

And he laughed. "Babe, I already own the land. I bought it under my company's name, thinking maybe I'd build a strip mall there one day, but I'm donating it to you as a wedding present."

"Your company's name?"

He nodded. "Badland Builders."

She pulled back from him on a gasp. "You! You're the one who stole my land?!"

"I bought it fair and square."

"I don't believe this. You've known all this time, and you didn't tell me?"

"I'm telling you now, aren't I?"

"Okay you two smile for the camera!" Barbra said.

"What?" Tabitha looked in the woman's direction and had a flash go off in her face.

TJ threw his head back and laughed. "Welcome to the family, babe. You'll have to get used to mom taking pictures at the weirdest times."

"And make sure you lock the bathroom door, or she'll probably take a picture of you on the crapper," Donald warned.

Barbra reached out and swatted her husband's arm. "You old coot! I'd never do something like that!"

Donald looked at his son and grinned. They both knew that had she thought about it while the children were growing up, she probably would have. They had enough pictures of their children taking baths to fill up half a scrapbook.

TJ stood up, pulling Tabitha right along with him. "We'll get it all settled later as we plan our life together. Do you have a date in mind for the -handfasting?"

"In a year-and-a-day from now," she told him.

"What?"

"Tradition. It's proper to handfast a year-and-a-day from the time of our decision to join."

"You're telling me I have to wait until next year, a year from today-"

"Plus one," she reminded him. "It's a time for learning about one another. And to decide, after a year, if we want to stay together."

"Are you trying to back out?" he questioned, although he appreciated the concept.

She laughed. "Not a chance, but I'm sure you'll want to learn about my major and minor sabbats and other traditions my parents and I celebrate. And I'll want to learn what holidays you like to honor so we can agree to what is important to us as a family."

"Samhain!" Abby's head bobbed. "It's my favorite day!"

"Of course it is," Tabitha agreed.

"That would be?" TJ asked, his head swimming.

"You would know it as Halloween," Tabitha explained. "Samhain only means summer's end and marks the be-ginning of winter."

"Apparently, I have a lot to learn."

She smiled at him. "I'll enjoy teaching you, and so will my mother." She slapped her forehead. "I need to call my mom and let her know we have a handfasting to prepare for! Thank the goddess she's a High Priestess and can perform the ceremony."

"High Priestess," TJ repeated, trying to grasp what that meant.

Tabitha nodded.

"A High Priestess to what, dear?" Barbra asked.

Now was the time to find out if these people would accept her beliefs. "My coven. I'm Wiccan. Or a witch. Whichever term you're most comfortable with using."

Barbra clapped her hands together. "Oh, my. I've always wanted to learn about that religion!"

Tabitha's heart soared. TJ hadn't lied when he'd told her his family did not hold prejudices against people's diversity of faith.

"Can we see the world's largest bear now, daddy?" Abby asked.

With heart swelling with love, TJ reached down and picked her up. "I think that's a great idea, munchkin."

There would be plenty of time to plan their future and learn all about handfasting, Wiccan Holy Days and whatever else there was to know about the woman he'd chosen to wed.

Chapter Twenty-four

1987
A year-and-a-day later
The F&L Ranch south of Medora

Jacqueline Fisher gazed at Tabitha's reflection in the full body mirror and told her, "Your dress is lovely. It almost reminds me of something medieval." She met the other woman's eyes. "I hope that wasn't insulting?"

Tabitha laughed. "Not at all. I always dreamed of being married in something like this as I enjoy Renaissance clothing."

The elegant dress, handmade by Tabitha's mother, was of ivory crushed velvet, edged with delicate silver trim with flowing sleeves that were shorter at the front, ending at her wrist, and swooped down in the back. The length of the dress brushed the ground.

"I'm eager to see how TJ looks in his attire," Jacqueline confessed, reaching for the slim package resting on the dresser. "And thank you for choosing to have your wedding-" she stopped, shook her head. "Handfasting, here. At the ranch."

"When I was trying to decide upon the perfect place, I couldn't get this land out of my mind. It calls to me, you know? That might be silly, but in some places among these buttes, it feels mystical," Tabitha looked back at her reflection, smoothed her hands down the sides of the dress.

"I know exactly what you mean. The first time I saw them, they called to me too."

Jacqueline stepped toward her. "Are you ready for me to open this? Your gift from TJ?"

Tabitha nodded, then watched Jacqueline take off the wrapper of the long jewelry case. When she opened it, Tabitha's eyes filled with tears when she saw the headpiece the love of her life had chosen for her and knew he'd had it custom made.

She would not think about how much he'd spent on it but would accept it for its intent.

To honor her.

The Celtic style headpiece was made from 14k white gold. At its center was a silver pentacle, adorned with an amethyst stone.

"Here, sit down so I can place it around your forehead," Jacqueline told her.

Tabitha watched in the mirror as Jacqueline set the piece in place and felt as though she'd been crowned a queen.

"I think that brother-in-law of mine knows how to make you happy."

Tabitha had no words but agreed wholeheartedly.

And even though the Fourth Circuit Court of Appeals ruled in favor of Dettmer v. Landon last year, that Wicca was a religion and should be protected by the First Amendment, TJ hadn't wanted to take the chance that someone would not recognize their union as lawful. He'd brought her to the justice of the peace last week, but they had told no one because it had only been a formality. This would be the day they would celebrate as their joining for the rest of their lives.

Tabitha stood up. "I have a gift for you and Colten," she told Jacqueline. "It's a thank you for hosting this day for us."

Walking to the dresser located across the room, she slid open the drawer she'd placed the item in earlier in the day. Taking the gift out, she turned around and handed it to TJ's sister-in-law.

It was Jacqueline's turn to have tears spring into her eyes. "Grant's drawing," she whispered, touching the glass of the framed photo. "I was under the impression it sold during your fundraiser last month."

Tabitha smiled. "We held it back, knowing it would mean more to you than some random person who would have bought it."

Stepping forward, Jacqueline wrapped her soon to be sister-in-law in her arms. "Thank you. I'll cherish it forever."

Abby came into the room dressed as a green garden fairy complete with wings. Her dress was embellished with leaves and flowers in shades of green tulle.

She stopped in her tracks when she saw her mother, and her mouth formed an O. "Mommy is pretty!" she exclaimed.

"Thank you, but so are you my baby girl."

Abby rolled her eyes. Why couldn't adults remember the difference between a baby and a four-year-old?

"Grandma Stevens told me to tell you it's time. The circle is made."

"I'm just waiting for TJ," Tabitha said. The two of them would walk to the altar together.

The words no sooner left her mouth when there was a knock at the door. When Jacqueline opened it, she had to admit TJ looked very fine in his attire. "Come on, Abby. Let's join the circle and give your mom and dad a moment to themselves." She reached out, clasped the child's hand, and ushered her out from the room.

Tabitha stared at TJ, scarcely believing how handsome he was. He was dressed in black jeans and a black silk shirt. Black boots covered his feet, and over the shirt, he wore a long red velvet coat that had black embroidery running throughout it.

"I want to devour you," he said as his eyes raked over her.

She smiled.

He held out his hand for her, and when she took it, he pulled her to him. Wrapping her in his arms, he said, "But since I don't want to chance your mother putting a hex on me, I'll refrain from ripping that dress off of you until we're given permission."

Tabitha laughed. "She wouldn't do that. She likes you."

"Let's keep it that way," he told her as he escorted her from the room.

Together, they walked around the side of the Fisher's house and up the path leading to the top of the hill behind the home where the Badlands' scenic view stretched out before them. Their guests stood in a circle with Tabitha's mother standing behind an alter contained within the center.

Here there would be no chairs for people to take sides, making everyone equal in their support of the couple about to be united.

Tabitha glanced around the sizeable number of people gathered, pleased to have each of them there to share this day with her. Along with their families, Grace and Gretta stood side by side with Mason Lafayette and his parents and young sister. TJ's brothers and sisters and their families could start a town all by themselves, they were so numerous. But they too stood along with everyone else.

"Who seeks to enter this ceremony?" Angela Stevens, dressed in her own medieval gown, asked.

"We do," Tabitha and TJ said together.

Angela inclined her head. "Then step forward for the blessing of the hands."

The couple moved forward, and the ceremony began.

When it came time for the binding of hands, Angela held out her hand to Abby, who promptly handed her the Handfasting ribbons that had beads, seashells, and other items attached to the end of the cords.

"The Handfasting," Angela explained, holding the different colors of ribbons up for everyone to see, "Is an ancient Celtic ritual in which we tie together the hands to symbolize the binding of two lives." She looked at the guest. "Will each of you who have been asked by Tabitha and TJ to participate in the ceremony, please step forward and receive your ribbon."

Colten stepped forward, as did his father and mother.

Grace and Greta each retrieve ribbons, as did Mason and Hunter.

"Join hands," Angela told the couple, and when they did, she said to the participants, "Begin."

Donald Fisher said to his son, "Will you be Tabitha's faithful partner for life?"

"I will," TJ answered.

Donald turned to Tabitha and asked, "Will you be Thaddeus's faithful partner for life?"

"I will," Tabitha said.

After the couple answered, Donald draped the first long ribbon over the couple's joined hands.

Barbra stepped forward. The tears in her eyes were for her overflowing joy that her youngest son had finally found someone to share his life with and whom Barbra already loved like a daughter.

Clearing her throat Barbra asked the question she'd been given to speak. "Will you both stand by one another in sickness and in health, and in plenty and in want?"

The couple smiled at each other and answered in unison, "We will."

Barbra added her ribbon to the first.

Each participant had been given a question to ask of the couple and once all were said, and TJ and Tabitha responded, they added their ribbon to the pile until all seven ribbons were placed. Once the ritual was completed Angela tied the ribbons together around the couple's hands effectively binding them together.

Angela said, "Your vows have formed this binding. It is up to you to ensure your hands remain bound, or break this union."

She then removed the bindings, placed them on the altar, and raised her hands as she said, "We ask the goddess for her blessing upon you. May your journey ahead be filled with happiness and beauty."

Lowering her hands, she told the couple, "I pronounce you lawfully and spiritually wed. May your souls continue to find each other through time and space."

Now she looked at TJ and said, "Kiss her already! And let's celebrate this union!"

And as their guests erupted into cheers, TJ pulled his wife to him and told her, "You know, I knew there was something magical about you the moment we met."

He lowered his lips to hers and sealed the declaration with a kiss hot enough to curl her toes.

Epilogue

Binghamton, NY
A few months later

On a Wednesday night, not long after TJ and Tabitha's handfasting, they joined Quinn, Ray, and their wives, for the weekly get together at Mindy's Over Yonder. Now that TJ's niece Melissa lived with them, having enrolled at Binghamton University to begin their Bachelor of Science degree program in Computer Science, finding a babysitter for Abby wasn't a problem. Melissa was more than willing to babysit. In exchange for helping Tabitha and TJ out with Abby, she didn't have to pay rent.

Melissa almost decided to stay at the dorms when she'd first applied at the college. But living with her favorite uncle and his wife the first year would help make the transition from having lived in the middle of nowhere all of her life to a bigger city a lot easier.

Perhaps next year, once she made friends at the college, she might consider moving into an apartment off-campus and finding a roommate while getting her bearings. For now, she was happy staying with her family.

Besides, she liked Abby. So, on Wednesday nights, Melissa would wave goodbye to TJ and Tabitha, and she and Abby would occupy themselves with reading a book, playing board games, or making homemade playdough. Or whatever else they felt like doing at the time.

And it gave Tabitha and TJ more freedom to have a night out together with friends, or a date night to be alone with each other.

"Hey, you two," Penny, Quinn's wife, waved to the newlyweds as they approached the table near the dance floor. "Glad you made it."

TJ pulled out a chair for Tabitha, then sat down once his wife was seated. "We stopped by the nursing home to visit Doris."

"Oh yeah," Quinn said. "The lady you purchased that gold mine of yours from."

TJ threw his head back and laughed. "I remember you singing a different tune when I first got it."

"Well, it sure as hell looked like a lost cause," Quinn grumbled.

Tabitha raised her hand. "I'm just as guilty as you are, Quinn. I've since learned my lesson." She reached her hand out, patted TJ's leg, then placed her hand on her husband's back to gently massage the Bindrune symbol resting there under his t-shirt. "I'll never doubt this man again."

"I had to pull some overnighters to make up the lost time, and hire a guy to help me, but I made a tidy profit."

"How much did you sell it for?" Ray asked as he tipped his beer up to his lips.

"I made five times on my investment." TJ grinned.

Ray nearly choked. "On that old dump?!"

"I told you it would be golden once I finished giving it a facelift. That house is part of the hot market right now."

"When will I learn to listen to you?" Ray questioned himself, disgusted.

"Anyway," Penny said, stirring the conversation in a different direction. "How's your clinic doing, Tabitha?"

"Business is booming," she answered. "I'm considering hiring another assistant, and perhaps another veterinarian who can help expand the procedures offered. Ever since my fundraiser for the dog sanctuary, I've gained a lot more clients."

"Probably because you now have photos of that Mason Lafayette holding some animals hanging up on the walls." Ray speculated, still peeved he didn't have the skills TJ did for making money.

Tabitha didn't care what the reason was. She was just happy to have a successful practice.

"So, who won the Date with Mason event you put on?" Penny asked.

"Doris," Tabitha answered without batting an eye.

"Doris?" Penny stared. "Doris?! That old lady won the raffle?"

Tabitha nodded.

"I don't believe it!"

"Where'd the porn star take her for their date?" Quinn wanted to know.

"He's not a porn star!" his wife exclaimed. "For heaven's sake, Quinn. He's a model."

"Who poses nude," Quinn tried to claim.

"Well, if that's true, I'd sure like to know where I can buy those photos. I wouldn't mind having a look at his-" Penny's husband scowled. "Navel," she amended.

"Could we not talk about Mason?" TJ wondered.

Linda reached into her purse, pulled out a book, and set it on the table. "Well, as long as he's on these covers, those books are flying off the shelves. Just look at him!" she gushed.

The image of Mason had him entwined with a female model in such a way it appeared as though he were about to pull the woman's dress off.

"I'm out," TJ said, pushing back his chair. Hadn't he gone through this before? "Someone order me a burger when our waitress arrives. I'll just be over by the jukebox looking for a song for my beautiful wife and me to dance to."

Penny and Linda watched TJ walking away from the table before looking at each other and laughing. "Now that we know Mason is his nephew, it will make teasing him so much fun."

"You two are bad," Tabitha chuckled with a shake of her head.

Linda put the book back into her purse. "So, to Quinn's question. Where did Mason and Doris go for their date?"

"He took her to the Italian restaurant on Chenango Street," Tabitha answered the question.

"Little Venice?"

Tabitha nodded. "That's the one."

"That place has been around since 1946, and still one of the best Italian Restaurants I've been too." Penny commented.

"Doris had a really great time," Tabitha continued. "Having a date with a hot guy and being the envy of every woman in the place gave her a great chuckle."

"I bet," Penny agreed.

Changing the subject Linda asked, "Tabitha, would you mind me asking about your ex-in-laws? What happened to them?"

"The judge sentenced them to twenty years, with no chance at parole." Tabitha suspected Cadman Benson had had a hand in that aspect of the verdict, and she was grateful to him for it. Thankfully, Abby did not seem to have any lasting nightmares from the trauma they'd put her through. She'd begun sleeping in her own bed within a week of returning from North Dakota, and she never mentioned them. She was all too happy to now have a dad who loved her and enjoyed taking her with him to run errands. And TJ was currently helping her build a birdhouse they planned to put on the side of the house where the living room was.

"And she loves telling people that her last name is Fisher now and does not care if they are strangers or not," Tabitha laughed, knowing her daughter reminded her of herself at that age. Never shy to talk to people.

"Excuse me," Tabitha told the group after a moment. "I need to use the lady's room." She pushed out her chair and began weaving around tables to reach the restrooms.

"I don't think I've ever seen TJ this happy," Penny commented, watching Tabitha as she walked away.

"I'm happy for them," Linda said. "It was a beautiful ceremony. I'm glad TJ invited us."

"Makes me wish I would have had a handfasting instead of a traditional wedding," Penny claimed.

"You wouldn't have gotten me into one of those costumes," Ray vowed.

His wife smiled at him, knowing full well he would have done it for her.

At the jukebox, TJ found a tune he associated with his new life, put in the correct amount of change into the slot and pushed the button for his choice so it would play once the current song was through.

Turning from the machine, intending to escort his wife onto the dance floor, he blinked when he noted she was no longer sitting at the table with their friends.

Now where, he wondered to himself, was she?

He no sooner had the thought when he heard her voice come from the hallway leading to the bar's bathrooms.

"Son of a bitch, you again?!"

TJ almost burst out into laughter as he headed that way. There was no way this could be happening.

But it was. The moment he entered the hallway, he witnessed Kip Bachmeyer crowding Tabitha's space.

"Come on, honey," Kip was saying as he leaned into her. "Just one kiss."

"Hey!" TJ said, not breaking stride. "That's my wife."

Kip glanced his way. Recognition dawned, and he backed away. "Hey, man. I don't want no trouble."

"Too late," TJ told him and planted his fist into the man's face hard enough to knock him out.

The big man's eyes rolled up, and he fell back into a heap onto the floor.

Tabitha's eyes grew enormous. "Holy smokes! Why didn't you do that the first time he crowded my space? You could have avoided that whole fight."

"Had I known at the time what would happen, I would have. But I learned from that and was not going to take the chance on another bar fight."

"What happens when his friends discover him on the floor?" she asked as TJ led her to the dance floor as the first beats of his song selection filtered through the speakers.

"They'll assume he passed out. Drunks do that some-times." He put his hands around her waist, moved with the tune of Starship's Nothing's Gonna Stop Us Now. "I love you so much, I ache."

Placing her hands around his neck, she told him, "Same here, Thaddeus. I'm the luckiest woman in the world."

"You know what your mom would say about that. She doesn't believe in luck."

"But she believes in destiny, and you were mine."

THE END

Keep reading for a sneak peek at The Dreamer. Mason's story.

TJ's Bindrune

About the author

Janette Walker, writing under the pseudonym J.R. Zimmer, is an author and artist. Born in Bismarck, ND, she is drawn to creative pursuits, and her passion for both literature and visual arts keeps her busy. The Badlands of ND are a source of inspiration for her. Her love of history and the fascinating characters of Antoine-Amédée-Marie-Vincent Manca de Vallombrosa, the Marquis de Morès, and his wife, Medora, inspired her to write the Fisher/Lafayette Series.

The Dreamer

By J.R. Zimmer

Book Six

Fisher/Lafayette Saga

Badlanders Press

Chapter One

May 1991
North Dakota

"Damn," she said, glaring at the computer screen. She'd just had the perfect dialogue pop into her head, and it fizzled before she could type it out because of the untimely interruption of the doorbell ringing.

"Damn it." Issuing a heavy sigh, Anastasia pushed the chair away from the desk as the doorbell sounded twice more. Apparently, whoever was outside was determined and not going away.

Briefly, before rising, she contemplated murdering the person responsible for this unwanted disruption.

It had taken her over thirty days to painstakingly work out the plot for the story she was writing. And now, just as the whole thing had come together, complete with the amazing opening sentence she'd crafted, some blockhead disrupted her creative moment.

"Damn it to hell."

Usually, Anastasia looked forward to a visit; they happened so seldom. People in this small community were afraid of being caught in her tiny house should her ex-husband show up. So naturally, it thrilled her that someone gathered enough courage to stop by. She just wished the person's backbone hadn't arisen at this particular moment.

"I'm coming!" she called out as she made her way through the tiny living room of her two-bedroom house. The moment she unlocked and opened the front door, a smile quickly replaced the frown on her face. "Gale!" she exclaimed with a laugh, then teased. "Good thing it's you. Anyone else would have been dead about now."

1

Gale Martin let out a very unladylike snort as she carried her bulk through the open doorway. "Let me guess. You're daydreaming again." Stopping in the middle of the small living room, she turned to face the twenty-four-year-old. "Honestly, Stasia. When are you going to get your head out of the clouds and become a member of the real world?"

With a roll of sky-blue eyes, Anastasia closed the door and locked it. "We've had this conversation countless times," she reminded her best friend. "You know how important writing is for me." She eyed the short, plump woman suspiciously. "Are you having PMS?"

Gale's mouth dropped open upon hearing that unexpected question, regardless of the fact she should be used to Anastasia's strange humor by now. "All right," she sighed, knowing there was no point continuing the conversation regarding Anastasia's fantasizing, "you win. And no. I do not have PMS, thank you." She settled her bulk onto the nearby sofa and ignored the groaning sound it made as it fought to accommodate her size. "However, since you haven't denied it, I will assume you were writing some tale or other and forgot what day it is." Seeing the puzzled expression cross Anastasia's delicate features, she held out the thick catalog she carried into the house with her. "Shopping day. Remember? You were going to help me pick out some new clothes."

Gale loved Anastasia as though she were her own daughter. However, that did not prevent her from secretly wishing she could have the younger woman's figure and looks. Good Lord. Anastasia would be attractive in just about anything. Including a gunny sack with cow manure stuck to it, she concluded, feeling a prick of jealousy sweep through her. But then she reminded herself that Anastasia's beauty had not guaranteed her a life filled with sunshine and happiness.

It totally slipped Anastasia's mind. Crap. Shopping day. How had she forgotten she agreed to have Gale come over today to spend time together?

"I'm sorry, Gale," Anastasia apologized, feeling guilt make its way to her heart. She hadn't meant to forget her promise to the woman who was ten years older than herself. Especially when the woman's husband

had probably saved her life a little more than a year ago, and the bond between the Martins and herself was worth more than anything to her.

"I can leave," Gale prompted, knowing Anastasia's writing was a therapeutic hobby. It was something she'd always enjoyed doing. But after what Anastasia endured over a year ago, it became a relaxation and kept her focused. It allowed her to switch off her mind every now and again whenever she began thinking about her ex-husband and the monster he'd become.

"Don't be ridiculous!" Anastasia gasped. "You mean the world to me. You and Jeff should know that." She crossed her arms under her ample breasts. "It isn't as though I can't continue my writing later and," she narrowed her eyes, "I don't want you to ever think you're not welcome. Understand?"

She met the woman's eyes and caught Gale's nod. "Good," Anastasia said, then walked into the spare bedroom, converted into an office, and turned off her computer. Moments later, after stopping in the kitchen to allow her poodle back inside the house through the back door, she returned to the living room.

"Now," Anastasia said, her voice filled with confidence as she extracted the magazine from Gale's hand, "Let's see what's hot for the fall season."

Gale watched Anastasia gracefully slide into the black vinyl recliner, placed a short distance from the couch, and begin paging through the home shopping publication. Grace and beauty. Gale sighed. There should be a law against having both. "So, what are you writing this time? Something about the woes of being a hairstylist and having to work with John Q. Public? Or did you begin that novel you've been talking about writing?"

Without glancing up from the page she stopped on, Anastasia laughed. "Now, that's an idea. Maybe I should write a book about hairdresser blues."

She looked back to the magazine, slowly paging through the women's clothing section.

A brief silence followed before Anastasia looked back at Gale. Her eyes twinkled as she revealed, "I heard from Redbook." She wiggled her light brown subtle brows. "Of course," she sighed wishfully, "you wouldn't want to know what they had to say." She averted her attention back to the wish book before the smile she was holding at bay got the better of her. She knew Gale's scolding of her daydreaming did not reflect the woman's interest in her writing.

"Well, for pity's sake, Stasia. Don't keep me in suspense!"

Giggling, Anastasia met the woman's eager eyes. "I won!" she cried. No longer able to contain her delight, she moved from the chair to dance circles about the small room. "Can you believe it? After months of entering writing contests, I've won!" She doubted if anyone in the world had ever experienced the amount of joy as she had when she received the congratulation letter from the magazine. And the hundred-dollar check awarded to the first-place winner of their short story contest. "They're going to publish the story in next year's January issue!" Reclaiming her place in the recliner, her face beaming as though she were a child who just received a pony for Christmas, she continued on zealously. "See, Gale. I told you. One of these days, I'm going to make it big. One of these days, it's going to be goodbye New Salem; hello Hollywood." A content smile formed on her face as she leaned back in the chair. "Yep. One of these days, I can close that beauty salon of mine and do what I love most and, best of all, get paid for it!" Her eyes took on a dreamy, faraway look. "One day, I'll join the ranks as a best-selling romance author. Just wait and see."

"Oh, Stasia, I'm so proud of you! I can't wait to see the story in print. But honey, you know not everyone becomes a best-selling author."

Hurt replaced Anastasia's joy. "You don't think I can do it?" she asked, feeling as though someone threw cold water on her. She knew the odds of a publishing house accepting her manuscript were astronomical, but that did not mean she had to give up her dream.

Gale softened her voice. "Listen, sweetie. I don't doubt for one minute you could be a best-selling author. You have the talent. Obviously, Redbook thinks so, too. But I just can't understand why you write stories of romance. Ever since Danny-" she broke off, shaking her head sadly. "You never act as though you want anything to do with men. You don't date. All you do is come home from work and lock yourself away in there," she pointed to Anastasia's office door, "and write. And the only man I've ever heard you talk about is that guy who happens to be almost every woman's impossible fantasy-"

"You should know by now that Danny is the reason I enjoy writing romances," Anastasia snapped, cutting Gale off. "Just because my ex-husband turned into a psychopath after his discharge from the Marines doesn't mean I have anything against men and romance." She sighed. "As far as dating, you know that's complicated. No guy in their right mind from around here would risk looking my way. Court orders or not, Danny still thinks I belong to him!" She bit her lip; forced back the tears. "For the time being, I'm stuck in this two-bit town. I can't change that instantly, but I am working on it. Writing romances keeps my hopes up. Can't you see that? Through them, I can escape Danny anytime and find a hero to take me away from here."

"I'm sorry, Stasia," Gale told her gently. "I didn't mean to upset you. Sometimes my mouth gets ahead of my brain."

"My stories keep me happy," Anastasia whispered. "And it helps to express my emotions through the characters I create. At least I no longer blame myself for Danny's choices. It was not my fault his personality changed once they released him from the military hospital, and they sent him home to me."

Gale stood up, reached out, and stroked Anastasia's arm to soothe her. "You did what you could for him, honey."

Anastasia nodded, then sighed. "I just wish I'd given up on him before he put me in the hospital."

Gale remained silent, as she didn't know what to say.

"At least during the short time Danny was in jail, the judge had no problem putting his signature on the divorce papers." Anastasia continued. "That was a silver lining since Danny was refusing the divorce."

Taking a deep breath, she pushed the unpleasant memory from her mind. Although Danny didn't seem to understand why she didn't want him around, it was in her past. Thankfully, his family convinced him to move to Minot. That, at least, put over a hundred miles between them. Unless he'd gotten drunk and came to New Salem. It was never a pleasant experience for the town, or her, when that happened.

"I'm going to continue to pray for you," Gale vowed. "I know the good Lord will bless you one day because of your suffering."

Though not religious herself, Anastasia thanked her, knowing Gale's faith demanded she beseech her god on someone's behalf. Besides, she was not opposed to the universe giving her a break for a change.

Anastasia waved her hand in the air as though trying to erase the conversation about her failed two-year marriage. "That's enough of that. Time to move forward, and besides, you're here to shop." She reclaimed the magazine from where she tossed it on the floor when she told Gale about her contest win. Flipping through the colorful pages, she stopped on the section containing men's fashions.

One page caught her eye, and she stopped on it when a silly idea formed in her mind unexpectedly. Pointing to the attractive male modeling a western shirt, she giggled and asked, "Think I could order him?"

Gale paled. "What?"

"You heard me. I think I'll just order that knight of mine from this here magazine."

Maybe she was joking.

Gale hoped she wasn't being serious. However, just in case, she tried to sidetrack her by saying, "Fine. You just go ahead and do that, young lady. I just didn't know you were fickle."

"Fickle?" Anastasia's brows drew together in her confusion.

"Yes. Fickle." Gale pointed to the calendar hanging on the wall next to the recliner. "All this time, since he's the only one you ever talk about, I thought you had your sights set on him."

Anastasia's eyes followed the direction of Gale's finger to the calendar on display. Her soft blue eyes met the unique cat green depths of the man whose likeness stared back at her from the image.

His name was Mason Lafayette. Actually, Mason Richard Fernando Antoine Albert Lafayette, to be precise though she could not remember when or how she'd found that out.

Regardless of it only being a photo, she sighed dreamily. The man definitely had an aura of sex appeal about him. It certainly drew her eye the first time she saw his image on the cover of a popular magazine that showcased the rich and famous last year.

Anastasia knew she would never forget the first time she saw him. She had been browsing at one of the bookstores in the Kirkwood Mall in Bismarck when she walked past the magazine rack. His handsome face was displayed on the cover for Hollywood Now!, and those uncanny green eyes of his, framed by masculine dark brows, drew her in. When she picked up the publication for a closer look, to determine whether she imagined the color of those eyes or if a photographer's trick caused them to appear like that, she felt as though she connected with him.

She knew if she told anyone that they would say she was being ridiculous. Or was crazy. Or both.

But she purchased the magazine, read the article, and wondered if there was more to Mason Lafayette than what the reporter revealed.

Not that she became obsessed over the man. She might have joined his fan club, but she limited the amount of information she read about him. She knew that articles were written to sell the publications and did not necessarily reflect who the man was deep within his soul.

Realizing Gale was staring at her, she broke the spell she'd fallen under when she'd looked at the calendar. "Yes, well…" she cleared her throat, feeling stupid for having just lusted over Mason's facsimile. "You're the one who said I need to face reality. Considering there are at least fifteen to twenty thousand women in the United States alone swooning over him, I doubt he would notice me. Which, mind you, is less likely to happen than a kangaroo trampling through my flower garden." Mason Lafayette in New Salem, North Dakota. Right. As if that could happen. "Now, here's a guy," she tapped the page of the shopping magazine with the back of her hand, "who isn't too bad. Granted, he's not Mason," not by a long shot, "But still…" She turned the pages until she found one of the two order blanks. "I'm going to do it," she declared, beaming.

"You're not!" Gale gasped, staring at Anastasia's Cheshire cat grin and knowing, from experience, that that particular grin said she would.

"Yes, I am," Anastasia confirmed without pause. Picking up the ink pen lying on the end table, she filled out the information the order form requested. Under the place marked description, she wrote, the guy on page eighty-five, and send him quick.

Looking up, she caught sight of the look of complete disbelief on Gale's round face and broke into a fit of laughter. "Oh, come on, Gale. It will be harmless fun! What's the worst that can happen? The company will just send back my check," I'll have to be sure to add the shipping and handling charges, she thought to herself and giggled. "Maybe they will add a note telling me they're out of stock. Or he's back-ordered!" That possibility amused her more than Gale's stricken expression, and she broke into another round of laughter.

Gale found nothing amusing about this hair-brained idea, and she watched open mouthed as Anastasia moved to her office to retrieve her checkbook.

"I wonder," Anastasia pondered out loud as she returned to the living room- Gale was still sitting there, staring wide-eyed- "Do you think the

four to six-week delivery will still apply? Since this is the end of May, there's a good chance he could be here before Christmas."

"You are being serious!" Gale blustered, coming out from her daze.

"Of course I am. Why not?" She wrote out the check, using the magazine's price for the shirt the man was modeling as the ballpark figure and ripped the check from the register. "Who knows?" she laughed, waving the check in front of a very ashen looking Gale, "I might have come up with a new merchandising idea for this company. "You've heard of find-a-friend. Why not, Male-Order-Guys?" She placed the check and form into the envelope and licked it shut.

"But… you can't…"

"Oh, Pooh!" Anastasia said, "Who's to say what will happen? If it works out, they just may thank me."

"You're more likely to get a free trip to the loony farm," Gale predicted.

Anastasia chuckled. "Where's your sense of adventure, my dear? Doesn't your bible say you have not because you ask not? Well, I'm just asking. No harm done. Besides, it will no doubt give those poor people in the order department something to chuckle over."

"I don't know about this." The doubt was plain in Gale's voice. "If I hadn't thought you had done some crazy things before, I do now. This has got to be one of the strangest stunts you've ever pulled."

"Stranger than the time I showed your six-year-old how to play walrus with straws at the café?"

Gale's eyes widened at the memory. "The place was packed! Twenty-five-year-old's do not go around putting straws between their lip and teeth as though they were tusks, cross their arms, and make seal sounds in the center of a public place!"

"Pattie liked it."

"Six-year-olds don't know any better! They don't know when an adult is crazy."

Patting the woman's arm, Anastasia grinned. "I'm not crazy, Gale. I'm a dreamer."

www.ingramcontent.com/pod-product-compliance
Lightning Source LLC
Chambersburg PA
CBHW060537180626
46817CB00002B/616